MW01222945

That's How You Know

A Novel

Julie Simmons

Copyright © 2023 Julie Simmons

All rights reserved
The characters and events portrayed in this book are fictitious. Any references to historical
events, real people, or real places are used fictitiously. Other names, characters, places, and
events are products of the author's imagination. Any resemblance to actual events, places, or
persons, living or dead, is entirely coincidental.
No part of this book may be reproduced, or stored in any form or by any means, without express
written permission of the publisher.

ISBN - 9798865094449

Cover design by: Signet Studios, Kamloops, B.C. Canada

That's How You Know
from ENCHANTED
Music by Alan Menken
Lyrics by Stephen Schwartz
© 2007 Wonderland Music Company, Inc. and Walt Disney Music Company
All Rights Reserved. Used by Permission.
Reprinted by Permission of Hal Leonard LLC

For my husband, Rod, who is, in so many ways, my Charles. So many of Charles' outstanding qualities are yours: your beautiful mind, your kind and gentle heart, your sensitivity, but most of all, your instinctive ability to always know exactly how to comfort me when the dark side of my mind sometimes gets the better of me. You love me fiercely, even when I'm a hot mess, and you always think I'm beautiful, even though I never believe it myself. You are my life, my soulmate, and my forever love.

Author's Note

As you read through this book, you will encounter references to many songs, most of them preformed by Tori and/or Charles. I urge you to take some time to look them up and give them a listen as you read, as they will enhance your reading experience. Most of the songs were not random choices on my part. In fact, I was quite deliberate in my selections, intending that they express the feelings of the characters, or foreshadow things to come.

"Perhaps the butterfly is proof that you can go through a great deal of darkness, yet still become something beautiful."
BEAU TAPLIN

Part 1

Before The Cruise

New York City

Chapter 1

The late March morning daylight shone through the airplane window, awakening twenty-four-year-old Tori Stewart, as the red-eye from Seattle began its descent into JFK. She gazed out the window overlooking the city below, just taking it all in. This was it. New York City: the greatest city in the world, the center of the universe. This had been her dream for as long as she could remember. She would only be here for six weeks while rehearsing shows for the upcoming Alaska cruise season for Dream Cruise Line, but the prospect of spending any time at all in this magical place was exhilarating for Tori.

A graduate of Carnegie Mellon University, Tori auditioned on a whim the previous fall when the cruise line held try-outs in her home city of Seattle, Washington, for entertainers for the next season, and to her astonishment, she was hired. She had always been intrigued at the prospect of performing on a cruise ship, and her fiancé, Evan, was very supportive of her doing a season this year before they were married the next summer. The timing was right, so she decided to go for it.

But now, as the airplane landed at JFK, she was filled with excitement and trepidation all at once, as her all-too-familiar insecurities took hold of her and she questioned whether she was good enough. Sure, she had done well in her Bachelor of Fine Arts program at Carnegie Mellon, one of the top schools in the country for drama and musical theatre, but her constant struggle with performance anxiety reared its ugly head far too often, causing her to spiral into crippling self-doubt about whether she would ever make it in her ambitions for a career in musical theatre on Broadway.

Tori, a tall, slender classic beauty with long, naturally curly strawberry-blonde hair and stunning large eyes the color of Caribbean water, stepped into the terminal and spotted her aunt Helen immediately. Tori would be staying with her in Queens for the time she was spending in New York ahead of the sailings, which were to begin in early May. Tori and her aunt were very close and were looking forward to this time together. Helen did not have any children of her own, so Tori had always been like a daughter to her. At fifty, Helen Brooks was still a strikingly beautiful woman, looking far younger than her years. They gave each other a warm hug when Tori reached her in the terminal.

"You didn't have to come here this early," Tori said. "I could have waited, or taken a cab."

"Oh nonsense," said Helen, dismissing Tori's concerns. "It's no trouble at all. Besides, I couldn't wait to see you, anyway," she said warmly.

"Thanks so much for having me," Tori said with a broad smile to her favorite aunt.

"Oh, it's my pleasure. I'm so excited to catch up with you. It'll be great company for me." Helen had been widowed two years earlier when Tori's uncle was killed in a car accident, and now, although she lived a vibrant life, she still felt lonely at times.

They walked to baggage claim to wait for Tori's luggage. "How was your flight?" Helen asked.

"Not too bad," Tori answered. "I didn't get much sleep, though. Some asshole kid kept kicking the back of my chair," she grumbled. "More than once I felt like turning around and belting the little brat."

Helen chuckled. "I see you still love kids as much as ever," she joked. It was no secret to anyone who knew her that Tori was not a fan of children, and while she was a warm and caring person, she possessed absolutely no maternal instincts.

On the drive to Helen's home in Queens, her aunt asked

Tori for more details on what she would be doing while in New York and later on the cruise ship.

"Well," Tori began, "we'll be based here in New York at a rehearsal space in Manhattan while we work up the stage shows we'll be performing on board. I don't know much about that yet. I'm sure I'll find out more on Monday when I get there. Then we set sail at the beginning of May and we'll be doing all the cruises from Seattle to Alaska for the whole season until the middle of September, when it shuts down for the year."

"How incredible!" cried Helen. "And how does Evan feel about it?"

"Oh, he's one-hundred percent supportive, and even encouraged me to do it before we get married next year," Tori responded.

"He's such a nice young man," her aunt said.

"I know it. He's a keeper," Tori concurred, already missing him. Tori had known Evan Bateman for her entire life. They had gone to the same school together in the same grade, and even lived on the same street when they were kids. They were best friends, so it only seemed natural when they started dating in high school and became engaged during their college years.

"I'll bet you're excited." Her aunt's comment broke into Tori's thoughts.

"Well, yes, for the most part," Tori replied looking pensive, "but I'm really nervous, too."

"Oh you're going to be great, Victoria. This is a wonderful opportunity for you." Her aunt and her mother both used her entire first name, which Tori had always thought sounded far too formal, so most people just called her Tori.

"How are things with your dad and Susan?" Helen inquired about her older brother and his second wife.

"Oh, they're great," Tori replied in answer to the question. "You know Dad, he's addicted to his work, and Susan is kept more than busy at the hospital." Tori's father, William Stewart, worked as a newspaper editor, and her stepmom was a nurse.

Tori was an only child and her parents divorced after

a disastrous marriage when Tori was twelve. Her mother, Catherine, was English and moved back to London when Tori started college. Her father still lived in Seattle, where he was raised.

By then they had arrived at Helen's home and Tori took some time to get settled, desperately trying to calm her butterflies about the next week and the start of rehearsals.

Monday morning, after a fitful night of sleep, Tori arrived at the rehearsal space. As she entered, she surveyed the scene around her. There were about thirty people in the large space, and it was an atmosphere of warmth, with many of them hugging one another as if they were long-lost friends. Tori quickly took a seat, and a few moments later, a middle-aged man with a friendly face and warm smile stood up in front of them and asked for their attention.

"Good morning everyone," he began in an English accent Tori recognized as being similar to her mother's. "My name is Steven Barrie, and I will be the cruise director on your cruises this summer. I see some familiar faces among you from previous seasons, so to you I say welcome back. And for those of you who are new, welcome aboard. We are going to have a great time for the next six months or so. I just want to give you an overview of how the entertainment works on our cruises. My apologies to those of you who are returning, as you already know this. In addition to your stage shows, which will be performed in our main theater, you will each have additional responsibilities on board as well. From what we learned about you from your application forms, auditions and interviews, we have a good idea of what might be a good fit for you, but we'll chat with you all individually in the coming weeks to finalize those things. You'll be performing in the various ship's lounges and nightclubs, as well as hosting events on the ship, so you'll all be kept quite busy. But we want you to have fun during your time with us, too, so we won't work you too hard," he said with a grin. "On behalf of everyone at Dream Cruise Line, I want to express my gratitude for you all. As entertainers, you are a huge part of our success in providing a quality product to our guests. Without exceptional entertainment, we would not be able to operate. And now, without further ado, I'm going to turn things over to our music director, Dr. Charles Ryan."

As Dr. Ryan made his way to the front, a cute little African American girl about her own age who was sitting next to Tori leaned over and whispered, "Girl, that man is fiiiine. Too bad he's married. What a waste," she said with a grin. She was a tiny sprite of a girl, with beautiful long dark curls and a pixie-like face.

Tori giggled and did not disagree with her in the least as she watched Dr. Ryan approach. She estimated him to be somewhere in his early forties, tall and lean, clean-shaven with clean-cut dark hair containing just enough gray peppered throughout to make him look distinguished, and very sexy, she thought to herself. She had to admit that he was one of the most compelling men she had ever laid eyes on.

"I'm Chanel Price, by the way," the girl said, introducing herself and extending her hand to Tori.

"Hi, I'm Tori Stewart. Great to meet you," she answered with a warm smile while shaking Chanel's hand.

Dr. Ryan began to address the group. "Welcome everyone. As Steven said, I'm Charles Ryan and I'll be overseeing the stage shows mostly. We'll be doing two shows for each cruise. One will be an original musical, which we'll tell you more about in the coming days, and the other will be a revue style show of Broadway songs, which will, for the most part, be familiar to a lot of the audience. We really want to provide an opportunity for everyone to shine in this show, and you'll all participate in solos and small ensemble numbers. Over the next couple of days, as we watch you perform, we'll finalize the roles for the other show," he explained. "As for me, you won't see me around here all the time. I am a teaching professor at Juilliard, so I'll only be here some of the time, depending on my schedule. And when I *am* here, I'll be working mostly directly with the musicians until all the pieces start to come together. My semester will end just before our cruises set sail. I do have an assistant music director and I'd like to introduce him now. Please say hello to Sean. He'll be working closely with the whole team in my absence. Now I'd like to introduce you to Alyssa, who will be acting as choreographer and dance captain for the shows. She's going to explain how these rehearsals will be organized. I'm very much looking forward to working with you all," he concluded, favoring the group with the most dazzling smile Tori had ever seen.

Next, Alyssa came forward. "Hey y'all," she said in a southern drawl. "Who's excited for this?" she asked enthusiastically. Everyone cheered as she continued.

"So, the format of these rehearsals will vary quite a bit. For the most part, you will have a dance rehearsal every day, so come prepared for that. The rest of the time in the day will be devoted to rehearsing ensemble numbers with a vocal coach. There will also be time set aside for you all to work individually with a vocal coach on any solo work you have in the shows. Depending on the day, you may find you have some of the time free, while other people are working on their parts. So use your free time wisely to prepare for some of the other things you will be doing on board."

They started rehearsing then and found out more about the two shows and what numbers they would be singing in the Broadway revue show. When they broke for lunch, Tori heard someone call her name and was dismayed to realize that it was Dr. Ryan.

"Victoria Stewart, may I speak to you for a quick moment?" he asked.

Tori's stomach lurched with nerves and she felt her heart starting to race. She hoped she wasn't in some kind of trouble already on her very first day. Hopefully she wasn't about to get reamed out for giggling with Chanel earlier during the opening presentations. But she soon found out that this was not the case.

"Hello sir, I'm Victoria Stewart," she said with a broad

smile by way of introduction.

Charles raised his gaze to find himself looking into the most stunning eyes and beautiful face he had ever seen. He was taken aback for a moment, unable to catch his breath. "Ah yes, Victoria," he finally said. "I wanted to have a quick chat with you about some of the other things you'll be doing on the ship," he began. "Based on what we've learned about you, you seem to have an incredibly diverse taste in music and the things you like to perform. So we think you'll be perfect for our main lounge and the ship's piano bar as well. We also think you'd be an excellent host for the karaoke on board. How does that sound to you?"

"That sounds great!" she said enthusiastically.

"So you'll actually be working with me quite a bit. I'll be accompanying you on the piano for the lounge sets. So I wanted us to set up some time to get together and pick out music and practice for that."

Tori hoped her anxiety did not betray her as she listened. She never imagined she would be working so closely with the actual music director. There's no way she could be anywhere close to his league, and she was instantly concerned about her ability to live up to the high standard that would be expected of her.

She nodded and he continued. "I'll be able to work with you here some of the time, but would it be possible for you to meet me at Juilliard sometimes when you're done here in the afternoons, or maybe occasionally on a weekend?"

"Yes absolutely. That's not a problem."

"Okay, let's see then. This is Monday and I've got some stuff going on for the next few days. You're finished here on Thursday at four o'clock and I've got a class until four as well. Could you meet me at Juilliard then?"

"Yes, that's fine," she confirmed.

"Alright, here's my cell number," he said as he wrote his number on a piece of paper and handed it to her. "Just so you don't get lost, call me when you get there and I'll come meet you. Sound good?"

"Absolutely," she said, sounding more confident than she felt as she entered his contact information into her phone.

"Thank you Victoria. I'm looking forward to working with you," he said with a warm smile.

"Me too, Dr. Ryan. Oh and please call me Tori. My name just seems so formal to me. My mom is British and just a little bit obsessed with the royals, so I ended up being called Victoria Elizabeth, but everyone calls me Tori."

"Oh, that's interesting," he said. "That's exactly the same way I got my names. My parents also love the royal family, so I ended up with Charles Edward. Then, without even realizing it, I did the same thing to my son. He's Andrew Philip."

They both laughed, feeling like they had broken the ice. "Was your mom devastated when Queen Elizabeth died?" he asked.

"Inconsolable," she answered with a smile.

"Yeah, same with my folks," said Charles, returning her smile. "And please," he said, "don't call me sir or Dr. Ryan. It's just Charles from now on."

"Okay, Charles," she said, feeling a little shy. "I'll see you on Thursday."

After the rehearsals were done for the day, Chanel asked Tori if she wanted to join her for a bite to eat. "There's a Shake Shack not far from here," Chanel said. "How does that grab you?"

"That sounds awesome! Bring it on," Tori enthusiastically accepted.

They walked to the Shake Shack, and once they were settled with their food, Tori asked Chanel where she was from.

"Portland, Oregon," she answered.

"Oh, no way, I'm from Seattle! We're practically neighbors!" Tori exclaimed. "I'm assuming that you're one of the returning performers. It seems like you know people."

"Yup, I've done two seasons before," Chanel confirmed.

"Do you love it?"

"Yeah, I really do. It's great fun. You get a lot of experience and make some awesome friends along the way," Chanel said. "So what did Charles Ryan want with you earlier?"

"He told me that they have me slated to perform in the lounges and that he would be accompanying me on keys. I'm super nervous about it. I never expected to be working so closely with the music director," she said with a nervous sigh.

"Oh, don't give it a second thought," Chanel reassured her. "He's a really great guy. He'll have you feeling comfortable in no time. He's really approachable. Not to mention hot, too," she observed about the handsome maestro. "Did I mention that?" she asked with a devious grin.

Tori chuckled and said, "Yeah, I think you might have mentioned that. I can't disagree with you on that. He must get hit on a lot."

"Oh my God, all the freakin' time. But I don't think he acts on it, or if he does, he's discreet about it. He has a spotless reputation and isn't the source of rumors on the ship at all. He's just a really decent guy."

"So, are you one of the women hitting on him all the time?" Tori asked, teasing her.

"Oh no, not at all. I'm not that kind of girl. Besides, he's too old for me. But damn, a girl would have to be blind or dead not to notice. And just wait until you see him in a tux with a conductor's baton in his hand. Yummy," she said dreamily.

"He mentioned to me that he has a son and you said he's married," Tori said, curious about him.

"Yeah, but word on the street is that it's not a happy situation. But I don't have that on good authority or have any idea what the circumstances are."

"That's sad," Tori replied. "He does seem really nice."

They moved on to other topics then. Tori learned that, at twenty-two, Chanel still lived with her mother and two younger brothers in Portland, and that her father died in Afghanistan when she was fourteen, leaving her mother a widow at age thirty-nine to raise three kids on her own.

"Wow," said Tori. "I can't imagine that. She must be an

incredible woman."

"Oh, she is," Chanel replied. "My mama is something special all right. We're really close. If I can be half the woman she is, I'll be happy."

"She never remarried?" Tori inquired.

"No," Chanel replied. "I mean, she's dated a bit but nothing really serious. She always says that after my daddy, nobody else could compare. They were the loves of each other's lives. He was a wonderful man. I miss him every day. I can only hope that someday, I find what they had."

"Aww, that's so sweet," Tori said.

They parted then and Tori made her way back to Queens. Her aunt couldn't wait for her to get home so she could hear all about Tori's first day. Tori told her about meeting Chanel and Charles and that she was apprehensive about working so closely with Charles, to which Helen replied that Tori had always been too hard on herself.

"I have a feeling, darling," said Helen, "that this experience is going to change your life."

Chapter 2

That week, rehearsals began in earnest, and by the time Thursday rolled around, Tori was feeling much more settled into the routines and had met several other people in the company. As usual with any show she had done, she was feeling a little overwhelmed with the dance element of performing, so she went to Alyssa to ask if it would be possible to spend some extra time on the choreography.

"Oh absolutely. We can schedule some one-on-one time for that. You're actually much more solid than you think," Alyssa assured her.

Tori smiled. "Well, thanks for that," she said. "But dance has never come easily to me. I've always struggled more with that than anything else."

"You're your own worst enemy," said Alyssa warmly.

"That's not the first time I've heard that," Tori replied. They scheduled a time and then Tori headed over to Juilliard to meet with Charles.

When she arrived, she texted him as he had instructed and a few moments later, he came out to meet her, looking far more handsome than Tori wanted to admit in a navy blue well-tailored full three-piece suit and tie. He led her though a number of corridors until they reached his spacious office. One wall consisted of floor-to-ceiling windows and another was lined with bookshelves filled with academic textbooks, music books and conductor's scores. The room was inviting and impeccably tidy and organized. There was a piano there as well. He took off his jacket and tie and loosened his collar, sat down on the piano bench and gestured to a nearby couch.

"Please, have a seat," he invited cordially.

Tori sat awkwardly in the chair, feeling her nerves start to overwhelm her once again. This was a familiar feeling she wished she could conquer. Charles picked up on it immediately. "You seem nervous, Tori. Are you okay?" he asked gently.

Damn, she thought. She hoped it would not betray her so obviously. She was usually better at concealing it. She decided to be straight with him about it. "I'm sorry. I really suffer from performance anxiety to the point where I even feel it in rehearsals," she answered honestly with a plaintive sigh. "It can be quite debilitating."

"Ah, that's rough," he said sympathetically. "So how do you cope with it?" he asked.

She smiled, "I whistle a happy tune," she said nonchalantly, referencing the famous Rodgers and Hammerstein song from *The King and I*.

Charles returned her smile, understanding the reference. He had the kindest, most gentle hazel eyes she had ever seen - eyes that looked as though they could see directly into a person's soul. She could easily get lost in them if she allowed herself to linger too long.

"Actually, it really is my go-to song when I'm anxious. You have no idea how many times I've sung that to myself. The lyrics are just so perfect. It's so simple, but Hammerstein really knocked that one out of the park. I just love it, despite the fact that I can't whistle. Sondheim got it wrong. Not just anyone can whistle." They both laughed at that.

In an effort to help steady her nerves and make her comfortable, Charles said, "Okay, so why don't we start with that one then? It would actually be a good one for our repertoire."

As Charles began to play the familiar opening notes, Tori felt herself relax, and knowing the song as well as she did, she sang it flawlessly.

"Beautiful," Charles said after she finished. "There's our first song," he said, jotting the title onto a piece of paper. "Do you have any others you'd like to do?"

"Well, speaking of 'Anyone Can Whistle,' how about that one?" she suggested. "We could do them together for a little mini theme of whistle songs. Do you know it?"

"I know it, but it's a little more obscure. I don't know it well, but I think I have a Sondheim volume here somewhere in my music." He got up from the bench, went over to the shelf and pulled out a large Stephen Sondheim anthology. "Here it is," he said. "Let's just look and see if it's in here. Ah, here it is," he said a moment later and flipped to the appropriate page, placing the book on the piano. He began to play it and, once again, she sang it perfectly.

"Wow!" he said. "You even knew all the words to that."

"My brain is a song lyric archive," she said. "But strangely enough, it's the fear of forgetting lyrics that is at the root of my performance anxiety," she confessed.

"I'll bet something like that happened to you sometime and it left its mark," he accurately assessed.

"And you'd be one-hundred percent correct," she confirmed. "I was a little girl and I forgot lyrics during a performance, and I've been battling it ever since. It doesn't help that I'm a perfectionist and I *do not* deal well with making mistakes. I have a major fear-of-failure complex. I know that's not healthy, but there it is."

"Well, you're right about that. It's not healthy, but it's not at all unusual," he said. "So what else do you think would work for us to do?"

"Well, I was thinking that you can't go wrong with some light pop songs. Stuff like maybe 'Love Will Keep Us Together' or something like that," she answered.

"That's a great choice. It's a good one for keys as well." He began playing the very recognizable opening riff and they went from there.

"That's another great one," he said, writing it on the list.

"How about 'Don't Go Breaking My Heart?' That's a duet, though. Do you sing?" she asked.

"I can get by," he answered. "Let's give it a try." They sang it though and added it to the list.

Tori was very impressed with his beautiful tenor voice. "I think you're being far too modest. You can do way better than 'get by,'" she said when they finished the song.

"Aww, shucks, you're too kind," he said and they laughed. She noticed he had an adorable dimple that appeared in his cheek when he smiled.

"I've actually always been in choirs ever since high school," he revealed. "And I'm equally comfortable conducting choirs as much as orchestras."

"So I'm curious," she began. "Why would a serious, accomplished musician like you want this cruise gig? I mean, this is usually something people do for a lark, or to get experience to add to their resumé."

"Well, I do this purely for my own enjoyment. It gets me away from the grind of the city for a few months a year. I mean, I love New York, but it can be a lot sometimes. So, I figure what better way to decompress than on a cruise ship in Alaska. The orchestra on the ship is such a scaled-back version of the large orchestras I'm used to working with that it feels like a working holiday for me," he explained.

"That actually makes a whole lot of sense," said Tori.

"Some people have vacation homes in the Hamptons, I have this," he said. "I actually love the way my year is broken up. I teach here from January to April, and then I do the cruise thing until the middle of September. I don't have an orchestra of my own, so I'm not tied down to a schedule for one particular orchestra. I spend a lot of time doing guest conducting gigs with various orchestras all over the place. I do that mostly from the time I get back from the cruise until I start back here again in January. It changes things up a bit for me."

"I can definitely see the appeal in that," Tori replied. "Keeps things from getting boring."

"It does indeed."

"Can you tell me a bit more about the types of venues we'll

be playing in on the ship?" she asked.

"Yes, absolutely. Because your musical genres are so varied, we're putting you in the main lounge a lot of the time. It's located in a busy traffic area and is wide open, so there will be lots of people coming and going. It's also a family friendly area, so there will be kids around," he answered. "We'll be playing there in the afternoons and early evenings quite a bit."

"Okay, so maybe we should put some Disney songs in for that location," she suggested. "I have tons of them in my repertoire."

"That's an excellent idea," he agreed. "Tell me some of the songs you do."

She explained that she did most of the princess songs and rattled off several titles, which they both agreed were good options. They went through several of them and Tori felt very comfortable with their selections.

"Your princess voice is perfect," Charles complimented her.

Tori smiled sheepishly. "It's my not-so-secret dream. I've always wanted to play a princess on stage. Either that or voice one in an animated movie," she confessed.

"Well, you have the ideal voice for it. You also have the perfect hair for it," he said with a smile. There was that cute dimple again. His smile was so warm, and it instantly made her feel at ease.

Tori's face flushed a little. "My hair is the thing I get asked about the most," she said. "People always want to know if it's naturally curly and if this is my natural color. Yes to both."

"No worries about having to wear a wig for that," he replied, grinning.

She continued to browse through his Disney music book. "Oh, I love this one. Would you sing it with me?" she asked, passing him the book open to "Once Upon a Dream" from *Sleeping Beauty*.

"Oh, I love this, too. Such a classic," he said, and they sang it together beautifully. She felt as though she had been waiting her entire life to find a singing partner that fit her as perfectly as he did.

"Well, you make a pretty decent prince yourself," she said.

"Why thank you milady," he said gallantly as he stood up from the piano stool and bowed in a courtly fashion.

"Well, chivalry is definitely not dead," she said with a chuckle.

Charles then went on to tell her that they would also be in the piano lounge sometimes as well. "That venue is for adults and doesn't open until nine PM. We'll only be in there on a couple of the nights when we don't have a stage show," he explained. "So maybe light standards and some showtunes would work best for that."

"I'm absolutely comfortable with that," she said. "That fits perfectly in my wheelhouse."

"We're actually going to have to put together a lot of music, based on how often we will be playing together during each cruise and the variety of genres we will have to tap into," said Charles.

They continued to throw around song ideas and he knew every one she suggested.

"I have to say, you are completely blowing all my preconceived ideas out the window," Tori said after she finished a sultry rendition of "I've Got a Crush on You."

"In what way?" he asked.

"I don't know, I've always had this idea that serious musicians and conductors are a bit, well, stodgy I guess, and that they aren't open to some of the more popular genres of music."

"Well," he said smiling, "that stereotype is not without merit. I know lots of those types in my business. But I've never understood it. I don't get why having an appreciation for the more classical forms of music somehow means you can't like anything else. I mean, why do the two have to be mutually exclusive? It's like, whenever I do a pops concert with an orchestra, there are always musicians who bitch and moan about having to do it. Meanwhile, I'm having a blast with it.

People just need to get their heads out of their asses and stop taking themselves so seriously, in my opinion. I love everything. I was heavily influenced by my parents' and grandparents' tastes in music, and I enjoy performing all of it. That's why we thought it was a good idea to pair us up, because you seem to be the same."

"I am absolutely the same," she confirmed. "I've always been an old soul. My parents and grandparents were a huge influence on me musically as well. I'm good with anything from the swing era to the present day. Most of my favorite music comes from long before I was born, but I love new music, too. I spend a lot of time with the radio, keeping up with what's current. I stream some radio stations from Vancouver as well, so I know a lot of Canadian artists that aren't necessarily very well-known here in the States. I also listen to a lot of BBC Radio and other stations from Britain, so I'm up on what's popular in the UK."

"The great thing about that is that it makes you a more versatile performer, and it gives you a much broader selection of music to choose from. It seems there's nothing you can't sing. I think you'll also really enjoy hosting the karaoke on board. It's in our family friendly area, so there will be kids and teens there singing as well. It's really fun."

"I'm excited for that. I'm glad it's family karaoke and not drunk karaoke," she said laughing. "Drunk karaoke is brutal."

"I agree one-hundred percent with that," he said with a chuckle.

They practiced some more songs and before they knew it, three hours had gone by.

"I think we've got a good start here today," he said to her as they were getting ready to leave. He walked her back outside and asked, "Do you feel a little more relaxed now that we've gotten to know each other a bit?"

"Absolutely," she answered with a broad, sincere smile. "Thank you for making me feel so at ease. Chanel told me you would." She noticed that his eyes and smile were not the only things about him that exuded warmth. His body language was very open and his entire demeanor relaxed and comforting.

She looked around her surroundings then. "This place looks amazing," she said. "It's so iconic. It's definitely somewhere I wanted to visit while I'm here."

"Well," Charles began, getting an idea, "why don't we meet here again to practice on Saturday?" he proposed. "Then I can give you a tour," he offered generously.

"I'd love that, but I'm sure you have better things to do with your Saturday than hang with me," she replied.

"Actually, I'd love it," he said sincerely. "So see you about one o'clock, back here?"

"Alright, see you then," she said, and as he watched her walk away, he couldn't help but notice the poise with which she carried herself. He smiled to himself, already looking forward to seeing her again.

Charles was waiting for her in his office on Saturday when she tapped on his door a few minutes before one o'clock. They greeted each other warmly and decided to do some work first before he took her on his promised tour around the campus. Tori noticed he was looking much more casual that day than he had on Thursday, in jeans and a gray turtleneck.

First they ran through the songs they had picked out on Thursday, and Tori was amazed at how solid they were already starting to sound. They had both jotted down some more song ideas since they last met and decided to add many of them to their repertoire, including duets of "They Can't Take That Away From Me" and "People Will Say We're In Love." Tori very much wanted to do "Meadowlark" from *The Baker's Wife*. It was a song she loved and she knew it had amazing piano accompaniment, so they gave it a try and both agreed it was perfect for their act.

After about an hour or so, they decided to take a break and go for their walk around Juilliard. He took her everywhere and pointed out all the highlights of the campus, and while walking, she asked him how long he had been doing the cruises.

"This is my fourth year," answered Charles.

"Do you ever get bored spending that long on a cruise ship?" she inquired.

"No, not really," he replied. "I'm not a person who gets bored easily. I usually bring things to do. Like, if I'm working on some arrangements or orchestrations, I'll take that with me and work on it when I have some down time. The good thing about being a performer on board is that we don't work during the days the ship is in port, so we have the freedom to leave the boat and explore. We don't resume performances until later in the evenings on those days, after we leave the ports. There's also a great camaraderie that develops among the members of the performing company, so it's always a great bit of fun."

"Your wife doesn't mind you being away all that time? Or does she come with you?"

"Oh, hell no," he answered emphatically. "Meredith is happy to see me go. She'd probably be overjoyed if I got tossed overboard and never came back."

Tori tried her best to stifle a laugh, but was unsuccessful. "I'm sorry," she apologized. "I don't mean to laugh."

"Don't apologize. It is what it is. If I didn't find a way to laugh about it sometimes, I'd probably drive myself insane." Tori felt sad for him. He was far too young and too nice a person to be living in an unhappy marriage.

He changed the subject then. He had noticed her engagement ring but was hesitant to ask about it, not wanting to get too personal or make her uncomfortable. "I see your engagement ring," he broached, "When are you getting married?"

"Next summer," she answered.

"Oh, so you're not going to be able to join us for another season next year?" he asked, disappointment evident in his voice.

"No, not next year, but I wouldn't rule out doing it again sometime, depending on how it goes this season. My fiancé, Evan, and I thought that this would be a good time for me to explore this before we get married next year. I've always been curious to try it. I met some people in college who had done it and they had good experiences."

"Am I remembering correctly that you attended Carnegie Mellon?" he asked. She confirmed that she had.

"The reason I ask is that my fifteen-year-old son, Andrew, has aspirations to pursue a career in musical theatre, like you, and Carnegie Mellon is one of his top choices. He's also considering Tisch at NYU, which is what I hope he chooses. I selfishly want to keep him close to home for as long as I can, but I'm supportive of whatever his choice is. Right now, he attends LaGuardia High School of the Performing Arts. I'd love for him to meet you and toss out any questions he has about your experience at Carnegie Mellon."

"I'd be delighted to chat with him any time you'd like," she replied graciously.

"Oh that would be so great. He'd love that. I'll check with him and see what he's doing, say next Saturday, if that works for you?"

"Yeah, that's perfect," she said with a nod.

"Okay, I'll confirm that with you this week. We can meet up for lunch. Have you been to Sardi's?"

"No, but I've always wanted to go there," she answered. "It's so iconic."

"So that's where we'll go then," he confirmed.

By then, they had reached his office once again. "Thank you so much for the tour," she said appreciatively. "It's amazing to be shown around by someone who knows it so well."

"It's entirely my pleasure," he responded with a warm smile. She couldn't help but notice how much his smile lit up his entire handsome face. "I did all of my degrees here. I've been a fixture around these halls for longer than I care to admit."

They went back to work then and by the time they wrapped up for the day a couple hours later, they had solidified several more songs for their lounge sets.

"I'm curious if piano was the instrument you specialized

in for your undergrad music degree." she inquired.

"Oh God, no," he replied. "Piano is just something I'm minimally functional at."

"There you go being all modest again," she said with a smile. "It's just that you are a natural accompanist, and trust me, those are few and far between. Most are really stiff and rigid in their timing, like they have a metronome in their heads. But you just naturally feel where I'm going and roll with it."

"Well, thank you, that's a huge compliment. Once you realize that the soloist should lead the accompanist and not the other way around, it actually becomes much easier. But you make it easy. You're a delight to play for. But my instrument is actually trumpet."

"Do you miss playing in orchestras now that you're leading them?" she asked, fascinated by him.

"Yeah, that's definitely the trade-off," he answered honestly. "In doing something I love in conducting, I have to sacrifice something else I love, which is playing. But I do seek out opportunities to play just for fun, like jazz and swing bands, brass quartets and things like that."

"You are just such a multi-talented person," she said, very impressed with his skills. "I am *so* nowhere close to your league."

"I wouldn't agree with that at all," he replied with conviction. "You're also nowhere close to my age either. When I was your age, I had just started my master's degree, I had a wife and kid, which was unexpected, and I was a working musician trying to make ends meet while doing coursework for my degree. I didn't have two dimes to rub together, but I kept my eye on the ultimate goal and plowed through until I finished my PhD. But for performers and actors, it's an entirely different story. The more time you spend in school, the more time you lose when you can be getting valuable experience and performing credits under your belt. So many performers don't go to college at all, or if they do go, they often drop out when an opportunity comes their way. I totally respect that. You can't waste your prime performing years doing extensive schooling or you could end up missing the boat completely. Whereas for what I do, that level of education is required. So really, it's just a different career path," he reasoned.

Tori looked contemplative as she carefully considered what he had said. "Yeah, I guess I never really thought of it that way before," she conceded.

They set another time then to meet for the next week. "I'll be at the rehearsal that day, so I can work with you there this time," he said. "And on Monday, the parts will be posted for the roles in the musical. I think you'll be pleased," he added.

"I'm just glad for the opportunity, regardless of what parts I play." She was modest and came with no expectations when she took the job.

"Well, I won't say any more. You'll see on Monday," he said with a knowing twinkle in his eye.

When Monday came, Tori was astounded when the parts were posted to see that she had been given the leading role. She and Chanel screamed and hugged when they looked at the list. They also saw that Chanel was playing her character's best friend, so they would have a lot of scenes together, as well as some songs.

Not so thrilled, however, was Simone Petersen, who was a returning member of the company and had her eyes on the leading role. When she saw the list, she turned to Tori and said, "Congratulations" in a less-than-convincing tone.

"What the fuck is her problem?" Tori asked Chanel later when they were in a more private place.

"Oh, just ignore her. She's a complete diva and expected the lead because she's done this before. Just do yourself a favor and steer as clear of her as you can," Chanel recommended. Simone's reputation clearly preceded her.

"Oh fan-fucking-tastic. I hate drama," Tori said. "That's a side of show business I could definitely do without."

"I hear you sister," Chanel replied. "But sadly, it goes with the territory."

When she next saw Charles, he congratulated her and she

thanked him for his faith that she could pull it off.

"Well, it wasn't just me," he said. "The entire production team agreed unanimously that you were perfect for it."

"I just hope I don't let you down," she replied, her nervousness creeping into her voice.

"I have no concerns whatsoever," he told her honestly.

They practiced for about an hour that day and when they finished he confirmed their plans for Saturday. "I spoke with my son and he's great with Saturday, if that's still okay with you?"

She nodded. "Yes, that's great," she confirmed.

"Okay then, Sardi's at noon?"

"See you then." She was really enjoying getting to know him, and now felt completely comfortable working with him. They were a natural fit as performers, and she couldn't deny she felt a definite connection with him. Meanwhile, Charles was thinking the exact same thing as he made his way home that day.

Chapter 3

The remainder of the second week of rehearsals went smoothly as things started to come together. Tori was spending some extra time with Alyssa working very hard on the choreography, and was feeling more confident with it every day.

She was still getting the evil eye from Simone, who was fairly rude whenever Tori tried to be friendly to her. But she was the only member of the cast who was in any way hostile. Tori was really enjoying getting better acquainted with everyone else and was making friends. She and Chanel were getting closer and had decided to sign up to be roommates on the boat when the cruise started.

On Saturday, she spotted Charles and Andrew as soon as she walked in the door of Sardi's. Charles got up to greet her and brought her to the table to meet his son. As soon as she saw Andrew, Tori did a double take and looked back and forth from one to the other.

"Oh my God, Charles, he's your mini-me!" she exclaimed. Andrew was indeed a younger replica of his father. "Seriously, if I saw you on the street, I'd know who you are," she said to Andrew. "But I'm sure this is not the first time you've heard that."

They all laughed and Charles introduced them. "Andy, this is Tori," he said. "I thought it would be great for you to meet her. She graduated from Carnegie Mellon a couple of years ago and I thought you'd have lots to talk to her about."

"It's great to meet you, Andy," said Tori warmly.

"It's nice to meet you, too," he said as he got up from

his chair and politely shook her hand. Tori thought that this was a behavior not common for kids his age anymore, and was impressed.

For the next hour, they conversed easily about everything from their mutual love of musical theatre and Andy's experiences at LaGuardia, to his career ambitions and her time at Carnegie Mellon. He asked her lots of intelligent questions, which she thoroughly answered, and they chatted at length about their favorite musicals.

"What would be your dream role on Broadway?" Andy asked her.

"Oh, that's easy," she said without hesitation. "Narrator in *Joseph and the Amazing Technicolor Dreamcoat*."

"Oh, you'd be perfect for that," Charles chimed in.

"That show is totally kick-ass," Andy said. "The part of Joseph is actually one of my most coveted roles." Tori thought Andrew was very well-spoken and mature. She didn't know many fifteen-year-olds who would use the words "coveted role."

"Okay, awesome," she said. "Next revival of that show, it's you and me, Joseph and the Narrator," she said laughing.

"You're on!" Andy said high-fiving her. "Thanks for meeting me, Tori," he said sincerely as they were getting ready to leave. "I really appreciate it. It's been great to hear about your experiences at Carnegie Mellon and to get the perspective of someone who actually went there. It was very helpful."

"It's my pleasure. I'm so glad I met you. You seem really focused on your goals and you know what you want. I'm sure you'll be successful wherever you decide to go." Tori thought he definitely had a good head on his shoulders.

Before leaving Sardi's, Tori just had to walk around the restaurant to view the world-famous caricature sketch portraits of theatre stars adorning the walls, for which Sardi's was renowned.

When they finally left, Charles asked her what she had planned for the rest of the day.

"I don't know really. I didn't make any plans other than

this. I've been seeing some of the sights with my aunt Helen since I've been here, but she's tied up today and Chanel is busy, so I'm on my own."

"What's still on your list of things to do?" Charles asked. "Have you been to the Empire State Building yet?"

"No, I haven't made it there yet, but it's definitely on my list," she replied.

"Well, why don't we all go there now?" he suggested.

"Oh, that's okay, I don't want to take up your time. I'm sure you're busy," she said.

"Actually, I'm very free today. I try my best to keep Saturday or Sunday open every weekend to spend time with Andy. So what do you say?" He turned to his son. "Are you up for it, Andy?" he asked.

Andy nodded. "Sure, it's been ages since I've been there."

"Well, okay then," agreed Tori happily.

Tori loved the Empire State Building and was captivated by the view, and Charles loved seeing the wonder of it through her eyes for the first time.

"It's so easy to forget how to be a tourist in your own city," Charles commented. "I can't remember the last time I did any of the New York attractions. You just start to take it for granted as you go on about your day-to-day life."

"Have you always lived in New York?" she asked him.

"No," he answered. "I grew up in New Haven Connecticut. I moved here for university and have been here ever since."

"Did you like it in New Haven?"

"Yeah, I really did," he affirmed nostalgically. "I had easy access to New York and all the benefits of that, but it was a lot quieter there with none of the hassles of the bigger cities. You're from Seattle if I recall, correct?"

"Yes," she confirmed, "and I feel the same way about Seattle as you do about New Haven. It's a wonderful city, but not so big that you have all the hassles of a city this size. Seattle is a great theatre town, too. We get all the concerts go through there and all the Broadway touring productions go there as well. I got to see so much theatre growing up. We also have an incredible regional theatre there. I've done several productions with them in the past, and it looks like I'll be doing at least two more for the next season: one in December and another in February. I also do some administrative work for them part-time."

"That's the 5th Avenue Theatre, if I recall correctly," Charles said.

"That's the one." She was impressed by his knowledge of the Seattle theatre scene. "But I agree with you about how easy it is to take things for granted in the place you live," she continued. "I can't remember the last time I did the Space Needle or Pike Place Market."

"I haven't been there in a long time, either. I visited Seattle briefly last fall when we did the cruise auditions, but I didn't do much while I was there. I had to get back to conduct a concert," he said.

"Well, I'll have to be your tour guide there sometime when we're docked between cruises this summer," she offered.

"I'd really like that," said Charles. "You must be really happy that it's based out of your hometown."

"That is definitely a bonus. I'll be able to visit with my dad and fiancé every week while we're there. And it'll be easy to pick up anything I forget to take with me, or drop stuff off that I don't need."

"So, your dad is in Seattle?" he inquired.

"Yes, he was raised there. My mother met him there while she was living in the States. My grandfather was a history professor in London and decided to come to America for a few years abroad. So he moved the family to Seattle and taught at the University of Washington for several years. He ended up staying far longer than he expected, and my mother met my dad and stayed after her parents moved back to England. They split when I was twelve, but my mother didn't want to go back until I left for college. She's remarried now to a lovely man from over there and my dad is also remarried to a great lady. I'm very fortunate to love both my step-parents."

"It's easy to see that you have some English in your background. I've noticed some dead giveaways in the way you talk sometimes," he observed.

"Oh yeah, like what?" she asked.

"You have some definite British-isms," he said. "Like just today when we were on our way up here, you said 'lift', and you said 'queue.' And every now and again, I hear a slight twinge of an accent on some of your words."

"Well, you're very observant, professor," she said with a grin.

"When did you last see your mom?" Andy asked.

"She came back for my graduation from Carnegie Mellon a couple of years ago." She searched her phone until she found a photo of her and her mother at the graduation to show them.

"Wow, you look like her," Andy observed.

"Yes, except for the eyes. I have my dad's eyes, and her hair is redder than mine. My dad is blonde, so I ended up with a color somewhere in between. I got her curls, though." She accessed a recent photo of her father on her phone then, and Charles and Andy found themselves looking at a very handsome man with aquamarine eyes, exactly like Tori's.

"I'll bet they were a striking couple," said Charles. Looking at her parents, it was easy to see where Tori got her breathtaking good looks.

"Oh they certainly were. They definitely turned heads. They were really good together in so many ways," she said. "It's just too bad my dad couldn't keep it in his pants."

"Wow, my folks are boring compared to that," Charles said. "They still live in the same house I was raised in. I like the fact that I don't live far from them. I can pretty much see them whenever I want."

"Be grateful for that," Tori said. "Trust me, boring is good. Be thankful you were raised by stable parents."

Just then, Tori's phone beeped. She checked it and said, "Oh, it's just a text from my aunt Helen letting me know she's back home now from whatever she was doing today. She's my

THAT'S HOW YOU KNOW

dad's sister and I'm staying with her in Queens while I'm here," she explained.

It was now late afternoon and they had all been together since noon. It was such an enjoyable day for all of them, and when they left the Empire State Building to go their separate ways, Andrew thanked Tori once more and she said she hoped she would see him again. She gave him her contact information and told him not to hesitate to reach out to her at any time if he had any more questions.

"Oh, you'll be seeing me this summer," said Andy.

"Andy will be joining me for two of the cruises," Charles elaborated. "He'll be on board at the end of June when he finishes school. Then he goes to a theatre camp all summer and will join me again after that in late August, before school starts up."

Tori was thrilled to hear it. She had really taken a liking to Andy and was happy she'd be seeing him again. "I'll be excited to hear about the camp when you get back," she told him.

"Yeah, I love it every year. It's a blast," he said enthusiastically.

As Tori made her way back to Queens that evening, she realized she was starting to consider Charles a friend. And on their way home, Andy commented to his father that he thought Tori was amazing. Charles agreed with him wholeheartedly. There was definitely something very special about her.

Chanel and several of the cast members she knew from the previous year were staying in a walk-up on short-term rental in Hell's Kitchen. It was crowded, but fun. She sat studying her script on Sunday afternoon while she waited for Tori to arrive. They planned to get together to run lines and go over some of the songs they would be singing together.

Tori arrived a few minutes later with her script and music in hand. Several of Chanel's housemates were home, while a couple of others passed her at the door on their way out as she was making her way in. "How many people live here?" Tori inquired as she looked around.

"Six of us," Chanel answered.

Tori's mouth dropped open. "Six!" she exclaimed in shock. "Oh my God, Chanel, what the hell? How can that possibly work in this space?"

"Welcome to the life of an artist in New York City," she replied. "Trust me, I'm glad I live in Portland." Tori was even more grateful to be staying with her aunt in Queens.

They ran lines and went over the songs for awhile and Chanel asked her how things were going with Charles.

"Oh, you were absolutely right about that. I was worried for nothing. I was so nervous when I first got there and he picked up on it right away. He made me feel so comfortable really quickly. We get along really great and we're a good match for doing lounge music. He likes so many different kinds of music, just like me. I was really surprised by that."

"I told ya he'd be great with you," Chanel said, flipping pages in her script. "Oh, by the way," she said, changing the subject. "My mama called today. She's coming to New York this week to spend a few days with me. I'm so excited. I knew she was trying to get the money together, but she didn't know if it was going to work out or not. Anyway, she's getting here on Wednesday and staying until Monday of next week."

"Oh, Chanel, that's so great! I can't wait to meet her. But please tell me she's not staying here," Tori said, rolling her eyes.

"No," Chanel laughed. "She booked a hotel nearby. I'm actually going to stay with her while she's here. One less body in this place will make everyone happier."

"I'll talk to Aunt Helen. Maybe the four of us can get together and do something. She's a great tour guide. She's lived here for many years and knows everything about the place."

"Oh, that would be awesome! Let me know what works for you guys."

"Yeah I will," Tori answered with a smile. "So have they told you yet what else you'll be working on during the cruise?" Tori asked.

"Oh yeah, yeah, they did and it's great news!" she

exclaimed excitedly. "I'll be working with you at karaoke. You're hosting it and I'm in the booth taking the requests and cuing up the songs."

"Oh, sweet!" Tori was as excited about this news as her friend was.

"I'm also going to be working in the dance club quite a bit and hosting some trivia in the daytime," Chanel continued.

"I honestly think this whole thing is gonna be a blast," Tori said.

They talked of other things for awhile then and practiced the lines again once more before Tori headed home.

When she reached Queens, she mentioned Chanel's mother's upcoming visit to her aunt Helen and suggested, as she had to Chanel, that they do something together while she was there.

"Oh, that would be delightful," Helen answered warmly.

She called Evan then for their daily check-in. She usually called him before she went to bed each night. It was three hours earlier in Seattle, so it was early evening for him.

"Hey babe," he said when he answered. "What's happening today?"

"It's Sunday, so it's pretty quiet today. I went to Chanel's to run some lines, but that's about it," said Tori in answer to his question.

"I miss you like crazy, especially on the weekends," he said in a forlorn voice.

"Aww, I know baby, I miss you, too," she murmured affectionately. "What are you dong now?"

"Working. Your dad has been giving me some higher profile stories lately and it's challenging, but I really want to prove myself. It's the opportunity I've been waiting for." Evan was a journalist and worked at the same paper for which her father was the editor.

"I'm so proud of you baby. You've worked really hard for this." Evan had stayed in Seattle to study journalism while she was in Pittsburgh at Carnegie Mellon. It was the only time in their lives, until now, that they had spent any significant time apart. She was so happy to see him finally getting his break. She suspected that her father had been a little overcautious where Evan was concerned, for fear of appearing to give him preferential treatment because he was his daughter's fiancé.

"I just hope I don't screw it up," he said. In some ways, he was as insecure as she was in his doubts about his ability to achieve in his chosen field.

"You won't Evan. You're amazing at what you do," she complimented him.

"Well, you've always been the president of my fan club," he said.

"And always will be," she said, smiling on her end of the conversation.

They chatted about various mundane things before hanging up a little while later. She truly felt like the luckiest girl in the world. How many people could say they were literally marrying their lifelong best friend? She fell asleep thinking of him that night with a contented smile on her face.

Chapter 4

Weeks three and four of rehearsals went by rather uneventfully, and Tori felt more confident each day and was having fun with the rest of the cast. However, despite her best efforts, she was unable to make any headway with Simone, and was still getting cold-shouldered by her. On Monday of the third week, she decided to broach the subject of their tension.

"You know, Simone, I'm not sure what your problem is with me. I've tried very hard to be friendly, but you seem to have an issue and I don't know what I ever did to offend you. I think you're an extremely talented person, and I'd like to get to know you better, but you're really not making it easy," she said sincerely.

"Then stop trying," Simone said haughtily and stalked away.

Charles spotted the tense exchange from across the room. "What the hell was that about?" he asked as he approached Tori.

"Oh, nothing. Don't worry about it," she said nonchalantly. "She just has some kind of grudge against me and I don't know what the actual fuck her problem is," Tori said in resignation.

"I'm actually not surprised," Charles responded. "She's very ambitious and a little full of herself. She's threatened by you."

"But why?" Tori mused. "I mean, I've been nothing but nice to her." She was mystified and felt more than a little defeated.

Charles was continually awed by her lack of ego. Not only was she completely unaware of her beauty, she also had no clue as to the degree of her immense talent. It was a quality that made her even more endearing, in his opinion, and was a refreshing change from a lot of the people he encountered in show business.

"You really have no idea how truly extraordinary you are, do you?" asked Charles. Her face flushed a deep crimson at his compliment. "She isn't half the performer you are and she knows it. Get used to it. I suspect it's not the only time you'll encounter her type throughout your career."

Tori was bowled over by his praise and didn't know how to respond. "I'm sorry," he said respectfully. "I didn't mean to embarrass you, but you really are that good and you need to know it."

Overwhelmed by the compliment, she settled on a simple "Thank you" and changed the subject. "I have some free time this afternoon if you want to run through some songs," she proposed.

"Yes, I do. I have to go back to Juilliard for a class at one o'clock, but we can meet up after that. I'm free for the rest of the afternoon," he answered.

"Okay, I'll meet you there at around three?" she proposed, which he confirmed was perfect for him.

As much as Tori was enjoying the entire process of working up the shows for the upcoming cruises, she had to admit to herself that the time she delighted in the most was the time she spent with Charles. They had developed such an easy rapport with one another that she no longer felt an ounce of nervousness when they practiced together. They also found that they were never at a loss for conversation and talked with ease about everything from music to politics and current events, as well as their musical influences, which they found were actually quite similar. They often found themselves in spirited discussions about which production of a particular musical was the best, and the merits of the original productions versus revivals.

"Oh my God, Charles, I don't think we can be friends anymore," she joked that afternoon when he revealed that his favorite actress to portray Eva Peron in *Evita* was Patti LuPone, as opposed to her choice of Elaine Paige.

"Elaine was one of my first musical theatre idols right from the time I was a kid," she said. "I even listen to her radio show each week on BBC Radio 2. I mean, I like LuPone in many things, but not *Evita*. Hers was the first recording of it I ever heard and I was not a fan of the show for a long time because of it. It wasn't until I saw the movie that I went nuts for it," she told him.

"I have no issues with Paige, but I just prefer LuPone," he replied.

"Well, I guess you're entitled to your wrong opinion," she countered playfully.

"You can always make me laugh," he admitted with a chuckle. "I do agree with you on the movie, though. It's one of my favorite film adaptations of a musical."

"Thank God someone else agrees with me. I thought Madonna was brilliant, but so many people trash her in it," she said. "And Antonio Banderas as Che was amazing. He's my favorite Che ever." He agreed with her on that, too.

They worked on some Andrew Lloyd Webber classics then and after they sang "All I Ask of You" from *The Phantom of the Opera* he exclaimed, "Jesus, is there anything you can't sing?" He was impressed by the depth and brightness of the more classical side of her voice.

"Sadly, I could never play the role of Christine because I'm a mezzo-soprano," she lamented. "I can sing a lot of the selections from it, but I wouldn't be able to do the whole part. You also won't hear me singing 'Glitter and Be Gay' anytime soon either," she said, making reference to the difficult soprano number from Bernstein's *Candide*.

"Nevertheless, you have an insane range, on the lower end, too. I think you could easily sing alto."

"I can't sing Olivia Rodrigo songs either. She's *waaaay* too angst-y for me. I mean, somebody must have majorly fucked her over in a big way to elicit such vitriol in her songs. I'd hate to be *that* guy. I think I'd be sleeping with one eye open and constantly looking over my shoulder if I was him."

Charles burst out laughing at that. "Well, even so, you're a total chameleon. You can adapt to so many different styles, and that's a huge asset when doing theatre."

"Thanks, I've worked hard on that. My biggest idols in theatre are like that, so I always worked my ass off to be that way."

"Well, it's definitely paid off. You've succeeded quite nicely." He was always so complimentary of her talents, and it really was a confidence booster for her. "Have you ever considered doing opera?" he asked her then. "I think you could totally pull it off."

"It hasn't really been a goal of mine, no." she responded. "Although I would do *Carmen* if the opportunity ever presented itself. It's my favorite opera. Plus, the lead role is in my range, and I'm also fluent in French. So that would make it easier."

"How did you get fluent in French?" he asked, intrigued. "I can't imagine you'd have much use for it living in Seattle."

"Well my mother was raised bilingual. Her father is from England, but her mother is French. Mom wanted me to be fluent as well so she spoke to me a lot in French while I was growing up. Even now, I converse with her in French quite a bit because I don't want to lose it, and as you pointed out, there's not much opportunity to use it where I live," she explained. "And I always speak to my grandmother in French."

"That's so cool. I'm not fluent in anything, but I'm not bad in German. I've picked it up a bit over the years, mostly from singing in choirs."

"It's a good skill to have, especially for singers," said Tori.

"Oh, I almost forgot to ask you," he said. "I've acquired three tickets for Wednesday night's performance of one of the hottest shows on Broadway right now. I know Andy will be excited to go, and I know it's short notice, but I was wondering if you wanted the other ticket and would like to join us." When he told her the name of the show, her mouth dropped in surprise. It really was the hottest ticket on Broadway right now.

"Oh my God, hell yeah!" She could not contain her excitement. "Two of my favorite performers are in that. I can't thank you enough for thinking of me."

"The composers are friends of mine, so they asked if I wanted the tickets."

Tori's eyes widened. "Wait, what? You're friends with *them*?" She was impressed. They were two of the biggest names in current musical theatre.

"Yeah, I've known Tom and Jerry since undergrad." Unlike most composer duos, Thomas Parsons and Jerold Edwards were never referred to by their last names, like Rodgers & Hammerstein, Kander & Ebb, Lerner & Loewe, and the more recent duo to take the theatre world by storm, Pasek & Paul. They were affectionately known as Tom & Jerry in the theatre community, despite the fact that they always listed their full names in all their credits. The Tom and Jerry moniker stuck, much to the chagrin of both gentlemen.

"We've been trying to work on a project together for years," Charles continued, "but the timing has never been right. They're currently working on a new musical and they've asked if I'll come on as music director and also do the orchestrations."

"No way! Are you going to do it?" she asked excitedly.

"I'm thinking about it," he confessed. "It's still early days in the project, but the timing might just work out this time."

"Wow!" she said in awe. "How cool is that? Do you compose as well?"

"Sadly, no," he answered regretfully. "I can arrange anything you put in front of me for whatever musical groupings you want, but I've never had the ability to come up with something original. It's one of my great disappointments, actually."

"It really shouldn't be," she said. "We all have our

individual talents to bring to the table. That's the beautiful thing about music, you know. It's so collaborative. I mean, you put a bunch of people together, all with their own abilities, and together they create something wonderful," she reasoned.

"Well, when you put it like that," he said contemplatively, "it makes a lot of sense."

The show was as extraordinary as Tori had hoped it would be and the three of them had a marvellous time. After the show, Charles surprised her by taking them backstage to meet the cast. Tori was starstruck and practically speechless when she met the two of her idols who were in the production.

"Oh my God, I'm so embarrassed," said Tori afterward. "I was a total fan-girl back there. Those are the most famous people I've ever met." Charles found her youthful enthusiasm quite refreshing, and was thrilled that he could give her this experience.

They stopped off for some quick Chinese food after the show. Tori and Andy were animated in their discussion of the performance, and Tori and Charles talked about some current world events that were unfolding at the time. They really could talk about anything and found they had similar views on most things. Charles always found Tori to be well-informed about whatever topic they were discussing. By the end of the meal, they were both in complete hysterics, quoting lines from a comedy film that they realized they both adored. Andy looked on, utterly confused as he had not seen the movie. "I gotta see this one," he said, amused as he watched his father and Tori.

They all reached for their fortune cookies then. Charles opened his first and read his fortune to himself.

"What does it say?" Tori inquired.

"Oh, I'm not saying," Charles answered secretively. "You're not supposed to say it out loud or it won't come true."

"Is that true? I didn't know that," she said. "Well, I was today-years-old before I learned that."

Charles chuckled as he reread his fortune. "If I add 'in bed' to this, it takes on a whole new meaning and kind of makes it wildly inappropriate," he said.

"Wait, you're supposed to add 'in bed' to your fortune?" Andy asked.

"Yeah, you've never heard that before?" Charles questioned his son.

"I thought everybody knew that," Tori added.

"Well, I guess *I* was today-years-old before I learned *that*. But I *am* only fifteen, remember," Andy pointed out.

"Oh yeah, sorry Andy," Tori apologized. "I honestly keep forgetting that. You seem so much older."

Tori opened her cookie then. "Oh, what a rip-off!" she exclaimed. "There's nothing in here."

"Oh, that's actually supposed to be a good thing," said Charles. "Apparently if the cookie is empty, it means something really great is about to happen to you."

"Well, alrighty then," said Tori, popping a piece of cookie in her mouth. "Bring it on. I'll take it. Boy you're just a real wealth of knowledge about fortune cookies now aren't you," she said to Charles with a grin.

"I ate a lot of Chinese takeout as a kid," Charles replied in explanation.

Next it was Andy's turn. He read his fortune to himself and grinned. "Okay, I see what you mean about the 'in bed' thing," he said, looking a little embarrassed. "It really does make it take on a whole new meaning." They all laughed.

By the time they left the Chinese restaurant, it was getting quite late. "Tori, it's late and I don't want you taking the subway home at this hour. I'm calling you an Uber," Charles said, taking out his phone.

"Oh, I'm sure I'll be fine," she protested.

"Nope, I'm not taking any chances," he insisted. "If something were to happen to you, I'd never be able to live with myself."

Charles and Andy waited with her until her car arrived, and on the drive home, she was beaming from ear to ear, thinking about their amazing evening. And Charles was having similar thoughts as he and Andy made their way home. He thought about the fortune in his cookie that he did not share, which said "A new relationship will blossom. You will be blessed."

When they saw each other the next day, Charles immediately picked up on the fact that Tori was much more subdued, and he questioned her about it. "You don't seem like your usual perky self today. Are you okay?" he asked gently.

Tori knew why she wasn't her usual self, but it was something she chose not to talk to many people about. "I'm fine, just a little tired," she lied, and despite his concern, Charles let the subject go.

When she spoke to Evan that night, he said, "I've been thinking of you today. I know this is a hard day for you."

"I keep wondering if it will ever get easier," she confessed grimly.

"I know," he said with his usual gentle concern. "I just really wish I could be there with you today and put my arms around you. You know I love you, right?"

Tori smiled. "I've never been more sure of anything in my life," she replied.

When she met with Charles again a couple of days later on Saturday afternoon, she was back to her normal self and he made a mental note of it, happy to see her in her usual upbeat mood.

She was a little early and he still needed to clue up something he was working on. "I'll just need a couple more minutes here, so make yourself comfortable and feel free to look though some of my music to see if anything strikes your fancy," he directed.

She pulled out his Sondheim anthology and his Andrew Lloyd Webber songbook, as well as the Disney collection they had been using, and a book of standards. She saw a bunch of his conductor's scores in the shelf and took one down, curious to see what one looked like up close. "Holy shit," she murmured under her breath.

Charles finished what he was doing then and came over to stand next to her. "Have you ever seen a full score like that before?" he asked.

"No, not this close up," she answered. "How the hell can you keep track of all of this?" she asked with amazement as she looked over the complex score.

"It's definitely an acquired skill," he admitted. "Why do you think I have a PhD?" he answered with smiling eyes and a laugh. Tori realized that this man always found ways to keep impressing her.

She replaced the score and spotted a display of his conductor's batons on the shelf then. She walked over to them and asked, "What's the difference between all these batons?"

He walked over and stood by her. "Well," he began, "they all have different uses depending on the size of the group you're leading." He picked up the shortest one. "This one is used for choral conducting mostly, while the middle-sized one is for smaller groups like jazz bands or concert bands. This is the one I'll use this summer on the cruise." He replaced that one and picked up another, which was considerably longer. "This one is for full-sized orchestras so that it can be seen by musicians from a longer distance."

"How do you hold it?" she asked, genuinely interested and hanging on his every word.

He moved behind her then and encircled her in his arms, taking her hand and placing the handle of the baton properly in her palm and adjusting her small delicate fingers into the correct position. She was acutely aware of his chest pressed against her back and realized she had never been in such close proximity to him before. As he guided her hand though the motions of the proper movement of the baton, she could feel his warm breath on her neck and realized she had been holding her own for what felt like minutes. Her heart was hammering so hard that she felt as though the entire drum section of a marching band had taken up residence in her chest, and she was amazed Charles couldn't feel her pulse racing as he continued to hold her hand in place on the baton. His touch sent chills down her spine.

Charles could feel the same electric current surge through his body that Tori had. His lips gently brushed her hair as he spoke to her from behind, and he caught the smell of vanilla emanating from her soft curls. He would have liked nothing better in that moment than to bury his face in her luxurious mane of hair and lose himself in her scent. Instead, he moved away and demonstrated the balance of the baton.

"Professional batons," he began, now facing her, "are made of wood, and they need to be perfectly balanced." He placed the baton on the top of his finger at the base of its handle and Tori could see that the handle was perfectly balanced with the rest of the stick.

"So," he said then as he replaced the baton on the shelf, "did you see anything else of interest in those music books?"

His question jolted her out of her trance, breaking the spell she had fallen under, and she was finally able to breathe properly again. "Yes," she said, "I did. Actually, I saw a few in here that I think would be excellent for you. I'd love for you to do more than just those few duets with me."

"Well, I guess I could do that," he replied, considering what she had said. "It would spell you off for a few minutes every now and then, if nothing else. What did you have in mind?"

"I think these are two of the most amazing songs ever written for musical theatre. 'Being Alive' from *Company* and 'Not While I'm Around' from *Sweeney Todd*," she said, handing him the Sondheim book open to "Being Alive."

"Oh, I know them well and also love them," he said. "Okay, I'll give it a try." He began playing the opening bars of "Being Alive" and just as she had thought, it was perfect for his voice. Then he went through "Not While I'm Around" and she thought he did an equally exceptional job on that one, stumbling only a couple of times on the keyboard over some of Sondheim's complex chord structures.

"Those are both keepers," she said when he had finished. Listening to him sing had set her heart beating in overdrive again. Then, she had one more song selection for him. She handed him the Andrew Lloyd Webber collection open to "Love Changes Everything" from *Aspects of Love*. "Another of my all-time favorites," she said.

He sang that one beautifully as well, and as he performed it, he found the words taking on a whole new meaning, and realized he was singing it directly to her. She closed her eyes as she listened to him, and allowed herself to get lost in his glorious dulcet tones.

"Another keeper," she said. "You could have a second career doing this any time you want."

"Oh you flatter me too much," he said modestly.

"No, I'm completely serious," she complimented him again. "You nailed those."

"So, anything new for you that you'd like to try?" he asked.

She passed him a Leonard Bernstein collection she had found on the shelf. "There are definitely some things of his I'd like to do," she answered. They went over some selections from *West Side Story*, and Tori wanted to try "A Little Bit in Love" from *Wonderful Town*, which was one of her favorite showtunes. As she sang it, she realized how perfectly the lyrics summed up the feelings she was developing for Charles.

"Beautiful," he said when she finished the song.

They went over some other songs then for awhile and finally, realizing the time, she said, "I'd better get going. Chanel's mother is in town this week and my aunt Helen and I are going to do some stuff with them tonight."

He was more sorry than usual to see their time together come to an end. "Have a great time," he said.

"Thanks, I will. See you on Monday," said Tori cheerfully, also sad to see their time together coming to a close.

After she left, Charles sat at his desk for quite some time, thinking of her and wondering what the hell had just happened between them. He was definitely developing intense feelings for her, but one thing he knew for certain: he could not give into them. His marriage was a complicated debacle that he could see no way out of, and she was engaged and much too young for him.

At the same time, while in transit back to Queens, Tori was asking herself the same questions about her feelings for him. This was insane. She was about to marry the most wonderful guy in the world - her best friend. She convinced herself that this was just a fleeting infatuation with a very attractive man, and knew she could not let it go beyond that.

Tori and her aunt Helen took an immediate liking to Chanel's mother. They went to Ellen's Stardust Diner for dinner that night, a New York institution that drew hundreds of tourists each day, and boasted queues far down the block at all times of the day. The environment in the restaurant was fun and lively, with servers performing showtunes while customers enjoyed their classic American dishes.

After dinner, they took a walk around Time's Square and the Theatre District, browsing in the various shops along the way and taking pictures of all the theater marquees. They stopped by the TKTS booth where Helen bought them all tickets to see *Chicago* that night, which they all thoroughly enjoyed.

"Helen, I can't allow you to do this!" Brenda Price exclaimed after Helen purchased the show tickets. "You already paid for dinner. It's just too much."

"Now don't you give it another thought. I'm not taking no for an answer," Helen replied vehemently to Brenda's protests. "I so rarely get a chance to treat friends to things like this. I've been having a ball spoiling Victoria since she's been here, and it's my absolute pleasure to treat you and Chanel to a night out on the town to make your visit more memorable. So I don't want to hear another word about it."

"Well, I can't thank you enough," Brenda gushed appreciatively. "You just met us and you're being so generous."

They agreed to meet the next day, Chanel's mother's last day in New York, to spend a Sunday afternoon at the Statue of Liberty. Brenda insisted on paying the additional fee to upgrade all of their tickets from the general admission, which would allow them access to the viewing deck in the statue's crown.

"Will you be going on one of the cruises this summer?" Helen asked Brenda once they were atop the statue. They all felt like they had known one another forever by then.

"Unfortunately not," Brenda said regretfully. "I've actually never been on one of the cruises in either season Chanel has done it. It's just not in my budget unfortunately. Just coming on this trip for a few days stretched my finances enough as it is. You know, a teacher's salary and all that," she laughed. It was spring break for her that week, so she didn't need to take any extra time off work to be there. "I'm just happy to be here with my baby girl for whatever time I can," she said, her pride quite obvious as she beamed at her daughter.

"Aww, Mama, I'm so glad you're here," Chanel said, hugging her mother. They had had a terrific week together, and Chanel was more than happy to get a few nights away from her crowded living arrangement.

When Tori and Helen got home that evening, Helen proposed an idea to Tori that had occurred to her that afternoon. "I just feel like I'd really like to pay for that amazing woman to go on one of the cruises this summer," she suggested. Helen was very well-off financially, although she didn't flaunt it in the least. "Do you think that's too forward of me? I wouldn't want to insult her pride. Do you think she'd even consider such an offer?"

"Well, she's a teacher, so she'd definitely have some freedom during the summer to go," Tori considered. "That's a lovely gesture, Aunt Helen. You are such a thoughtful and generous person. I just love you to pieces."

"I just believe that if you have it, you should share it," Helen said. "I like her and Chanel a whole lot, and I'd love to do this for her."

"Well, you guys said you were going to keep in touch.

So why don't you do that and see what you think in a couple of weeks or so? You might get a better feeling about her receptiveness to it when you get to know her better," Tori suggested. Helen was planning to take one of the cruises that summer as well. "Maybe you could bring it up by proposing that she go on the same sailing as you're on, and that you'd like her to go with you for company. Your treat," Tori mused.

"That's a good idea," Helen agreed. "I can really see us becoming good friends."

"We can get you a decent discount as staff members, too," said Tori. "They offer it to staff for family members. Charles Ryan is doing that for his teenage son. He's on two of the sailings this summer: one at the start of his school vacation, and another at the end."

"Oh, that would be wonderful. It might help soften the blow for her if she knew I didn't have to spend as much money to take her along."

Tori hugged her aunt and, once again counted herself lucky to be related to her.

Chapter 5

During the final two weeks of rehearsals, things amped up quite a bit as all the elements of the shows started to come together. In the last week, they began rehearsing more with all the musicians, rather than just the piano accompanist, and it suddenly felt like things were all falling into place. Charles was present more regularly by then, as classes at Juilliard had ended for the semester. Also in the final couple of weeks, Charles began to assemble the musicians who would be playing in the big band for the weekly formal ball that would happen on each sailing. Tori also needed to attend those rehearsals, as she and Matt, the male lead in the stage show, would be singing several numbers with the band for that as well. Things were made even busier with final wardrobe fittings and decisions about hair and makeup. But as rehearsals revved up, so too did Tori's butterflies, and she noticed her anxieties had begun to creep in again as the time for the sailings drew closer.

At the end of the last week, Tori and Charles got together for the last time to go over their music and finalize their lounge sets. They both had come to cherish their time together and were sad to see it end, but they knew they would still be spending a lot of time together once they started working on board the cruise ship. After they finished their rehearsal together, he looked out his office window and said, "It's a beautiful afternoon out there and I don't have anything else going on today. It seems a shame to waste such a lovely spring day, so what do you say we blow this joint? Do you want to go to Central Park with me for a walk?"

Tori couldn't think of anything she'd rather do. "I'd love

it," she answered with a broad smile.

They took the quick cab ride from Juilliard to Central Park. It really was a lovely spring day and warm enough that they only needed light jackets.

"So, will you get some down time on the few days we have before the cruise sets sail?" she asked him as they walked.

"A bit," he answered. "The semester is winding down and I'll only have some exams to mark. I'm going to go to New Haven for a couple of days to visit my parents. I won't see them for months once the cruise gets underway."

"Tell me more about your parents," she requested, always eager to learn more about him.

"My mom is a psychologist, and my dad is a lawyer, and neither one of them is in any hurry to retire. They are amazing people and just as in love with each other as the day they were married. They have something really special. I always hoped I'd find that in my own life, but sadly, it didn't work out that way," said Charles regretfully.

"I'm so sorry Charles. You deserve so much better."

"I've made my peace with it. For the most part, my life is great. I love what I do and, at forty, I can honestly say that my career is in a good place, and I have a son I adore. I can't ask for more. My marriage is the only missing piece to my ideal life."

"So, if I'm getting too personal, just say so," she said, carefully broaching the subject, "but when did things go sour between you two?"

"I don't know if they ever weren't sour, to be honest." He took a deep breath and continued. "Meredith got pregnant when we were dating. It was never a deep love between us or anything. We were kind of on-again, off-again during my undergrad degree. We never had a lot of interests in common. She didn't share my passion for music and performing, and I didn't care about fashion and social status. When she got pregnant, I wanted to do the honorable thing, so I married her. It was really important to me for my child to grow up in a stable home with two parents, like I did. Once I got used to the idea that we were having a baby, I was thrilled. She, however, definitely was not. When Andy was born it was love at first sight for me, but she never bonded with him. She had really severe postpartum depression and she resented me after Andy was born. She was starting to really emerge in the field of interior design, and she had to give it up for awhile because of the depression. She blamed me for ruining her life. Things never did get any better for us and all we have in common is our address. She lives her life and I live mine. We never see one another and we're barely civil when we do. I always wanted so much more out of marriage than that. The only good thing that came out of it was Andy." He paused, smiling at the thought of his son. "You asked me when we first met why I wanted to do the cruise thing, and what I told you is all totally true, but the other element to that is that being on the cruise for four months a year gives me a break from my shitstorm of a personal life for awhile. Once Andy started doing summer theatre camp a few years ago, I figured I had nothing to stay around for."

Tori was quiet for a moment, taking in all he had said. "Why have you never ended the marriage?" she finally asked.

"A lot of reasons," he began. "First there was Andy. I didn't want to put him through that. Besides, I didn't want him living, even part of the time, with a mother who barely acknowledged his existence. Essentially, I'm the only parent he has and we're so close. I couldn't risk losing him. The other reasons," he continued, "had to do with her constant threats that she would destroy my life if I left her, just like I destroyed hers. She said she'd see to it that I never saw my son. She also threatened me financially and professionally. Her spending habits have gotten quite extravagant over the years. She spends money faster than I can make it, and she says she'll take me for everything I have if I leave her. Also, her father is a very important man. He's the president of a major bank." When he told her his father-in-law's name, she instantly recognized it. "He is a major supporter of arts programs, both personally and on the corporate level," he continued. "He also sits on the boards of several arts organizations in New York, so his name pulls a lot of weight in this town, not to mention his money. He did help me get my foot in the door when I was starting out, and Meredith takes great joy in reminding me of that. She says her father made me and he can just as easily break me. I've worked hard to get to where I am and I just don't want to risk it."

"So it sounds like she comes from money, so why does she need to threaten you about yours?" asked Tori.

"Because she can. She's vindictive as fuck," he said, defeated. "Yes, she has access to as much money as she wants from her old man, but she delights in torturing me and making me suffer. She'd like nothing better than to take me down when she takes everything I have. But at the end of the day, it has nothing to do with money and everything to do with control. In her mind, it's all my fault that she ended up with a kid she didn't want and married to a man she didn't love, so she's hell-bent on making me pay for it for the rest of my life."

"I guess the one piece of good news is that Andy is growing up and will be out from under her influence in a few years," Tori pointed out. "So she won't be able to hold him over you anymore."

"That is true, but there's still all the other stuff. Like I said, I've made peace with it and as far as Meredith is concerned, I have zero fucks left to give. She's a menace, but at least I hardly ever have to see her. That makes it a little easier to cope with. Looking back on it all, I should never have married her. I should have just taken Andy and raised him on my own. I've pretty much done that for all these years anyway. But I guess hindsight is twenty-twenty."

"I think you're giving her way too much power over you," Tori said. "I mean, you've established yourself now and are well respected. Maybe the fallout wouldn't be as bad as you think," she suggested. "It seems a high price to pay for your happiness." They had stopped walking by then and were sitting on a secluded bench.

"You may be right," he conceded, "but I've always just

thought it would be easier to avoid the mess and ugliness and not upset the proverbial apple cart."

"That's a very sad situation," Tori said. "My parents had a really volatile marriage and ugly divorce as well, so I understand where you're coming from. My dad screwed around excessively on my mother in his younger days. I swear, I've thought many times that I could have siblings out there that I'll never know about. It was horrible for my mother. Anyway, my mother did the same thing you did. She stayed with him for our sake, but we saw the tension and the fighting. It wasn't a great situation for us either."

"Us?" Charles questioned. "You have siblings?"

"No, I..." she hesitated, not intending to let that piece of information slip. This was a part of her life that she assiduously avoided talking about. "I don't anymore," she finally said sadly. "I had an older brother," she clarified, nervously fiddling with the buttons on her jacket.

"What happened?" he asked gingerly, sensing this would not have a happy ending.

Tori pursed her lips and drew in a deep, thoughtful breath before she continued. "He died when I was twelve," she volunteered. "He was fifteen. He committed suicide," she revealed, her eyes clouding with unshed tears and her voice quivering.

"Same age as Andrew is now," he observed.

"Yes, same age as Andrew, a fact that was not lost on me when I first met him," said Tori.

"Oh my God, Tori, that's terrible!" he said in astonishment.

"James was the center of my universe. I absolutely idolized him," she said with tears now brimming in her eyes. "He was relentlessly bullied, and I guess he just couldn't take it anymore. He hung himself in my dad's garage. My mother found him." She paused for a moment to compose herself. "I don't talk about it to anyone. I just tell people I'm an only child," she continued. "The only people who know are the people who knew us back then. That's when my friendship with Evan, my fiancé, really started to deepen. We've been best friends since we were four. We went to the same school, same grade, and even lived on the same street when we were kids. We are literally the boy and girl next door. Then it's like he filled the void my brother left in my life. Anyway, James' death was the final blow to my parents' marriage. They blamed themselves and each other for what happened, and by the end of that year, they were split. I went back and forth between them during junior high and high school, and I will say, my father did grow up after that. He's remarried now to a wonderful woman and treats her like gold. If he had been the kind of husband to my mother that he is to her, maybe they'd still be married. They actually get along better apart than they did when they were together."

"I've actually heard that before from other people I know who have divorced," he said.

"Well, there you go then. Maybe if you and Meredith finally made the break, you'd actually start getting along."

Charles rolled his eyes. "Somehow I doubt that," he commented dryly. "But Tori, I can't tell you how sorry I am about your brother," he said sympathetically.

Tori sobered again. "Thank you," she said. "I'll never get over losing him. I keep waiting for it to get easier, but it sits in my heart like a dull ache all the time." She felt immense relief in finally sharing the sad story with someone.

"I can't even imagine what it must be like," he said, unable to comprehend carrying the weight of such a heavy burden.

"Remember a couple of weeks ago when you said I didn't seem like myself and you asked me what was wrong, and I just told you I was tired?" she asked.

"Yes, I remember," he replied in a quiet, sympathetic tone.

"Well, that day was the anniversary of his death. I barely function through it every year, even all these years later," she admitted, her eyes swimming with tears.

"Oh, Tori, I knew you weren't right, but it seemed like you wanted to drop the subject, so I let it go," said Charles, his voice filled with concern, his eyes full of compassion.

"Well, like I said, I don't talk about it." She wasn't even sure what had possessed her to open up to him about it that day. She was openly crying now, and buried her face in her hands.

There was so much to unpack to this story, and Charles sat digesting it for a moment, visibly moved by all she had told him. Tori was crying harder now and he could not resist the urge to take her in his arms and hold her as she sobbed. He drew her into his embrace as she fumbled for tissues in her purse.

"It's okay, just let it out and cry as long as you need to. I'm here. I'm not going anywhere," he consoled softly, his voice a soothing caress, as he kissed her forehead and smoothed her hair back from her face. He took her hand and threaded his fingers through hers, giving her hand a reassuring squeeze. She clung tightly to him as if she were drowning and he was her life raft. At that moment, he knew without a doubt that he loved her with everything in his soul, and also knew that all he wanted to do for the rest of his life was kiss away her tears, take away all her hurts, and do everything in his power to make her happy. She was an extraordinary young woman, and such a paradox in so many ways: bubbly, yet quiet and shy, confident, yet modest, strong, yet vulnerable. He found everything about her so alluring, and he loved every single facet of who she was. He knew with certainty that he had never felt like this before, but also knew he could never act on it.

They sat like that for a long time, and he held her until her tears finally subsided. The late afternoon sunlight kissed her hair and highlighted all of its natural red and golden hues, and even with her tear-stained face and puffy eyes, Charles thought she was the most beautiful thing he had ever seen in his life. "Thank you," he said looking deep into her sorrowful eyes with all the love he felt for her, trying to convey just how honored he was that she had opened up to him about this very tragic and painful detail of her life.

"Why are you thanking me?" she asked, puzzled. "I'm the one who should be thanking you." She bowed her head in order to avert her eyes, feeling a little embarrassed for letting down her defenses and allowing herself to be so emotionally exposed with him.

"Hey, hey, look at me," he whispered as he placed his hand under her delicate chin and tilted her head toward him so their eyes met. He took her face in his hands and tenderly stroked her cheeks with his fingertips. Their faces were so close together that he could feel her warm breath on his lips, and he ached to kiss her at that moment, but knew it would be inappropriate. "Thank you for being so open, and for sharing such a raw part of yourself with me. I'm truly honored."

Tori's heart raced as Charles bent his head slightly so their foreheads were touching, their lips mere inches apart. In that instant there was nothing in the world she wanted more than to feel his lips on hers. *Oh please kiss me*, she silently implored him. She looked into his warm hazel eyes and knew she could no longer deny what she felt for him. "I'm so sorry, Charles, I never intended to unload all of this on you today," she said mournfully. "I guess when the floodgates opened, I just couldn't stop it."

"Don't apologize," he said sincerely. "You needed to let it out. It's not healthy to keep things bottled up like that. I'm just glad I could be here for you. And I want you to know that I'm here for you any time you need a shoulder."

"Thanks Charles. You've been a huge comfort to me today. I can't tell you how much you... I mean, *it*, means to me," she said, quickly covering her blunder and mentally berating herself for almost saying too much.

"You've become very important to me, Tori," he said, trying not to be too obvious about his feelings for her. "I really value your friendship."

"Ditto," she said with a smile. She desperately wanted to tell him the full extent of what he meant to her, but didn't dare betray her feelings.

They left the park then, arm in arm, in companionable silence, each consumed with their own private avalanche of emotions for one another. They both were acutely aware that their relationship had progressed to another level that day, and both were at a complete loss as to what that meant for their future.

The next day was the final day of rehearsals and they basically ran both shows in a dress rehearsal fashion. There was nothing else they could do now until they were able to access the ship's theater when they boarded in a few days.

On her last night with her aunt Helen, Tori inquired about how things were going for Helen and her developing friendship with Chanel's mom.

"Oh really well. We have contact most every day. We call or text and we're friends on Facebook now," her aunt replied enthusiastically.

"I take it you haven't broached the subject of the cruise with her yet."

"No, not yet. I'm getting there, but I want to make sure it's the right time," Helen explained.

"Yeah, I totally get that," said Tori. "But don't wait too long. I'd hate for you to lose your chance to book. Do it before it's too late," she cautioned.

"Yes, I've been thinking that, too," Helen replied. "Don't worry, I'm going to discuss it with her soon. I'll let you know as soon as I have any news for you."

The next day, Tori bid farewell to her aunt and boarded a plane back to Seattle for her final weekend at home before leaving for the cruise season to Alaska. She thought of Charles as she sat on the plane, wishing life didn't have to be so complicated.

She spent the weekend with Evan and visited her father and stepmom, packed her things and wondered what the upcoming months held in store for her.

She spent a quiet evening with Evan on the night before she left, and when he made love to her, she was ashamed to admit to herself that she was fantasizing of Charles. And when she finally fell into a restless sleep, she dreamed of him.

Part 2

The Cruise

Chapter 6

The Dream Cruise Line ship *Aurora* set sail the next day, and everyone was in a jovial mood as they boarded and got settled into their quarters. The first night, a meeting was called for the entire cast in the ship's theater to discuss the itinerary for the next few days.

As soon as Tori saw Charles, her heart soared. Even after only a few days, she had missed him desperately. He brought the meeting to order and told everyone that they only had a few days to get settled into the theater and run some full dress rehearsals before shows began. "Our shows will run every Wednesday and Saturday evenings. We will run two performances each night: one early and one later, in order to allow everyone an opportunity to attend," he told them. "So, first thing tomorrow, we all need to be back in here, ready to go to do a tech run-through of both shows, which will just be a cue-to-cue rehearsal. Wednesday morning we'll do a full dress rehearsal of the first show and Saturday morning we'll do the dress for the second show. Wednesday night it's show time. It's going to be a very busy week and we need to hit the ground running, so make sure you get your sleep. We need you at your best."

With those words, Tori felt the familiar nervous lurch in her stomach. After the meeting was adjourned, she went out into the main part of the theater to acquaint herself with the surroundings and get a feel for the space. Seeing the sets all in place suddenly made it all seem real to her and she felt slightly sick. It was there where Charles found her a few minutes later.

"Hey, you okay?" he asked gently.

"Yeah, it's just, well, this is starting to get real right now," she answered, looking panicked. "For the last six weeks it's been something we've done in a rehearsal space, but now..." her voice trailed off and she was at a loss for words.

Charles came over to stand beside her and placed a reassuring arm around her shoulders. "You're going to be fine. You're spectacular in this and you're going to do a wonderful job," he said in his most soothing voice, knowing her anxiety was probably raging. "I have complete faith in you."

"That makes one of us. I just don't want to screw this up and give you guys any reason to regret giving me this opportunity," she said with a plaintive sigh as her mouth curved into a strained smile.

"I don't think there's much chance of that happening," he said. "And if you need a little moral support, you can look over at my head sticking out of the pit and know how much I believe in you."

Tori thought that was one of the sweetest things he'd ever said to her, and she smiled, feeling much better. "You always know just the right thing to say," she said, wishing more than anything that she could tell him how much she loved him.

The next couple of days were hectic. When they weren't in rehearsals at the theater, Tori and Charles had to race to the lounge to do their sets. The rehearsals over the next two days went pretty well considering it was their first time in the theater, and in the blink of an eye, Wednesday night arrived and she found herself standing in the wings in full costume, ready to go.

In an effort to settle her nerves, Tori inhaled deeply while counting to four, held her breath for a count of seven, and then exhaled slowly, while counting to eight. This was a breathing exercise she had learned in college, and had always found to be helpful for lowering her heart rate and calming her nerves. She heard the voice of the stage manager backstage calling "Ten minutes" and her heart started beating faster again. It was then that she saw Charles approaching her in his full tux, and her heart skipped a beat as she realized how right Chanel had been on that very first day when she told Tori how striking he looked in it. She felt herself go weak in the knees, and was no longer certain if the butterflies in her stomach were due to nerves or from seeing Charles looking so devastatingly handsome. For a fleeting moment, she wished she could discover what lay beneath his well-groomed exterior, but quickly banished her fantasies of exploring his sensational body from her mind, as she forced herself to return to the present moment, and concentrated on the task at hand.

"So, how are you doing? I knew you'd be nervous so I wanted to make sure I saw you before we start," said Charles. "So, are you whistling a happy tune?" he asked with a grin.

She laughed in spite of her nerves. His presence was such a comfort to her, and he always seemed to know exactly what to say to make her feel better. "I can't whistle, remember?" she replied.

"Oh that's right," he said. "Well are you humming a happy tune?" he asked, his grin broadening into a full smile that warmed Tori from the bottom of her heart.

She chuckled again. "Oh trust me," she said, "I've been singing that all day."

"Five minutes," announced the stage manager. Tori took another deep breath.

"Hey, don't worry, you're golden," he said, resisting the tremendous urge to kiss her, but giving her a peck on the check instead. "I gotta go get in place, but I wanted to check in with you first. Good luck. You'll be wonderful," he said in his most comforting voice. He would very much have liked to add "I love you" to the end of that, but caught himself.

"Places," called the stage manager a moment later. She heard Charles start the overture, and as she stood listening to the orchestra, she thought of him and felt her tummy start to settle.

The curtain rose and she looked directly at him. He caught her glance and smiled encouragingly at her. She relaxed and gave an awe-inspiring performance. Everything went perfectly and the audience applauded and cheered their appreciation at the end as the cast took their bows. They did the second performance of the show later that night to equal accolades from the crowd.

After the show, Charles approached her, flashing the most dazzling smile she had ever seen on his face. "Brava!" he said, squeezing her tightly in a warm congratulatory hug. "I told you you'd be brilliant."

She beamed back at him. "It's all thanks to you," she said. "I couldn't have done this without your encouragement and belief in me."

"No, that has nothing to do with it," he said, diminishing his role in her success. "You've done lots of shows in your life without me and done just fine. This is all you, and I'm so very proud of you," he praised her, with all his pride in her evident in his eyes.

The atmosphere backstage afterward was very celebratory and jubilant. There really was no feeling like that of a successful opening night. Tori saw Chanel then and they ran to hug each other, ecstatic over their first performances. Chanel had been incredible as well. They all had.

During that first week, they didn't go off the ship in the ports of call at all. They were all too busy getting settled into their jobs on board. Tori enjoyed everything she was doing and realized that this job was allowing her the opportunity to tap into all her favorite musical styles and genres. Her lounge sets with Charles all went well and the guests loved them. Right away, she was being stopped in the corridors by passengers who said they really enjoyed her and Charles, and commented that they were a wonderful duo.

But the family karaoke was the thing Tori found to be the most fun. She hosted it every night when they didn't have a stage show. It was great fun, even despite the sometimes horrible singing by the guests. But occasionally, someone really great got up to sing and astonished everyone. The kids were the sweetest part of it. Sometimes they'd get up, very shy at first, with their parents urging them on, and by the end of the song, had completely broken out of their shells. Tori loved working the event with Chanel in the tech booth at the back of the room, and she enjoyed kicking off the show each day by performing a selection of her own, which helped to warm up the crowd and gave people a chance to get their requests in to Chanel. She would start off by singing a showtune, Disney song, upbeat pop classic or hot new hit by the biggest current artists. Sometimes she would sing a song that secretly perfectly articulated her feelings for Charles. One night it was Dua Lipa's "Break My Heart," while on another she sang "Clumsy" by Fergie. She realized soon after they set sail that she had moved past denial about her feelings for him. Now she was more focused on the challenge of concealing them.

Charles often stopped by karaoke, mostly out of interest to check out what number Tori would open with. Sometimes he'd even sing a song himself or a duet with her. One night, he sang "Somebody's Baby" by Jackson Browne, and on another occasion he did Hall & Oates' "Rich Girl," which made Tori giggle when she realized who he was singing it about.

"Oh my God, that was hilarious," she said as they laughed about it later. "I bet I know who that was for."

"I honestly think that song should be subtitled 'Meredith's Song,' that's how perfectly it fits her." They both laughed at that.

"You seem really relaxed at karaoke," he observed. "It's the least nervous I've ever seen you."

"That's because the lyrics are on the prompter if I need them," she explained. "I hardly ever need to look at them, but it's sort of a security blanket kind of thing, just knowing that they're there."

One night in that first week, she opened with a song she loved, "That's How You Know" from Disney's *Enchanted.* Every little girl in the room was literally enchanted watching this young woman who looked and sang so much like a real princess, and while he listened to her singing the lyrics, Charles got an idea.

Before they knew it, the first cruise was drawing to a close and they were getting ready for their Broadway revue show on Saturday. While still struggling with her ever-present nervousness, Tori was much more relaxed and the show went as well as the first one had, and was just as well received by the audience.

When they docked in Seattle on Monday for the turnover, she met up with Evan for lunch. She excitedly talked about the first week and how well everything had gone.

"I honestly think I'm finally starting to come into my own as a performer," she told him. "I've struggled for so long to feel like I'm equal to everyone else, but Charles has been so encouraging and complimentary to me. I think he's actually starting to make a difference in how I see myself."

"Well, I'm glad someone else sees what I've always seen in you. It's about time you clued in," he said with a grin as he leaned in for a kiss.

"So what's new with you?" she asked.

"Not a whole lot really," he answered. "I had dinner at your dad's a couple of times this week. They want to make sure I don't starve. They had me over a bunch while you were in New York, too. Between your parents and mine, I've hardly had to eat at home for months." Truth be told, Evan was quite capable in the kitchen and always did his fair share of the cooking.

"How are they?" she asked.

"They're fine, the usual."

"I should try to meet up with Dad next week when I'm here."

Tori's phone rang then and she saw it was her aunt Helen. "Oh, I need to take this," she said, answering the call.

"Hi Aunt Helen," she said, happy to hear from her. "I miss you."

"Hi sweetie, I miss you, too. I just couldn't wait another minute to hear how your first week went."

Tori filled her in and Helen was overjoyed to hear how happy Tori was sounding. Before they hung up, Helen said, "I've got good news for you. I convinced Brenda Price to accompany me on the cruise." She sounded elated.

"Oh my God, that's amazing!" Tori shouted. "How did she react?"

"Well, it took a few tries. The first time she refused outright, but I held my ground. I told her I didn't want to go all by myself, so she'd be doing me a great favor because I would have so much better a time if I had a buddy with me. Then, when she found out about the discount, she finally relented. She was overwhelmed by the gesture."

"Oh, I am over the moon! Chanel will be so excited. She doesn't really let on how disappointed she is that her mom can't afford to go, but I know how much she'd love for her to come and do the cruise with her and see her perform. You really are an angel on earth, Aunt Helen. I'll send you the discount code right away, so you can get it booked. Let me know your dates as soon as you have the info."

"I will darling. I can hardly wait."

"I know, me neither," she said before they hung up.

It was time for her to get back to the ship then. All aboard was at four o'clock and it was now three-thirty. Thankfully, they were not far from the dock. She kissed Evan and hastily made her way back.

When she got back to her room, Chanel was there and greeted her with a giant hug. "My mama called," she said excitedly. "She told me about coming on the cruise, and it's all thanks to your aunt. Oh Tori," she gushed, jumping up and down, "I don't know what to say. This is amazing! There's no way I can thank her enough."

"You don't have to," Tori reassured her friend. "She really wanted to do it. She spoke to me about it right after we came home from the Statue of Liberty. She liked your mom so much right away, and it seems like they're becoming great friends."

"I know. Mama loves your aunt, too. The friendship has

been really good for her," Chanel beamed. "Oh, I can't wait!"

Chapter 7

The second week was much more relaxed as everyone started to settle into their various routines. Tori was really excited to explore the ports of call, which were Skagway, Juneau, and Ketchikan. Chanel was already quite familiar with each place from the last two seasons that she had been on the cruise, so she acted as a tour guide for Tori, who had never been to Alaska before. Tori had a great time exploring the shops and tourist attractions, and hoped to get to know the ports better as the months went by.

Performances of the shows went well again in the second week and Tori was in the best vocal shape of her life, singing multiple times a day, between the stage shows, the lounges, and karaoke.

As Charles had predicted, a camaraderie between the cast and crew developed once everyone was under one roof. The staff lounge was always an entertaining place to be. It is always fun when musicians get together in a social setting, as a jam session can break out at any time. Such was the case one day when Charles was looking for Tori to inform her of a slight change to their schedule in the lounge, and walked in to an impromptu performance of "Boho Days" from *tick, tick... BOOM!* being sung by Jeremy, a member of the show company, while everyone else provided the accompanying clapping parts contained in the song.

"This looks like fun," Charles said to Tori, grinning.

"Do you have your trumpet on board?" she asked him.

"Yes, I do," he confirmed. He always brought it along in

case he needed it. Sometimes he would need to sub in for a sick trumpeter for a show, and often the brass players would get together and form a quartet or quintet.

"Go get it," she encouraged. He did and joined in on the jam.

Quite often, the gang would go to the dance club on board later in the evenings when Chanel and a couple of the others were working there. Neither Charles nor Tori were big drinkers, but they always had a great time, and the mood was always lively.

Charles adored watching Tori interact with the passengers on board. When she encountered French cruisers, she would frequently converse with them in her fluent French, making friends on every sailing. Little girls would often approach her in the lounge or at karaoke when she sang princess songs, which Charles found to be very sweet. And Tori was always so good with them, engaging them in conversation.

On one particular occasion, a little girl of about six came up to Tori after she finished their lounge set with "Let It Go" from *Frozen*, which was always a favorite with the younger set. "Are you a real princess?" she asked Tori shyly.

"Do you think I'm a real princess?" asked Tori.

"Yes," said the little girl. "You look like one, and you sing like one."

"Oh, thank you. You're so sweet," replied Tori. "Are *you* a real princess?" she asked the child then.

"No," she answered, giggling.

"Why not? I think you're a real princess."

"Why?" the little girl asked, bemused.

Tori bent down so she was at eye level with her and whispered, "I'm going to tell you a secret. I think that we're all princesses in our own special way."

"Really?" the child said, wide-eyed.

"Really," Tori confirmed.

"Why?" she asked quizzically.

"Because," Tori began, as if she was letting the little girl in on a secret reserved only for her, "there's something about every one of us that makes us really special. There's nobody else in the world like you, and that makes you unique. We all have something special about us that nobody else in the whole world has, and that, in my opinion, makes us all princesses."

"Wow, that's cool," she said. "I'll remember that forever."

"What's your name, sweetheart?" Tori asked her.

"Brittney," she answered.

"Okay, Brittney," said Tori, "whenever I see you around this week, I'll call you Princess Brittney. How's that?"

"Awesome!" she cried. "What's your name?"

"Tori."

"Then I'll call you Princess Tori from now on." Brittney hugged Tori then and left the lounge with her parents, smiling broadly as she waved goodbye.

"Oh my God," Tori said to Charles as she watched the child walk away, waving to her as she went. "How freakin' adorable was that?"

Just when Charles thought he couldn't love her more, he witnessed an exchange like that one, and he fell in love with her all over again.

Perhaps Charles' favorite interaction he observed between Tori and a passenger in those first few weeks happened at karaoke. A young teenage girl named Erica, got up and sang "Home" from *The Wiz,* and she blew everyone away. After karaoke that night, Erica approached Tori to tell her how amazing she thought she was.

"Forget about me," Tori said, *"you're* amazing. You blew my mind tonight. How old are you?"

"Thirteen," she replied.

"Oh my God, *thirteen*, wow!" Tori said. "Well let me tell you, when I was thirteen, I wasn't anywhere close to as good as you are right now."

"Really?" Erica said, overwhelmed by the compliment.

"Yeah, really. So I assume you probably do musicals and

stuff like that at school."

"Yes, and community theatre as well," Erica confirmed.

"Well, you just keep doing what you're doing. You can only get better and better as you mature as a performer. I know you're going places, girlfriend," Tori said encouragingly.

"Thank you so much," Erica said with a blush at Tori's approval.

"Where are you from?" Tori asked with genuine interest.

"Pittsburgh," she answered.

"Oh, I spent a lot of time in Pittsburgh," Tori said. "I went to Carnegie Mellon."

"Seriously?" Erica's eyes widened. "That's where I want to go."

"Well, it's a great school. I think you'd do well there. If you have any questions this week while you're on board, just let me know. I'd be happy to chat with you."

"Oh, wow! That would be amazing."

Erica came to karaoke every night during that week and Charles observed Tori talking to her every time. On her last night, Erica asked Tori to sing a duet with her at karaoke and they sang "I Know Him So Well" from *Chess*. They did an amazing job and high-fived each other after they finished. When karaoke was done that night, Erica and her mother came over to say goodbye.

"Tori, I just want you to know that you really made this cruise extra special for me," Erica said sincerely.

"Oh, thank you. I've really enjoyed getting to know you, too," Tori replied.

"You're an idol for her now," Erica's mother added. "She couldn't stop talking about you all week and loved you in the stage shows as well."

"Oh, that's so sweet of you. I know you're going to do well Erica," said Tori. "But I have one piece of advice for you as you go into this business."

"What is it?" Erica asked, listening with rapt interest.

"Don't let it change you. You're such an awesome girl, and

show business can be brutal. Be confident, but don't get too full of yourself. Stay real, okay?"

"I will," she promised, hanging on Tori's every word.

"I'd really love to keep in touch with you if you'd like that." Tori said.

"Are you kidding? YES!!" Erica shouted with glee. They exchanged contact information and Erica hugged Tori before she and her mother left the room.

"That girl is a friggin' prodigy," Tori said in awe to Charles after they left.

"You probably changed her life this week, you know that?" Charles said, feeling his own awe at her, as he did every single day he spent with her.

"Oh, I didn't do anything much. Just encourage her and let her know how awesome she is," Tori said, downplaying the impact she'd had on the young girl.

"She idolizes you, Tori. It's obvious. She'll remember you forever, I can guarantee it. I hope you keep in touch with her. You could be a real mentor to her."

"Oh you bet I will. I can't wait to see what she does," she said, and Charles knew she meant it.

During the first few weeks, Tori had the pleasure of meeting the cruise director, Steven Barrie, again on several occasions. He and Charles were good friends and he often joined them at the end of the day in the lounge after Tori and Charles finished performing for the day. She and Steven hit it off, and she found out he was originally from London and grew up not far from where her mother did. Steven often made his rounds around the ship to check out what they were all doing for entertainment and see how the guests were enjoying themselves. Such was the case one night at karaoke a few weeks in. Tori got up to start the show and saw Steven and Charles hanging out at the back, chatting.

"Hey everyone," she said. "Welcome to karaoke. Who wants to have some fun tonight?" Everyone cheered and she continued. "For this number, I'm gonna need some audience participation. Are you ready to help me out with this one?" More cheers. "Okay, so I think you'll all know this one, and if you know what to do when this song starts, I want you all to come up front with me and help me out, okay? Alright, roll it, Chanel."

The opening notes of Meghan Trainor's "Made You Look" burst through the speakers, and Tori began to sing the boppy pop song. Almost immediately, a dozen or so little girls and teens rushed up to the front and started doing the well-known dance they all had learned from the song's music video. Some others who were a little more shy also joined in as the song went on. It was pure magic as Charles and Steven looked on at Tori and the kids doing the dance in perfect unison that had become such a sensation on the internet. When the song was over, the kids all cheered and some of them hugged Tori. She decided she wanted to do that song once on every cruise from then on.

That same night, Charles decided to sing a song again. Tori got up and introduced him. "Give it up for Charles Ryan, everyone. What you may not know is that Charles is our music director here on the cruise, but you might not recognize him because you only see the back of his head from the orchestra pit at our shows. He also plays piano for me in the lounge. Okay, Charles, it says you're singing 'Tempted' by Squeeze. No pressure or anything, but that happens to be one of my all-time favorite songs, so you'd better bring it." With that, she turned the mic over to him. He smiled at her and sang a perfect rendition of the song.

She even managed to urge Steven to get up to sing that night. "Are you here to sing too tonight, Steven?" she asked from the front of the room.

"Oh, no, no," he protested, shaking his head vigorously. "You don't want to hear that," he said with a chortle.

"Well, Steven, I'm a karaoke host. I can guarantee you I've heard worse." Everyone laughed. "Come on up. Give it up for Steven, our cruise director, everybody."

Everyone in the crowd started chanting "Ste-ven, Ste-ven, Ste-ven." Finally Steven relented and came up to perform a very passable version of Tom Jones' "It's Not Unusual."

After karaoke was over and all the guests filed out, Steven and Charles hung around for awhile to relax in the now empty room with Tori and Chanel.

"So Charles," Tori said. "That was an amazing rendition of 'Temped' you did tonight," she complimented him. "It really is one of my favorite songs of all time."

"Well, thank you," he said. "But I have to ask, which version do you prefer: the original 1981 or the 1994 re-recording they did for the *Reality Bites* soundtrack?"

"Oh God, here they go again," Chanel said as she and Steven looked at each other and shared an eye-roll. "The last time I got subjected to one of these conversations, they were debating which cover versions of songs are better than the originals."

Steven chuckled. He had also been subjected to similar discussions between Charles and Tori. "The last one I heard was about which version of *Company* was the best, the original or the gender-swapped revival," he said and they both laughed. "And then there was the detailed debate about the merits and drawbacks of jukebox musicals," he added.

"Oh the 1981 for sure," Tori replied in answer to Charles' question.

"They're so similar, though," Charles observed. "A lot of people wouldn't even be able to tell them apart."

"No, a lot of people wouldn't," Tori agreed, "but when you know that song as well as I do, you just know," she countered. "There are subtle differences in Carrack's lead vocal and he embellishes more on certain lines in the second half on the '94 version, which is where it really starts to sound different from the original. But for me, it comes down to the vocal every single time. Yes, I'll grant that the '94 version has a better mix. The drums are better and the bass is tighter, but again, it's all about the vocals for me. Anyway, I noticed that you sang the '81 original when you did it tonight."

"Yes, I did," Charles confirmed. "I actually prefer that one, too," he concurred.

"I think it always comes down to what version you hear first," said Tori. "The one that made you fall in love with the song in the first place will probably always be your favorite."

"Totally," Charles agreed, "but you weren't even born when either one of those came out."

"It's always been one of my dad's favorite songs, so I grew up listening to it," she said. "Besides, you weren't born either when the original came out in 1981."

"True," Charles conceded. "But I was born not long after that. Christ, I'm older than dirt," he lamented.

"Oh Charles, you are *not* old. Now that expression on the other hand, *that's* older than dirt," Tori said with a smirk, "but you aren't."

Charles responded with a broad grin. "See, that's how old I am. I'm dating myself with my expressions."

"Are you guys *done*?" Chanel finally yelled with a good-natured laugh. "Jesus, you guys are such music nerds."

"I know, I know," Tori said. "Sorry, it's just something we do."

"We know!" Chanel and Steven shouted in unison, causing all of them to shriek with laughter.

"You guys remind me of one of those morning radio show teams who have this incredible rapport with each other," said Steven. "It's actually fun to watch you two banter back and forth."

"Well there you go, Charles," said Tori. "That could be a whole new career option for us if we ever get sick of this music racket, or maybe a side hustle."

Charles grinned. "That would actually be a lot of fun."

"I know. I'd love a career in radio. God knows I listen to enough of it," Tori said. "Anyway, on that note, I think I'm going to call it a night, guys. I'm tired."

"Me too," agreed Chanel. The two girls bid good night to the guys and headed out. The two men remained.

"Tori is quite an outstanding girl," Steven commented

while watching them walk away.

"She certainly is," Charles concurred.

"And not to be crass or anything," Steven began, "but it's not hard to notice what she does to that outfit, or anything else she wears for that matter. She looks equally good coming and going," he observed.

"Yes, she does indeed," agreed Charles. "But she has absolutely no clue whatsoever how beautiful she is, which makes her even more special, in my opinion."

"So, mate, if I'm overstepping here just tell me to bugger off and I'll take no offence whatsoever," Steven began, "but I'm sensing a lot of chemistry between you two. So am I totally off base, or what?"

"We're good friends," Charles answered cautiously, "but there's nothing going on there, if that's what you mean. We got close in New York during rehearsals, and yes, we definitely have a connection, but not like that," he said dismissively. He wanted to be careful not to reveal his true feelings for her.

"I don't know," Steven mused. "I'm not buying it, mate. You appear to be quite smitten with her and it seems as though there's definitely something flourishing between you. So what are you going to do about it?" he asked.

"I'm doing absolutely nothing about it," answered Charles adamantly. "She's an amazing young woman, but 'young' is the operative word there. I'm way too old for her. I have students her age, for God's sake."

"So does that mean that if you weren't too old for her, you'd be interested?" Steven pressed.

"It's a moot point, Steven. I'm married anyway."

"Yes, but your marriage is complete rubbish," Steven reminded him.

Charles certainly didn't need reminding of that fact. "It doesn't really matter, though does it? I'm trapped in it and I have no right to drag her into the clusterfuck that is my life. Crossing a line with Tori would be inappropriate on so many levels."

"You are an honorable man, Charles, and you always do

the right thing. But here's how I see it. Doing the noble thing has cost you so many years of your life being stuck with the wrong person. Don't repeat that same mistake now that you just may finally have a shot with the *right* person," Steven counselled.

Charles sat silently for a moment as he considered his friend's sage advice. "I get what you're saying Steven," he finally said with a sigh, "but I just can't disrupt her life. Besides, she's engaged anyway, and she's known the guy her entire life. Seems like the real deal," Charles said, resigned to the fact that he could never be with her.

"That's unfortunate. She really is extraordinary."

"I know, and like I said, she is totally oblivious to it. Her talent is incomparable. She can sing anything. Her pitch is fucking perfect every single time and she can even sing opera. She's a total chameleon, and not just musically, either. Like, when she's with Andy, she's a total teenager. She has this infectious energy about her. She can be the center of attention and the life of the room, but then it's like she flips a switch and can be so introverted and shy." Charles exhaled a breath and continued. "She's been through a lot in her life and is a true survivor. There are so many layers to her. She's deep beyond her years, but so much fun. She makes me laugh. I've laughed more since I met her than I have in years. She truly is a remarkable woman. She just lights up any room she's in," he finally concluded.

"Boy, you really do have it bad, don't you mate?" Steven said when Charles had finished extolling Tori's virtues.

"I'm forty years old and I feel like a lovesick fourteen-year-old boy," Charles confessed wistfully.

"I don't envy you in this dilemma, but I'm here for you anytime. And don't worry, I'll keep this to myself," Steven reassured him.

"Thanks man, you're a pal," Charles said appreciatively.

Meanwhile, back in their room, Chanel was asking some of the same questions of Tori that Steven was asking Charles.

"Karaoke was especially fun tonight, I think," Tori said. "I really like Steven. He's a riot."

"I know," agreed Chanel. "He's really funny when he makes his announcements over the PA every day, too."

"Charles did such a great job on that song. He really amazes me. I mean, he talks about how I can sing anything, but so can he. He's so multi-talented and versatile."

"He is. We're very lucky to have someone of his caliber here."

"Yes, we certainly are," Tori agreed wholeheartedly.

"So, what's the deal with the two of you anyway?" Chanel probed.

"What do you mean? There's no 'deal.' We're just good friends," Tori insisted, trying to sound casual.

"Is that all it is?" Chanel pressed her friend.

"Yeah totally," Tori protested. "We've shared some really important things about our lives, and we got close during all those rehearsals in New York." There was no question that since that day in Central Park, when he shared the details of his marriage and she told him about her brother's death, the bond between them had grown deeper. "He's really special to me, but just as a friend," she lied.

"It just seems like there's this really intense chemistry there, that's all," observed Chanel.

"I mean, I'm engaged to my best friend, Chanel, and Charles is married. Yes very unhappily, but still married nonetheless. So it's not like it could become a thing anyway."

"Aha, so I'm right then. You do have feelings for him," Chanel deduced.

Tori started nervously playing with a throw cushion on her bed. "Well, maybe a little, but I can't act on it. I'm getting married next year. It's just an infatuation."

"If you say so," Chanel said.

"Yes, I say so," Tori answered, wishing she could convince herself of that.

"'The lady doth protest too much, methinks,'" said Chanel, accurately quoting the frequently misquoted line spoken by Queen Gertrude in *Hamlet*.

"Cha-*nel!*" Tori exclaimed, laughing as she threw the cushion at Chanel. She covered her face to conceal her deepening blush from her friend.

"Alright, alright, I'll let it go," Chanel relented. "But I'm not buying a word of it."

Chapter 8

During the last cruise in May, Tori fell very ill with a terrible cold, and had to miss karaoke and her sets with Charles. Luckily there was no stage show for a few days, so she hoped she would be better in time for the next one. She barely left her room for several days for fear of spreading whatever she had to others. She spent her time reading and listening to music while she rested.

She was getting a little restless one evening and decided to venture out of her room for a little while to get some air. She found a note in her mail slot outside her door from Charles.

Dear Tori:

So sorry you are under the weather. I just wanted to let you know that I'm thinking of you and really missing you in the lounge. But don't worry about a thing. I've been covering it on my own and Chanel has been doing the karaoke. But it's not the same without you. I'll check in on you tomorrow to see how you're doing.

My Best,
Charles

She smiled and folded the note, thinking of him and missing him, too.

The next day was a port of call day, which was a relief for Tori because she wouldn't have to perform in the lounge that day anyway. However there was a stage show on the schedule for that evening and she still wasn't feeling much better when

Charles stopped by to check on her, just as he'd promised he would. He knocked on the door, and when she answered, there he stood, holding a bouquet of yellow roses and a teddy bear with Alaska embroidered on it. She smiled in spite of how badly she still felt.

"Oh Charles, you are so kind," she said, taking the flowers and bear.

"I thought that your one poor lonely bear could use a buddy," he said with a smile. Tori went to place the new bear next to the one Evan had given her that she had brought with her. As he looked at her, wearing pajamas with Snoopy on them and a pair of bunny slippers, her long hair in a messy ponytail, Charles thought she had never looked more beautiful.

Tori sneezed. "You probably shouldn't be anywhere near me," she warned, blowing her nose. "You seriously don't want whatever this is."

"I'm willing to take my chances," he said, grinning. "How are you feeling?" he asked.

"Like I got run over by this boat," she answered, and they both laughed. "But at least it's not in my stomach. That would be way worse."

"Well it would seem you are not in any condition for doing the show tonight," he observed.

As much as she didn't want to admit it, she knew he was right. "I'm so sorry, Charles," she apologized sincerely. "I thought I'd be better before now."

"Hey, don't give it a second thought. That's what understudies and swings are for," he reassured her. "I've got your back."

"Thank you. If I could just get a good night's sleep, it would probably make a world of difference," she said miserably.

"So, I have an idea," he said. "These rooms down here are definitely not very conducive to resting, what with all the comings and goings and noise all the time." Staff quarters were located below decks and were of a dormitory layout. "Why don't you come up to my stateroom tonight and rest while I'm doing the show? I'll be gone for hours anyway and it'll be much quieter up there. You can have a nice long nap." Charles had the advantage of having his own accommodations on one of the upper decks.

Charles' suggestion sounded glorious to her and the thought of a few hours uninterrupted sleep sounded like heaven. "Oh Charles, thanks, but I can't possibly impose on you," she protested.

"It's no imposition," he insisted. "Really, it's my pleasure. Like I said, I'll be at the show for hours anyway."

"Charles, you really do have the kindest heart," she said, accepting his offer.

That evening, before he left for the theater, she arrived at his room, and when he left, she lay down on the top of the bed and was out like a light in minutes, enjoying the best sleep she had had in days. This was exactly how Charles found her hours later when he returned. He sat on the bed for a moment, just watching her sleep and listening to her deep, even breathing, which was interrupted occasionally by a gentle sigh or an adorable soft cooing sound. He looked at her peaceful face adoringly, his heart overflowing with everything he wished he could tell her, but vowed he never would. She was sleeping so soundly that he didn't want to disturb her, so he covered her up with a blanket, kissed her on the forehead, and pulled out the convertible sofa bed, where he spent the night.

She was still sound asleep the next morning when he woke. He got up, showered, and ordered her a nice breakfast from room service, anticipating that she would be starving when she finally woke. She awakened a little while later and was disoriented by her surroundings for a minute when she first opened her eyes. She saw Charles then, already up and about, wearing a bath robe and holding the room service tray.

"Good morning sunshine," he said, smiling at her as she stirred. "Looks like you had one hell of a good sleep. How do you feel?"

Tori sat up, rubbing her eyes. Her mouth fell open

momentarily when she saw him in his bathrobe. She wondered if he was wearing anything underneath, and desperately wanted to strip if off of him and find out. "Actually, much better," she answered. "The last thing I remember is you leaving and then lying down here. Then I was out."

"You were sleeping so peacefully, I didn't have the heart to wake you up when I got home, so I just left you alone and slept on the couch. Are you hungry?"

She realized that she was for the first time in days. "Famished," she answered.

They ate breakfast together and she brushed her hair and got ready to leave when a thought occurred to her. "Oh God, what are people going to say when they see me coming back like this after not being home all night? People will get the wrong idea and talk. You know what the rumor mill is like?" she said, mortified.

"I let Chanel know last night what was going on so she wouldn't worry when you didn't come back," he told her.

"It's not Chanel I'm worried about, it's everyone else," she said with growing concern.

"Don't let it get to you. We didn't do anything wrong," he said, although a very big part of him definitely wished they had. "People will always find things to talk about."

"I know, but you know as well as I do that perception is everything. It's not good optics for you if people think you're messing around with a member of your show company. As the music director, you need to be above reproach. I don't want your relationship with me to reflect poorly on you, or put you in an awkward position," she said sensibly. It was yet another solid reason why she could never pursue a relationship with him, as if his marriage and her engagement weren't already reason enough. "You did a very kind and thoughtful thing for me last night, and I'd hate for it to come back and bite you on the ass. But you know what they say, no good deed goes unpunished."

"Don't you concern yourself with that. You let me worry about that," said Charles, absolving her of all responsibility for any potential fallout that their relationship might befall him. "Besides, I don't think it will be an issue. At least not with anyone who truly matters," he said reassuringly.

"Okay fine," Tori relented. "I just don't want to be responsible for tarnishing your image. I want you to maintain your stellar reputation around here. Anyway, I do feel a lot better. I even think I can perform today. This did me a world of good."

"I thought it would," he said. "I could tell you really needed it."

She went back to her room then, showered, and got dressed in nice clothes for the first time in several days. But her concerns about people talking about her whereabouts the night before were founded later that day when she and Chanel overheard Simone and Tanya, a friend of hers from the cast, gossiping as they were about to round the corner outside the staff lounge. They had not spotted Tori and Chanel, who stayed behind the corner when they heard the two women's voices.

"So, she didn't come home last night. Apparently she was in his room all night. I saw her coming back this morning, looking very, shall we say, dishevelled, from whatever she was up to last night," Tanya said.

"Well, well, well," Simone scowled. "I wonder what raises his baton every night? And I don't mean his conductor's baton."

"Yeah, I wonder?" Tanya chimed in with a smirk. "I wouldn't mind a shot at a piece of that action myself if I'm being honest," she said, licking her lips. "That's some serious eye candy right there. I mean, the man just oozes sex appeal."

"I'll bet she's been sleeping with him the whole time." Simone accused. "I wonder why she got the big part in the show." It was not a question.

"It's obvious he's into her," said Tanya. "I'll bet in more ways than one," she added suggestively.

Tori bristled with anger at their not-so-subtle accusations. At that moment, she had finally had enough and found a strength within herself she did not know she possessed.

"Okay, fuck this," she muttered as she rounded the corner, revealing herself to Simone and Tanya. Simone's mouth dropped open when she saw Tori come into view.

"Well, good afternoon ladies," Tori said as she sauntered up to them. "And I use the term 'ladies' loosely. You know, Simone, I've been putting up with shit from you for far too long and I've had quite enough. First of all, what I do and who I do it with is absolutely none of your damn business, but just to be clear, Charles Ryan and I are just good friends and that is all. He's been nothing but a perfect gentleman. I've been sick, so last night, he merely offered me a quiet place to rest while he was out anyway. He slept on the couch. Again, not that it's any of your business."

Simone interrupted her. "It's just funny that he never does that for any of the rest of us when we're sick. I wonder why?" she said with a sneer, the accusation sharp as a knife on her lips.

Undaunted, Tori continued. "Oh bloody hell, Simone. For fuck's sake, grow up," she said, her eyes shooting daggers at Simone. "As for why I got the part, I was as shocked as everyone else, but I can assure you, I didn't sleep my way into it. I didn't even know Charles until I first saw him when rehearsals began. And as for why you didn't get it, I have no idea, but I could hazard a guess that your shitty attitude may have had something to do with it. Whatever the case, it's not my fault."

"What's wrong with having ambition?" Simone challenged.

"Nothing, Simone. Not a damn thing. We all need to have a certain amount of that to be in this business. But I can tell you this. If this business turns me into a backstabbing bitch like you, I don't want it. And I'd hope that someone who cares enough about me would smack me upside the head and let me know that I've become someone I never wanted to be."

Simone opened her mouth to speak, but Tori shut her down. "Nope, I'm not done yet," she said as she forged ahead, her fingers clenched tightly into fists at her sides. "So, I've tried to be nice to you, Simone, but I'm fucking done. So here's the deal. I have no intention of telling Charles, or anyone else for that matter, about our little chat today. But if I hear so much as a single syllable out of your mouth again about me, or gossip and lewd comments about Charles and me, then all bets are off and I won't be so nice the next time. So I'd advise you to keep your nose to the ground and your mouth shut from now on. Do we understand each other?"

Stunned, Simone could only nod.

"Excellent then. *Now* I'm done here. Have a lovely day," she said, pivoted on her heel, and stalked away.

When they were out of earshot, Tori finally let out the breath she was unaware she had been holding. She finally unclenched her fists and realized she was shaking.

"Oh my fucking God!" Chanel exclaimed. "That was amazing! I didn't know you had it in you, girl!"

"Neither did I, actually," Tori confessed, her heart still thrashing in her chest.

"Well, just so you know, I recorded all that on my phone in case you need to call it in sometime in the future," Chanel said. "As soon as I saw you waltz up to her, I knew it was going to be good, so I hit the record button."

"Seriously? That's awesome," Tori replied. "Sometime after I calm down, I'll have to listen to it, just to remind myself that I really did that. Fuck, that actually felt incredibly good."

"You go, girl!" Chanel said, putting her arm around her friend.

True to her word to Simone, Tori did not say anything to Charles about the encounter, but Chanel did. The more she considered it, the more she thought that it was something that Charles should know about, so she vowed to tell him if the opportunity presented itself, and a couple of days later, it did.

Chanel was walking alone on deck one Wednesday when she spotted Charles leaning against the railing, looking out at the glaciers.

"It never gets old does it?" she asked him.

"No, it certainly doesn't," he agreed, awestruck by the scene in front of him. The fact that he got to experience such majestic beauty weekly for several months each year was not lost on him.

"I'm actually glad I ran into you alone, because there's something I really think you should know about, but I know Tori will never tell you," Chanel said tentatively, feeling badly for betraying her friend.

She had his attention. "I'm listening," he said with keen interest.

Chanel proceeded to explain to him what had gone down between Tori and Simone and played him the recording from her phone. Charles was as flabbergasted by Tori's outburst as Tori herself had been, and as he listened, he was fiercely proud of her, but also just as fiercely protective of her. "Wow!" was all he could manage to say after he finished listening to it.

"I know, right? I was blown away. Girl was *fierce*. Simone pretty much got her ass handed to her by Tori. It was freakin' amaaaz-ing," Chanel said, equally proud of her friend.

"Thanks for letting me know about this, Chanel," he said finally. "You're right, it is something I should know about."

Later that evening while they were relaxing after that night's show, Charles broached the subject with Tori of the escalating tensions between her and Simone. "So," he began, "were you ever planning to tell me about your little set-to with Simone the other day?"

"Oh, you found out about that, huh? News travels fast around here," said Tori. "I wasn't keeping it from you for any reason really, I just thought you didn't need to know, and anyway, I handled it."

"I'll say you did. Soundly," he said, his pride in her obvious. "Truth be told, I thought you were pretty damn badass," he said, grinning broadly.

Tori chuckled at his comment. "Well, I'm fairly mild-mannered most of the time, but I can pick up for myself when I have to. But yeah, I *was* pretty livid that day. So who told you about it anyway?" she asked curiously, but was somewhat certain she already knew who it was.

"It's not important."

"It was Chanel, wasn't it?" she asked.

"It was," he confirmed. "Don't be mad at her. She thought I should know, and she's absolutely right."

"I'm not mad. I told Simone I wouldn't tell you, so I wanted to honor my word."

"I really should have her fired over this," he said, galled by Simone's treatment of Tori. "Her behavior isn't at all acceptable."

"No, please don't," she pleaded. "I just feel like she has a lot of insecurity and that's how she takes it out. I know about insecurity, trust me. She and I just deal with it differently. I turn mine inward, whereas she lashes out."

Not for the first time since he'd known her, Charles was struck once again by Tori's sensitivity and empathy for others. It was yet another of her beautiful qualities that he loved so much. "Okay fine, have it your way," he acquiesced. "I won't do anything. But I'll be watching her like a hawk."

"I just don't understand why people find it so goddamned difficult to grasp the concept that a man and a woman can be just good friends," said Tori in frustration. "They can't resist reading more into it and spreading gossip. It just really pisses me off." As much as she secretly wished her relationship with Charles could move to another level, she knew she could not allow it to happen.

"I know, me too," Charles replied, wanting far more than friendship with her but remaining steadfast in his resolve to never reveal his feelings to her. He would cherish his relationship with her, even if it could never move beyond what they shared now.

Things were tense whenever Tori and Simone were in the same room after their confrontation, and most of the time Simone would quickly leave whenever Tori appeared. But to Tori's absolute shock, she was approached by Simone, looking nervous, a few days later when Tori was lounging in a secluded porthole in a quiet part of the ship she liked to retreat to sometimes when she just needed some time to herself.

"Um, Tori, I'm glad I ran into you," she began awkwardly. "I've been wanting to talk to you, but didn't know how to start."

Intrigued, Tori got up and made some room for Simone to sit with her. "Have a seat," she said. "What's up?"

Simone sat next to her in the large porthole seat. "Well, I..." her voice faltered as she struggled to find the right words. "It's just that, I've been thinking a lot about what you said to me, and I wanted to apologize to you for gossiping, and for the way I've treated you since the very beginning. For... all of it," she said with genuine remorse. "I don't know what's wrong with me. I've always been under so much pressure to be the best and get the big parts, and it's turned me into someone I don't like. But I want to change that. I want to be more a part of things around here and get to know people. It took guts for you to confront me like that, and I admire that so much. You told me a lot of things I needed to hear, and I wanted to thank you. Can we please clear the slate and start over?" she asked sincerely.

"You bet," Tori answered with an encouraging smile. "And Simone, it also took guts for you to do this today, and I admire *that*."

"Thanks for that," Simone smiled. "I'm really embarrassed about how I behaved. I wasn't raised like that. Friends?" she asked hopefully, extending her hand.

"Absolutely," Tori said warmly, accepting the truce and shaking Simone's hand.

Simone didn't just stop there. As soon as she had an opportunity, she approached Charles to apologize to him as well. She found him sitting backstage one night after the show, gathering his things together.

"Professor Ryan," she said tentatively, addressing him formally.

"No need to be so formal, Simone," he said stiffly. "What can I do for you?"

"Well," she began, feeling just as awkward as she had with

Tori. "I really wanted to clear the air. I'm not sure if you heard about what happened between myself and Tori the other day."

"I did," he confirmed. "But it wasn't Tori who told me, though. It was someone else."

"Well, I was gossiping about you and Tori and insinuating some things that I'm ashamed of. That's why she told me off that day. I just wanted to apologize to you for it. I already spoke to her and she was very gracious about it. I'm hoping you'll accept my apology as well," she said, truly remorseful.

"Well, that's really big of you, Simone," he said, and genuinely meant it. "That takes a lot of courage, and I absolutely do accept your apology." Charles only hoped that Simone's intentions were sincere and not duplicitous. A part of him was skeptical about whether her sudden change of heart was genuine or motivated by some other agenda to save face now that the cat was out of the bag regarding her conflict with Tori. But he reasoned that her endgame would be revealed soon enough, so he decided to give her the benefit of the doubt for now.

"Thank you," she said shyly. "I can't tell you how much I appreciate it. I promise you, you'll have no trouble with me again. I really want to be a better person and I owe it all to Tori. She told me things I really needed to hear, and I'm grateful to her for it."

"Well, here's another thing you should thank her for," Charles said. "When I first heard about all this, I told Tori I wanted to fire you, but she begged me not to."

"Really?" Simone said, aghast. "I was so horrible to her. Why would she do that?" she pondered. "She could have totally thrown me under the bus, and I wouldn't blame her if she had."

"Tori is a very special person," he said by way of explanation, and not for the first time since Simone had met her, she was beginning to see just how special Tori really was.

Chapter 9

During the second week of June, Charles asked Tori if she felt like changing up their sets a bit and introducing new music into their act. "I brought all of our favorite music with me if you feel like taking a look," he proposed, grasping to find any excuse to spend more time with her.

"Yeah, sure, changing it up a bit will keep it fresh," she agreed.

"The piano bar is free during the day, so we could go there and work on some stuff," he suggested.

So they began to meet up after their afternoon lounge sets to practice again as they had for all those weeks in New York. Tori loved having a reason to be with him as much as possible.

They decided on some new songs for Tori, including "La Vie en Rose," which she wanted to do in its original French, "Both Sides Now," and "Dream a Little Dream of Me," as well as a few duets for them both. Tori particularly loved their rendition of "I Have Dreamed" from *The King and I*.

"You sang 'New York State of Mind' one time at karaoke and it was wonderful. You should do that," she suggested one day.

"I could play Billy Joel songs in my sleep," he said. "He was one of the first musicians I ever idolized. That was the main reason I wanted to learn to play the piano in the first place, to be honest," he admitted.

"Yeah, I love him, too," she said as he began playing the song. "Yes, that one should definitely be in," she said when he finished it. They also settled on "If I Can't Love Her" from *Beauty and the Beast* and Josh Groban's "You're Still You" as solos for him, which Tori thought was her favorite of Charles' songs to date.

"I wish I had the confidence of Maria von Trapp," she said with a woeful sigh after she finished singing "I Have Confidence" from *The Sound of Music*. "Maybe if I did, I wouldn't have so many hang-ups."

"But even Maria wasn't very confident at the beginning of that song," Charles observed. "You're really too hard on yourself," he told her, not for the first time. She was not in any way boastful about her talents and was always so self-depreciating. He hated to hear her put herself down. "Whenever I was down on myself, my dad would say, 'Get off your own back, Son. Throughout your life, you'll have too many people on it as it is, there's not enough room for you up there, too.'"

"Wow, that's very sound advice," she said, reflecting on that for a moment. "I'll have to remember that."

"Well, it's served me well over the years," he reflected.

"I just really wonder if I have what it takes to make it in this business," she began. "I seriously think I have a bad case of Imposter Syndrome or something. Sometimes I think this racket will just chew me up and spit me out. I mean, I'm generally a fairly meek person and I'm not totally full of myself. I lack confidence, I have performance anxiety and body image issues, and I'm not a strong dancer," she said, listing a litany of her weaknesses. "Sometimes I think I'm just a hot mess of insecurities," she confided. She no longer had to put on a brave facade with him and could be completely herself, imperfections and all.

"Lots of people in the business struggle with performance anxiety. It's more common than you might think. I mean, look at Barbra Streisand. Her anxiety was so bad that she had to take beta blockers to control her physical reactions whenever she performed live," he pointed out.

"Yes, I've read about that and it actually gives me encouragement," she said. "I guess if Babs can deal with it, so can

I."

"Just the fact that this is enough of a passion for you to make you deal with your nerves and work so hard on choreography tells me that you are meant to do it. You really are exceptional at what you do, and I think you're way more competent with the dance stuff than you give yourself credit for."

"That's what Alyssa said. But make no mistake, no one will ever confuse me for a dancer. I mean, I'm not getting cast in *A Chorus Line* in this lifetime."

"Maybe not, but you're doing it, and doing a fantastic job, I might add," he complimented with an encouraging smile.

"I just don't want show business to turn me into someone I don't want to be. I mean, look at Simone. I'm just glad she realized it before it was too late." The changes in Simone had been drastic over the last couple of weeks and Tori and Charles were both very happy to see it. Charles was relieved that his initial doubts about Simone's sincerity were unfounded, and to Tori's surprise, she and Simone had actually started to get friendly and comfortable with each other.

"Tori, you have tremendous strength of character, and I hope you never, ever change," said Charles. "But I really don't think you have anything to worry about," he reassured her. "You're very grounded." Her down-to-earth nature was yet another thing he loved about her. Despite her enormous talent and staggering good looks, she did not possess an ounce of arrogance or pretentiousness.

"Well, thank you. I really do try to keep it real," she said, appreciating the compliment. "There's also so much pressure on performers, especially women, to look perfect all the time and I don't know if I can handle that. I mean, I'm a size six and that's practically considered plus-sized nowadays. It's ridiculous."

"Yeah, that's freakin' crazy," he agreed.

"I also have an ugly scar from an emergency appendectomy I had a couple of years ago that I'm gong to have to deal with at some point if I have to wear costumes that expose my midriff."

"Aren't those kinds of surgeries way easier now and less invasive?" he asked.

"Yes, normally you would be correct, but mine ruptured."

"Ouch! So you got the old fashioned slice-and-dice?"

"Yup, complete with the eight inch incision to show for it. It was a shit show of epic proportions. It happened just after I graduated from Carnegie Mellon, and it took me out of commission for quite a while."

"That's horrible," he said sympathetically. "But scars are proof that you survived something and that you're stronger than whatever hurt you. You should wear it like a badge of honor," he reasoned.

"I guess I never really thought of it like that," she said, considering his words.

"I'm just really grateful that in the line of work I do, all I have to do is be well groomed and show up in a tux and it's all good."

"Yes, you are lucky," she agreed. "It also helps that you're a man. If the conductor was a woman, I can guarantee you that there would be a lot more expected of her as far as her appearance is concerned. The world has come a long way, but that's a huge double-standard that is still very prevalent in our society, unfortunately."

Charles considered her observation for a moment and realized she had a point. He hadn't really thought of that before. While it was true that the profession had traditionally been very male-dominated, the tides had been turning in that respect for some time, and Charles now knew of several female conductors who were very successful and well-regarded in the field. "Yeah, I guess you're right about that," he said in response to her remark.

"When I was a teenager, I struggled with eating disorders and, while you can recover from it, I guess the mentality never really leaves you completely. It's kind of like being an addict. It's a one-day-at-a-time kind of thing," she confided.

"Wow, you never told me that before." He kept

discovering new facets to her character as he learned more about her. She had been through so much darkness in her young life, yet she radiated such an ebullient aura about her, which was obvious to everyone who encountered her. As beautiful as she was physically, this was the essence of her true inner beauty. She was resilient, and it was yet another of her impressive traits that he admired more and more as he uncovered more of her many layers.

"It's another thing I don't talk about much," she said, wondering why it was so easy for her to reveal so much of herself to him. His calm temperament was such a comfort to her and she found herself opening up to him in a way she rarely ever did to anyone. "I spent a lot of time in therapy working through that, and James' death. It helped me understand a lot more about the nature of eating disorders. It's only partly about poor body image, and just as much about control. Many people with eating disorders feel like they have no control over anything in their lives, so they turn to something they *can* control, which is what they put into their bodies. That was definitely the case for me. I had no control over James' death, or my parents' divorce, so I turned it inward. And through it all, there was Evan. I swear, that guy has been to hell and back with me. He's always been my rock."

"Wow! Was it Anorexia or Bulimia for you?"

"It was actually both, but primarily Anorexia," she replied. "I didn't eat, but then, when I'd get to the point where I couldn't take it anymore, I'd binge and purge. It's left me with lasting issues with my upper digestive system. I have a lot of scarring from acid. I'm very lucky I can still sing," she revealed.

"Jesus, Tori!" Charles exclaimed in shock.

"I know, I know, it was really stupid. I get it. But I was sixteen, seventeen years old," she said in her own defense.

"So was it under control by the time you went to college?"

"Yeah, for the most part. I was definitely still in recovery at that point, though."

"You know, your self image issues are completely

unwarranted," he began. "And that's not just coming from me. I hear comments from people around here all the time about how beautiful you are." Tori's face flushed, and she felt suddenly shy. "I don't want to be in any way inappropriate, or make you feel at all uncomfortable," he continued respectfully, "but you really are stunningly beautiful, Tori, and everybody sees it except for you. The fact that you are so completely oblivious to it is even more endearing."

"Well, I could tell you a thing or two about what people say about you around here, too," she teased, and immediately regretted saying it.

"Yeah, do tell," he said. She had his undivided attention.

"Forget it," she said. "I should *not* have said anything."

"Oh come on, Tori, you can't just open up a can of worms like that and then not tell me," he protested.

Tori mulled over her next words carefully. "Put it this way," she finally said. "There are a lot of women around here who would love to find themselves in your bed. I've been hearing those kinds of comments since the very first day of rehearsals in New York."

Now it was his turn to blush.

"Oh come on Charles, now who's being oblivious," she said, laughing. "Women hit on you all the time."

"I know, but I never act on it. That's just superficial attraction. Those women don't know anything about me, and I really don't believe in casual sex. I'm not a fuck-and-chuck kind of guy." This was just another perfect example of what an upstanding human being he was, Tori thought. It seemed to her as though good men like him were an endangered species in today's world.

"That's an admirable quality in a man," she said. "Especially the way women flaunt themselves these days. A lot of men would be all over that."

"Can I ask you a question? I'd like the opinion of someone younger than me."

"Sure, shoot," she replied.

"So, I don't know if I'm just getting old, or what, but it seems to me that everywhere I go these days, all I see are young women, and even teenage girls, looking like harlots. I see it all the time at the university and when I'm at Andy's school. I can't believe the clothes they wear. I mean, I'd never let any daughter of mine go out looking like that. Is it just me?" he mused.

"Nope, not at all. It blows my mind all the time as well," she agreed. "But one thing I can tell you is that if you didn't allow your daughter to go out like that, she'd probably just change her clothes when she left the house."

"Good God, I'm glad I don't have daughters," he said with relief. "I mean, I'm all for a woman's right to choose what she wears without having to worry about being attacked and ogled by guys, but when you go around with everything on display, it just seems to me to be indicative of a total lack of self-respect. But I've noticed you're not like that at all. You always dress appropriately for whatever the occasion, and your outfits when you perform are always classy." She took his breath away every time he saw her. When she performed, Tori always wore clothing that was becoming, never anything excessively short, tight or revealing. But even wearing a hoodie and jeans, as she was that day, he thought she was gorgeous. At performances, she wore little makeup and usually none at all otherwise. He actually preferred her without it. "You're a class act, Tori," he added.

"Well thanks. I really appreciate that. I like to wear pretty clothes and things that are complimentary, but I could never dress the way girls do now. Then again, I do have body image issues, so I'd never wear anything very revealing anyway. But no, Charles, it's not just you who feels that way. And no, you're not old."

"Okay, good to know," he said with a relieved smile. "I'm not ready to be a dinosaur yet."

"You are anything but," she reassured him.

"So, what are your plans for the rest of the afternoon?" he asked, changing the subject as they were getting ready to clear out.

"I'm going to go for a nice walk on deck," she answered. "One thing I do miss since I've been on the ship is actually getting to take nice walks. I mean, I walk laps around the deck all the time, but I miss nice long walks somewhere in nature, peaceful and quiet," she answered. "I confess that I do feel a little cooped up at times, even though it's a big boat."

"Hmm, I think I might know just the place for you," he said. "Next time we're in Juneau, I'll take you there," he offered.

"Okay, you're on," she said as they walked out together.

The next time they were in Juneau was only a couple of days later. It was a lovely mid-June day, but there was still a little chill in the Alaskan morning air, so Tori made sure she wore layers to ensure that she could be comfortable as the day warmed up. She met Charles at the gangway and they headed off to a beautiful park that he had discovered during his wanderings the previous year.

"So is this what you had in mind?" he asked.

"This is just what the doctor ordered," she confirmed appreciatively.

"I thought it might be," he said as they started walking, falling easily into step beside each other. "One thing I've learned over the years is that when you're on a boat for long periods of time, as we are, it's really important to get off the ship and walk on solid ground as much as possible."

"Yeah, I'm already starting to figure that out myself," said Tori.

"So, now that we've been underway for a month or so, how are you liking this cruise experience?" he asked.

"You know, I think it really suits me well. I love the variety of performing I get to do. I mean, what other gig would give me the chance to tap into all my musical passions? I get to do showtunes, I get to do standards and pop stuff, and the people are so appreciative. It's such a laid-back environment," she said enthusiastically.

"I love that about it as well," he agreed. "And one thing I really like is that people unplug while they're on the cruise. Connectivity tends to be rather costly and can be unreliable, so people actually take their faces out of their devices for once in their lives and communicate with other human beings. Call me old fashioned, but I believe devices should be used as a tool, not a way of life. I want to *be with* someone, not texting them all the time."

"Oh, I couldn't agree with you more," she concurred as they strolled through a walking trail surrounded by dense trees. "I fear that we're headed for a world where entire generations of people are completely incapable of communicating with each other anymore. It's already started. Today's teens are so detached, and are terrible at making conversation."

"I know," he agreed. "That's one thing I really love about Andy. He doesn't have his face in a phone all the time. He's very engaged when he's with people, and he's really interested in having meaningful conversations," he said, beaming with pride about his son.

"Yes, I took note of that whenever I was with you guys," Tori observed. "He's very mature and articulate. He communicates exceptionally well. You should be very proud of him, Charles. He's an outstanding young man. I guess he's his father's son that way," she complimented.

"Aww, thank you," Charles said with a heartfelt smile that melted her heart. "I guess I did something right where he's concerned," he said. "However shitty my marriage ended up, I *am* grateful to Meredith for bringing him into the world, if nothing else."

"You've done an incredible job raising him, Charles," she said sincerely, "And I guess he followed your example when it comes to wanting to actually talk to people, rather than just texting on a phone. It's so rare these days, especially in people his age, and very refreshing."

"Yes it is, and I'm really happy about that with Andy," said Charles. "That is definitely one of my major pet peeves about people these days. I mean, I hardly ever talk to my brother anymore. He never answers his phone and he texts all the time," he complained. "Sometimes I just want to have a chat."

"I never asked you before if you have siblings," she realized then.

"An older sister and a younger brother," he replied.

"Oh, so you're a middle child."

"Yup, I think I turned out pretty well-adjusted all things considered. I'm actually very close to both of them."

"Where do they live?" she asked.

"My sister, Anne and her family live in New Jersey and my brother, Albert and his wife live in Philly, so they're not too far away. We get together fairly regularly."

"Oh, Charles and Anne, that's cute," she said, making the connection. "You really weren't kidding about the royal names in your family."

"Nope," he said. "We all have them. Even my parents are Margaret and George."

"Same with us. My parents are William and Catherine, so they were Will and Kate long before there was a royal Will and Kate," she revealed.

"Oh, that's just too funny," he said with a chuckle.

They walked and chatted for quite a while before arriving back at the park where they had started. There were benches and fire pits all around. They sat down for a rest and Charles opened his backpack and took out some food. "I thought I'd order up a little lunch to take with us," he said, offering her a sandwich.

"Well now, you just think of everything, don't you?" she said, taking the sandwich from him and unwrapping it.

"Well, it helps that I'm buddies with one of the chefs on board, so I asked him to put together something for us."

"That's so thoughtful." In addition to the sandwiches, there was fruit, bottled water and brownies for dessert. They got a little fire going and it was perfect for the chilly day.

"So," she said while they enjoyed their lunch, "If you weren't a musician, what would you have done as a career?"

"Oh, that's easy," he said. "I would have been a chef. I absolutely love to cook. New Yorkers generally have a bit of a take-out mindset, so a lot of people don't even have a kitchen, or if they do it's barely functional. But I made sure I got a place with a fully kitted out kitchen."

"Seriously? They don't have kitchens?" she asked quizzically.

"Some don't. Space is at such a premium that a lot of people gut the kitchens and use the space for something else," he explained.

"Okay, that's crazy," she remarked in astonishment.

"Oh, I know. I think so, too. I can't imagine that. I'd be lost if I couldn't cook. It's actually something I really miss during the months I'm on the cruise."

"Really? Well you're just full of surprises aren't you? So what got you interested in cooking?" she asked, hungry for any tidbit of information she could learn about him.

"My mother," he replied. "She's an excellent cook. I used to spend a lot of time with her in the kitchen when I was a boy. That's where we'd talk and just hang out together. When I was young, she started getting me to prep food for her. I was kind of like her sous chef. Then as I got older, I picked up on a lot of stuff by watching her, and I got really interested in it. I'd ask her questions about whatever she was making, and she'd teach me more complicated things. Then I started watching cooking shows on TV and I got interested in particular chefs and started following them. I have so many fond memories of my mom and me cooking together. It was amazing bonding time for us," he said with love and nostalgia. "Even now, whenever I go home for a visit, it's her and me in the kitchen."

"Aww, I love that," said Tori. "So what's your signature dish? If you were on *Beat Bobby Flay*, what would you challenge him to make?"

He thought about that for a moment before he answered. "Hmm, good question," he said. "Probably fried chicken and waffles."

THAT'S HOW YOU KNOW

"Oh, God, marry me. A man who can cook is every woman's dream," she said laughing, only half kidding. Her love for this man was deepening with each passing day. "You can make that for me any time you want."

Charles thought there was nothing he'd rather do. "I'd love to. Hopefully I get the opportunity to do that for you sometime."

"So what else do you like to cook?"

"I make a good chili and I love to make soups, too."

"Yum, well I like to *eat* soups. It's actually one of my favorite things. Do you also like to make desserts?"

"Yeah, I make a good chocolate raspberry souffle, and I love making cream pies."

"So where did you get your love for music? Does anyone in your family have musical talents?"

"Actually, no, not really. My father has a beautiful baritone voice, but there aren't any musicians in my family. My parents have a deep appreciation for the arts and are ardent theatergoers, so they took me to symphony concerts and Broadway shows from a very young age. So I guess that's where my own love of music came from," he answered. "So what about you, what would you have done if you hadn't chosen theatre?" he asked her then.

"I considered teaching," she answered.

"Really? Why didn't you pursue it?"

"Okay, you'll laugh if I tell you."

"No I won't," he insisted. "Try me."

"Yes you will, I know it," she said, still reluctant to share the reason with him.

"I won't, I promise," he persisted.

"Okay," she relented. "The reason I didn't go into teaching is that I really hate kids."

Charles bit down on his lower lip in an effort to stifle a laugh, but couldn't help himself, her confession eventually causing him to break up laughing.

Tori swatted his arm playfully. "Asshole," she said. "See, I told you you'd laugh."

"I'm sorry, I'm sorry. It's just that hating kids is a really good reason not to go into teaching. Wait, did you just call me an asshole?" he asked ruefully, a playful smile lighting up his handsome face.

"Yes," she said, chortling, "I did indeed call you an asshole."

"Well, I'm hurt," he said with a pout. "You've never called me an asshole before."

"I call 'em as I see 'em," she said, teasing him.

"I'm actually really surprised to hear you say that you don't like kids, though," he mused as they cleared away their lunch and started walking again.

"Why?" she asked.

"Well, you're so great with all the kids at the karaoke and they just love you," he observed.

"That's different, though," she began. "They're not in my care. I don't have to deal with them when they're being irritating little brats. Oops, did I say that out loud? I meant to say adorable little darlings," she joked.

He laughed at that. "You're so great with Andy, too," he remarked.

"That's also different. I have a great rapport with teenagers, but anything under, say, twelve, forget it. And I absolutely can't tolerate really little ones, like toddler age. As for babies, they're cute but they scare the fuck out of me. I have no clue how to look after them and probably wouldn't know one end from the other."

"So, I guess no kids for you then?"

"Nope. Absolutely not," she said definitively. "I've known that for as long as I can remember. I have zero maternal instinct, and I'm only half joking when I say that if I had kids I'd be in jail. And orange is *not* my color," she confessed, and he laughed.

"Well, you're still young, you might change your mind."

"Oh *please*," she said, rolling her eyes. "If I had a dime for every time I've heard *that*."

"Okay, fair enough," he said with a chuckle. "I actually really admire anyone who knows themselves well enough at a young age to know what they want from life, as well as what they don't. So many people have kids because they think it's what they're supposed to do, only to realize later that they never should have had them in the first place. That sucks for everyone involved. Better to know beforehand and prevent a whole lot of misery."

"My point exactly," she affirmed. "Anyway, as for teaching, I figured I could teach high school, but then I thought that it would really limit my job prospects, so I decided against it. Musical theatre is my passion, anyway."

"What subject would you have taught?"

"Literature," she answered without hesitation. "I just love books. All kinds of books. I've always been an avid reader."

"What's your favorite book?" he asked.

Again she answered without hesitation. "*To Kill a Mockingbird*. I'd love to teach it."

"Oh, I love that one, too," he agreed. "Did you read the book that Harper Lee wrote before *Mockingbird* that was released a few years back?"

"*Go Set a Watchman.* Yeah, I did, as soon as it came out."

"What was your opinion of it?"

"It was okay. It's definitely not on the same level of *Mockingbird*. But considering it was written earlier, but takes place after the events of *To Kill a Mockingbird*, I guess it's understandable. The masterpiece that is *Mockingbird* didn't exist yet when she wrote *Watchman*. I thought Uncle Jack was the hero of that one. But it kind of shattered my opinion of Atticus a bit. Atticus Finch has always been one of my absolute favorite literary characters."

"I would agree with you on all of that," he concurred. "I thought the exact same things when I read it."

It was now well into the afternoon and they had returned to the boat by then. "Thank you for a wonderful day, Charles. You were right, that was exactly what I needed," said Tori.

"Well, I'd be happy to do this again whenever we're in Juneau," he said.

"Me too," she agreed, favoring him with her brightest smile. "Hey, I told you once that I'd do some of the Seattle scene with you sometime. We should do that on one of the Mondays when we're there," she suggested.

"I don't want to take away from your time with Evan," he said graciously.

"No, seriously, we don't always see each other every week anyway. Sometimes, he's got something going on for work, so I'd really love to do that with you."

"Okay, well, Andy will be on board soon. Maybe we can do something there with him then, either on the day he sails or the day he gets back a week later. Just let me know how Evan's schedule looks and if one of those Mondays will work for you."

"Okay, I definitely will," she promised and made a mental note to check with Evan.

She got back to him a few days later. "So I'm good for the day Andy's cruise finishes," she confirmed. "I'm all yours for the entire day."

"That actually works out really well because Andy has a later flight from Seattle on that day," he said.

"Perfect, we'll have the whole day to show him around."

"Sounds like a plan." He was already looking forward to it.

"So I'm planning to lighten my workload a little bit when Andy is on board," said Charles. "I'm still going to do my sets with you and the stage shows because Andy will want to see those anyway." Andrew always enjoyed watching his father at work. "But I'm not going to lead the swing band at the formal ball that week. I'll get Sean to do it this one time. I never get to go to it because I'm always working." The same was true for Tori as well, as she always sang several numbers at the ball with the band. "So I was thinking I'd just go to it this time and take Andy with me. How about we get Matt to sing all the songs that night and give you the night off, too, so you can join us?" he suggested.

Tori loved the idea, but was concerned she didn't have

anything quite that formal to wear to an event like that. "I have no idea what to wear," she mused. "I don't have anything that formal with me."

"You'll look great in whatever you wear," he said, but then an idea came to his mind. "Actually, talk to Kayla about that," he recommended. Kayla was in charge of the costumes for the shows. "I've seen some formal gowns in the costume room from other shows they've done on board in the past. Maybe you can find one that will work for you. I'm sure it won't be an issue for you to borrow one."

"Okay, I'll do that."

"So, is that a yes, then?" he asked hopefully.

"It's a yes," she confirmed.

The next day she spoke to Kayla about the possibility of using one of the dresses. "Oh sure, that would be doable," Kayla replied. "Let's go take a look."

"So is this a date?" Kayla inquired as they looked through the gowns.

"Oh, no, not at all," Tori quickly clarified. "Charles' son is on board that week so he's taking the night off and we're all going together."

Charles was correct. There were some beautiful gowns hung in plastic covers in the costume room. She looked at several until she found the perfect dress: a full-skirted aquamarine princess-style gown that matched her eyes to perfection, and happened to be her favorite color.

"Oh, good choice," Kayla said when she saw which gown Tori had chosen. "I actually made that one with my own hands. I put a lot of blood, sweat and tears into that, and it's probably my favorite of my own designs."

"It's amazing," Tori said, awestruck.

"It was Cinderella's gown a few years ago when we did a production of Rodgers and Hammerstein's *Cinderella*. Try it on," she urged.

"Oh my God," Kayla said when she saw Tori in it. "That was made for you." Tori agreed, and luckily, it fit her to a tee.

After Tori left, Kayla found the tux accessories made from the same fabric as the dress and passed them on to Charles to wear so he would match her.

As Tori fell asleep that night, she was giddy at the thought of the beautiful dream dress she had found that day, and the prospect of spending a formal evening with Charles. Yet she was apprehensive at the same time. The depth of the feelings she had developed for him over the past months filled her with both excitement and fear all at once. She was getting married after all, and knew there was no way she could have a future with Charles, as much as there was a big part of her that wanted one, if she was being completely honest with herself.

Chapter 10

On the day Andy arrived, Charles left the *Aurora* as soon as it docked in Seattle to go meet him at the airport. Once he completed the embarkation process and got settled in his room, Andy asked about Tori and told his father he wanted to go hang with her.

Tori was thrilled to see him and they gave each other a warm hug when they all met up in Charles' room. "So, what's the plan?" she asked him.

"I have absolutely no plan," he said, stretching out on the couch and propping his feet up on the coffee table. "And that's exactly how I like it."

That night, she and Charles took him to karaoke. She opened the show with "Victoria's Secret" by Jax, with the crowd shouting "Dude!" in all the appropriate places in the song. As Charles listened to her sing the lyrics about body image issues and eating disorders, he remembered their earlier conversation and realized the song had to be very personal for her. She confirmed this when he asked her about it afterward.

"That song has become my anthem," she said.

"I figured as much," said Charles. "It's kind of neat, too, that your name is Victoria."

"Yes," she chortled, "but I can guarantee you that *this* Victoria was definitely *not* made up by a dude. I'm also not an old man who lives in Ohio." They both laughed at her witty reference to the song lyric.

Tori encouraged Andy to get up and sing, but he was a little shy about it. "Oh, come on," she urged. "I haven't heard you yet and I'm dying to."

"What should I sing?"

"Well, you told me you'd love to play Joseph, so how about 'Any Dream Will Do?' You probably know that inside and out," she suggested.

He got up to sing it and as soon as he finished the first line, Tori started cheering and jumped up and down. "He's fantastic!" she said to Charles, enthusiastically.

When Andy finished the song, she said excitedly, "Oh my God, you are *crazy* good! You're going to be sensational in whatever shows you're in."

"Aww, thanks," he said sheepishly. Then a while later Charles got up to sing "You'll Be Back" from *Hamilton,* which went over great with the crowd. It had been a long time since he had done a number at karaoke.

They had a great time that night, and for the next couple of days, the *Aurora* was at sea with no port of call until Thursday. They all spent some relaxing time together in between shows and lounge sets, just hanging around on deck and enjoying the ship.

Charles and Andy were at the pool on Tuesday morning, when Tori and Chanel happened to walk by. Tori's jaw dropped and her heart skipped a beat when she caught sight of Charles, looking staggeringly delectable in nothing but a pair of swimming shorts.

Chanel elbowed Tori and said with a giggle, "Tori, your mouth is hanging open."

"I can't help it," Tori said, closing her mouth. "Good Lord, how is that man not on the cover of a magazine or a romance novel?" She couldn't take her eyes off of his impressive body, which could rival Adonis. "He's got abs for days," she observed as Charles got out of the pool, with water running down over his muscular body. He was a perfect specimen of a man.

"I know," Chanel agreed. "That's a GQ cover if I ever saw one."

Charles spotted them then, and approached them while

draping a towel around his neck. "Hey," he said in greeting, his megawatt smile lighting up his face. "What are you ladies up to this morning?"

"Not a whole lot," Tori answered, still flustered. "Just taking a morning walk."

"You girls should join Andy and me," he invited.

Tori hesitated. "Um, well, I..." she stumbled awkwardly, feeling rattled. "Sorry Charles, I don't think so, but thanks anyway," she said, finally regaining her composure.

"Why not?" Charles said ruefully, looking disappointed.

Tori shrugged. "Oh, you can probably guess," she said with a sigh. "You know my issues about wearing anything tight or revealing. There's absolutely *no* chance I'm ever wearing a bathing suit in a place this public," she answered honestly.

"Well, I can understand your reservations," he said kindly. "But please think about it. You're letting your inhibitions keep you from doing something you'd really enjoy. Don't let it run you, Tori. The only person you're hurting is yourself, and it pains me to see that. You have no reason to feel so self-conscious."

"I'll think about it," she conceded, knowing he was right, and wanting desperately to join him. "You guys have fun and I'll see you in the lounge this afternoon."

She and Chanel kept walking and sat down at a table on deck a couple of minutes later. "So," Chanel said, "have you recovered from seeing him looking like that?"

Tori blushed. "Holy fuck, he is definitely well put together," she sighed. "He's so friggin' perfect in every way. You'd think he'd be an egotistical ass, but he doesn't have a conceited bone in his body. He is a truly remarkable man, so kind and genuine. Oh, I love him, Chanel," she said with a wistful expression on her face. It was the first time she had ever uttered those words out loud. "I don't know if I can keep fighting it for much longer. He's so gentle and compassionate, and he always sees the very best in me. But not only that, he also brings out the best in me, too. He's very free with his compliments and encouragement, and for some reason, I can tell him anything. He knows things about me that only Evan knows: all the things that I'm insecure about, my deepest fears, my triggers, my frailties, and every miserable thing that's ever happened to me in my life. I don't know why I find it so easy to open up to him, but I just do. I feel so safe with him."

"Do you think he feels the same way?" Chanel questioned.

"I doubt it," Tori answered dubiously. "He probably sees me as a kid, or at best, a good friend. And even if he did reciprocate my feelings, he's totally unavailable, and so am I. What am I going to do, throw away everything I have with a guy I've loved my entire life for a man I've known for a hot minute? I can't do that."

"So where does this leave your feelings for Evan?"

"I love him to pieces, but what I feel for Charles is totally different," Tori confided to her friend. "Evan's my best friend, but Charles is so much more. I've never wanted a man this badly in my life, but it's about everything he is, the whole package. The sexual attraction is just the icing on the cupcake."

"Yes," said Chanel with a suggestive grin, "but we all know the icing is the best part."

"Maybe, but the real substance is in the cake," Tori answered. "And Charles is all substance."

"Tori, I really think he feels the same way," said Chanel. "I mean, he lights up whenever you walk into a room and he looks at you like you hang the moon in his world. He looks like a man in love," she observed. "The chemistry between you two is palpable."

"Well, even if he does, there's no way this could work between us. I can only see it ending badly if we did get together, so we're better off just not going there. I'd rather have him as a friend than nothing at all."

"I can totally understand your position on this," Chanel said. "But that kind of love is so rare, and I'd hate for you two to miss out on it just because it's complicated."

"I know," Tori said regretfully. "I guess if it's meant to be, then it will work out. But I'm not going to be the one to act on it," she vowed with determination.

"But what if *he* did? Would you tell him how you feel at that point?"

"Yes, I probably would," she replied after mulling the question over for a long moment. "But I'd have to see how I felt in that moment, if it came to that," she said indecisively.

"Well, I love you two together and I'd be so happy to see it work out," Chanel said hopefully.

"Me too," said Tori.

The rest of the week while Andy was on board passed merrily. Tori made a point of giving Charles and Andy some time together, so she didn't go ashore with them in Skagway, their first stop for the week.

That night was the night of the formal ball, and it happened to fall on July fourth, Tori's twenty-fifth birthday. She and Chanel were in their room as Tori got ready and Chanel did her hair and makeup. Tori put on her dress and Chanel looked at her approvingly after zipping her up. "Girl, you are going to be the belle of the ball," she said, giving her friend a big hug.

"I feel like such a princess in this," she said, blushing. Tori was captivated with the gown. She had been obsessed with princess dresses since she was a little girl.

"Enjoy every minute of it," Chanel beamed.

When she entered the ballroom, Charles and Andy were already there. Charles' breath caught in his chest and his entire face lit up when he saw her in the entrance to the ship's most opulent room. She was a vision in her sleeveless floor-length aquamarine gown with its sweetheart neckline, sequined bodice and full-flowing shimmering skirt in ruffled layers, which was almost iridescent, like abalone shell, in the ballroom lighting. She wore a rhinestone heart necklace with matching earrings, and a pair of shiny silver flats completed the ensemble. Tori rarely wore heels. She had never learned to feel comfortable in them, and she was tall enough without them anyway. She thought the flats would be the safe choice that evening for ease while dancing. Chanel had done her hair in an elaborate up-sweep, with several loose curls framing her delicate face and neck.

Charles was dumbstruck as he walked toward the door to greet her. "You look stunning," he said, offering her his arm in a courtly gesture. She linked her arm in his as he led her to a table where Andy was already sitting.

"Wow! Just... Wow," Andy said when he saw her. He could not think of any other words in his vocabulary at that moment that would adequately do her justice.

"You're not lookin' too bad yourself," she said, smiling at Andy, who was looking sharp in his suit.

Charles pulled out a chair for her. "I don't even know if I can sit down in this," she joked, "there's so much crinoline under here," she said as she settled the large skirt of her dress around the chair. Charles was looking dashing in his tux, as usual, and she was surprised to see him wearing the tie, cummerbund and pocket square to match her dress. "I didn't know you were wearing matching accessories," she said, pleased at how striking he looked.

"Kayla found them with the dress and passed them on," he explained. "She thought it would be a nice touch."

Charles went to the bar then to grab them each a glass of champagne. He stopped off to check in with the band for a moment to see how Sean was feeling and to request a special song for them to play for Tori.

He returned with the champagne as Sean got up to introduce himself and the band and kicked off the night with an upbeat rendition of "Fly Me To The Moon." Charles, Tori and Andy sat for awhile, chatting and enjoying the music until finally Sean got up to introduce the song Charles had requested.

"Okay, I've got a special request here from Charles. He's normally the guy up here doing this, but he's taking a well-deserved night off tonight. He requested this number especially for Tori on her birthday tonight."

The band started playing his request, "The Way You Look

Tonight," and Charles stood up and extended his hand to her in an invitation to dance with him. "Would you do me the honor?" he asked chivalrously. She took his hand, feeling slightly shy and awkward as he led her onto the dance floor.

"Happy birthday," he said once they had begun dancing.

"How did you know it was my birthday?" she asked. She hadn't recalled ever telling him.

"I saw it in your personnel file once. It stuck in my mind because I thought it was cool that your birthday was on the fourth of July," he answered.

"Yeah, it's kind of neat. I could always count on fireworks on my birthday," she said with a smile.

As they danced, he held her intimately and they fit together like two pieces of a puzzle. He gazed lovingly into her eyes and was unaware of anyone else in the room but her. Charles was mesmerized by everything about her. They were such a striking couple and all eyes were on them, although they were both completely oblivious of the attention they were drawing. They were absorbed only in each other, and as Charles listened to the words of the song, he thought about how perfect they were for her and how he felt about her, which was why he chose it in the first place. The band finished his request then and dove right into "A Kiss To Build a Dream On," so Tori and Charles continued dancing.

"Who says you're not a wonderful dancer?" he said to her as he whisked her around the dance floor.

"I'm totally fine with ballroom dancing," she said. "I'm way better at ballroom than I am at big show production numbers." Tori could feel herself becoming completely lost in him, and she felt like Eliza Doolittle in the "I Could Have Danced All Night" scene from *My Fair Lady*, or Belle gliding around the dance floor in her iconic yellow gown in *Beauty and the Beast*.

Charles held her even closer to him, and as her full sensual lips parted, he felt as though they were beckoning to him to kiss her. It was the closest he had ever come to doing just that, but he forced his attention away from her inviting mouth before he gave in to his urges and ended up doing something he would regret.

When the dance finally ended they returned to their table where Andy sat watching them. His father's captivation with Tori did not go unnoticed by him.

Steven stopped by their table then while making his rounds, greeting all the guests at the event. "How is everyone doing here?" he asked.

They all smiled and confirmed that they were having a wonderful night. Steven asked Tori if she would like to dance with him then and she accepted, leaving Charles and Andy alone at the table.

"I gotta say, I really like Tori, she's amazing," Andy told his father. "I hope we can keep in touch with her after this is over."

Charles looked at his son with a mischievous grin. "So when you say 'like' do you just mean 'like,' as in friendship, or do you mean *like*, as in, in a crush kind of way?" he asked.

"No, not a crush. I mean, she's drop-dead gorgeous, but I just think she's fantastic," Andy replied. "Besides, I think you've got the crush thing covered all on your own, Dad," he said, teasing his father, causing Charles' face to flush a little bit.

"What are you talking about? We're just friends," Charles said evasively, denying his feelings for Tori.

"Oh come on Dad, I've been watching you all week and it's obvious just in the way you look at her, especially tonight. I thought you were actually going to kiss her right there on the dance floor. You've fallen hard for her. Admit it."

"It wouldn't matter if I had. She's engaged to this guy she's known all her life. Anyway, I'm way too old for her, and in case you've forgotten, I'm married to your mother."

"Seriously, Dad, you can't call that a real marriage. I can't even remember a time in my life when you shared a bedroom. It's not hard to tell that there's nothing there. I'm not a kid anymore, Dad, and I know a lot more than you think I do. Mom treats you like shit, and she's really not a nice person."

Charles was taken aback by his son's candor, not to

mention how observant and wise he was for his fifteen years. "Don't disrespect your mother," he warned his son.

'Why not?" Andy protested. "She doesn't deserve my respect."

"But whatever she is, or is not, she's still your mother, and I won't have you saying disrespectful things about her," Charles admonished him.

"Dad, that's just another example of you being the upstanding guy you are. You've always done the right thing, and I know one of the reasons you've stayed all these years was because of me, but I'm not a child anymore and it's about time you did something that makes you happy for once. Dad, it's obvious that Tori is perfect for you and I honestly think you need to seize the day and go for it," Andy urged. "You'd be nuts to let her get away."

Charles looked at his son and arched his eyebrow. "Wow," he said, "I never thought I'd be having this conversation with my fifteen-year-old son."

"Almost sixteen," Andy reminded him. "Besides, someone's gotta set you straight," he said with a lopsided grin.

Just then, Tori and Steven returned from their dance. "This guy can really dance!" Tori exclaimed. "Who knew?"

"Well, thank you... I think," Steven said, and they all laughed.

"Okay, Andy, it's your turn," Tori said, holding out her hand to him for a dance.

Andy got up and Charles shot him a say-anything-and-die expression. Andy winked at him and escorted Tori to the dance floor. Tori was impressed by how smoothly and naturally Andy danced, and she said so.

"They teach us all this at school. It's the advantage of going to a performing arts high school," he replied.

"True," Tori agreed.

"Tori, I've never seen my father as happy as he is right now." Andy decided to broach the subject with her. "You've been really good for him."

"Well, I don't know how much of it has to do with me exactly. He's so much more relaxed when he's on the cruise. He told me it's one of the reasons he does it: so that he can unwind and get away from the city."

"That's true, but I've done this with him every year since I was twelve, and he's different this time," Andy observed.

"Don't read too much into it, Andy. I adore your father, but we're just very good friends. I'm getting married next summer," she told him.

"Yeah, my dad told me that. I'm just glad you're in our lives and I hope you always will be," Andy said shyly.

"Oh Andy, that's so sweet," she said, touched by his honesty. "I've gotten very attached to both of you, and you have no worries about that. I'll always want you guys in my life as well."

Meanwhile, back at the table, Steven was grilling Charles once again about Tori as he watched her dancing with Andy. "Holy shit that girl is beautiful!" he observed, not for the first time. "So mate, anything new on that front with you?" he asked.

"Nope, but it's getting harder and harder not to act on it. I almost kissed her when we were dancing," Charles admitted.

"Yeah I saw that actually. I thought you were going to as well."

"Fuck, am I that obvious? Andy said the same thing," Charles said, berating himself for his obvious slip.

"To be honest, I think she feels the same way about you," said Steven. "It's as written all over her as it is you," he observed.

"Well, I'm still not planning to go there," said Charles with determination.

"She sure does look amazing in that dress, though," Steven commented.

"Yes she does." Charles agreed, an idea coming to him. "So, Steven, about that dress. I have a question for you about that."

By the time the evening ended, Charles and Tori had danced together several more times and Tori's feet were actually tired by the time they left the ballroom. On their way out, Charles noticed that several of the ship's photographers were outside the ballroom, taking photos of guests dressed in their finest by some lovely backdrops. "We need to commemorate this evening. Let's go do this," he suggested as the crowd began to disperse. He wanted some photos of Tori, looking as magnificent as she did that night, to keep forever.

They chose a beautiful Alaskan scenic backdrop with mountains and aurora borealis, which was a breathtaking picture taken from the ship's deck. The photographer took several photos in a number of groupings: Tori by herself, Tori and Charles, Charles and Andy, and the three of them together. After the photos, Andy thanked them for a great night and made his way back to his room. Charles walked Tori to hers.

"Come with Andy and me around Juneau, tomorrow," he requested while they walked.

"Oh, I really don't want to horn in on all your time with him, Charles," she objected.

"You haven't, but honestly, Andy adores you. I think he secretly likes you better than he likes me," he said, grinning. "We can go for a walk in our favorite place, and I'm planning to take him up on the tram. Have you done that yet?" he asked.

"No I haven't," she replied as they reached her door, "but I've been meaning to."

"So come with us, then," he pleaded, and she finally relented and agreed to join them.

"Thank you for a wonderful evening," she said.

"I'm the one who should be thanking you," he replied as he took her hand and gallantly kissed it, while once again fighting the overwhelming urge to kiss her, and wondering how much longer he could conceal his love for her. "I'll see you tomorrow."

Tori opened her door and felt like she was walking on air as she floated into the room.

"So Cinderella, did your coach turn into a pumpkin?" Chanel asked, smiling at her friend.

Tori looked at her, glowing.

"Girl, you are literally swooning right now. I take it you had a good time," said Chanel.

"It was amazing," Tori said with a sigh. "We danced together so much, and it felt incredible to be in his arms," she said as she took off her dress and hung it up, ready to take back the next morning. "Oh, I hate to take this off. I'll remember this gown and this night for the rest of my life." She went to bed then and fell asleep dreaming of Charles and her fairy tale evening.

The next day was clear and beautiful, the perfect conditions for the observation area atop the tram. Then, as Charles had suggested, they took Andy to their favorite walking spot, which Charles and Tori had revisited since he first brought her there. It was a very enjoyable day for all of them.

Andy's last few days on the ship flew by. He and Charles went to karaoke on all of the days Tori was hosting it, and she got to hear Andy sing a few more songs. One evening he asked Tori to sing a duet with him and they performed "Love is an Open Door" from *Frozen*. He really was very talented and she was excited to see where his career would take him in the future.

Before they knew it, it was Andy's last day, and as she promised, she took them around Seattle for the day. They went up in the Space Needle and walked around Seattle Center, which was a favorite spot of Tori's. They had lunch at a cafe Tori loved, and Charles and Andy really enjoyed it as well. They then walked down to Pike Place Market and explored the various shops and vendors there. Andy had never had a chance to look around Seattle before and it was one of his favorite days of his trip. The day passed much too quickly and soon it was time for Andy to go to the airport. Tori made her way back to the ship, while Charles accompanied Andy to the airport to make sure he got off okay. Tori was tired when she got back. She had put on more miles that day than she had in ages.

Meanwhile, at the airport as Andy was about to go through security, he looked seriously at his father and said, "Think about what I said, Dad. Don't let her get away."

"I'll give it some thought, Son, but I really don't see how it could possibly work out," Charles answered, deflated.

"It will if you want it bad enough," Andy said, wisely.

Charles hugged him goodbye then. "See you in August," he said. "I'm going to miss you, but I can't wait to hear all about camp." As he left the airport, he did consider all his son had said to him that week and wondered how he'd gotten so lucky to have such an incredible kid.

Chapter 11

The day after Andy left, Tori sat in her room deciding on the songs that she would open karaoke with for the rest of the week. She was a perfectionist so she liked to choose her songs beforehand and practice them a few times before she sang them at karaoke, to ensure she would give a good performance.

She looked over a list of some of her favorites and spotted one she hadn't done in a long time. "Oh, I haven't done this one is ages," she said to herself as she settled on "That's How You Know" from *Enchanted*. She started to sing it and stopped dead in the middle of a word. She sat with her mouth gaping open as a realization hit her square in the face. Charles had done every single thing that the lyrics of the song listed as things a man would do to show a woman he loves her. She mentally went through the lyrics, checking each thing off the list as she went.

Well, does he leave a little note to tell you you are on his mind?
Send you yellow flowers when the sky is gray?
Well, does he take you out dancing just so he can hold you close?
Dedicate a song with words meant just for you?
He'll wear your favorite color just so he can match your eyes.
Plan a private picnic by the fire's glow.

Omigod, this is crazy. Does this mean he loves me, too? Tori wondered as she sat there, dumbfounded, trying to process what she had just realized. This was how Chanel found her a minute later when she entered their room.

Chanel took one look at Tori's face and asked, "Tori, what the fuck?"

Tori turned the lyrics on her laptop screen toward Chanel, "Charles, he did all of it."

"All of what?" said a puzzled Chanel. "Girl, you're not making any sense."

"All the things in this song," she replied. "See, look at this." She pointed out all of the relevant places in the song lyric and told her what Charles had done to carry them out. "When I was sick, he left me a note and brought me yellow flowers. He took me for a walk in Juneau and brought a lovely picnic lunch that we ate by the fire pit. Then he took me dancing at the ball, where he dedicated a song for me and wore the accessories that went with my dress, which happens to be my favorite color and matched my eyes. Chanel, there's no way that could all be a coincidence. I sang this at karaoke, like, the first week and he was there when I did it."

"Holy shit!" Chanel cried out. "You know what this means, don't you? The only question now is what you're going to do about it."

Tori's head was spinning. "I think I know," she said mysteriously as a plan began to surface in her mind.

Later that afternoon when she met up with Charles in the lounge for their set, she casually asked, "So are you planning to hit karaoke tonight?"

"I thought I might," he answered, curious as to why she was asking. "Why? Is there any particular reason you ask?"

"Actually, yes," she answered. "But I'm not telling you. You'll find out tonight."

Her answer intrigued him and he decided he would definitely be there. "Hmm," he said. "Should I be scared?" he asked tentatively.

"I'll let you be the judge when you get there," she answered cryptically.

She was nervous that night when she got up to sing her opening number and saw him standing there in his usual place at the back of the room, leaning against the sound booth. *Well, here goes nothing*, she thought.

She started the song and while singing it, she made her way back to him, grabbed his hands and dragged him up front while she continued to sing directly to him. As the last line approached, she looked him squarely in the eyes and changed the lyrics slightly from "That's how you know he's your love" to "That's how I know he's my love." After the song finished, she kept a tight grip on his hand, introduced the next performer and song, and quickly led him out into the deserted hallway outside the venue. She was happy that the next song was "Bohemian Rhapsody," which was very long, because she needed the time to confront Charles immediately.

When they were finally face-to-face in the hallway, she was momentarily lost for words as she stared at him, stupefied, not knowing what to say. Her mouth opened and closed several times as she struggled for words. "You...I..." she babbled, tongue-tied.

He grinned then and eventually broke the silence. "So you finally figured me out, huh?"

"You did all of those things in the song," she said, finally finding her tongue. "How did I not figure this out earlier? I was going over the song this afternoon and it all hit me. But what I really need to know is if this was just a cute little game to you, or if you really love me, too," she questioned, her heart racing.

"Too?" he asked with a mischievous grin, picking up on her slip. "Does that mean that you love me?"

"I asked you first," she said, her heart beating wildly as she awaited his answer with bated breath.

He moved closer to her, looked at her with adoring eyes, took her face in his hands and finally kissed her for the first time, making her feel giddy. She felt his arms encircle her and a rush of adrenaline surged through her body as she gave herself up entirely to the kiss. "Yes, I've fallen desperately in love with you,

Tori, hook, line and sinker," Charles declared. "So can I assume then that I'm not alone in this?" he asked and kissed her soft sweet lips once again. It was a long, sensual kiss and was what he had been yearning to do for months.

Tori's heart leapt as she lost herself once again in the kiss she had also been longing for for such a very long time. "No, Charles, you are definitely not alone in this," she answered. "I've known that I'm in love with you since before we left New York," she confessed when they finally broke apart, "but I didn't want to admit it to myself for quite a while." It felt good to finally profess her feelings to him openly. She realized then that "Bohemian Rhapsody" was about to end. "Damn, I have to get back," she said. "But we have a lot to talk about. Things just got way more complicated for us. Can we talk after karaoke is over?" she asked him.

"Yes, come to my room when you're free," he said, kissing her gently once again and running his fingers through her luscious mane of soft curly tresses.

She appeared at his door as soon as karaoke was over, her head reeling from what was happening. He took her in his arms and kissed her again with all the hunger he had left unsatisfied for months. His kisses and his touch sent shivers through her entire body.

"We have two big problems right now, Charles," she said when they finally got a hold of themselves, "and their names are Evan and Meredith. What the hell do we do now?"

Charles was silent for a long moment. "I honestly don't know," he finally said. "I've been trying to fight this for so long. It's been taking every bit of energy I have to try to conceal my feelings from you, and I just couldn't do it anymore," They sat down on his couch and he took her hands in his. "Tell me what you're feeling right now. I want to know where your head is at where Evan is concerned."

She took a deep breath and slowly exhaled. "Honestly, I'm all over the place with that," she began. "Until I fell in love with you, I thought my future was all settled. The thing is, I've known Evan since we were four, and we've been best friends our whole lives. He's been through the wars with me and I genuinely love him. It just seemed like a natural progression for us to become a couple and get married. It's what everyone, our friends and family, always assumed would happen. We have a great relationship, but I've come to realize that it's comfortable and familiar, but really does not go beyond friendship, at least not for me. It's nothing like the kind of feelings I already have for you. I just can't bear the thought of hurting him and losing my best friend. I know he'd be very good to me. I could marry him and have a wonderful life, but I wouldn't be married to the love of my life. I know that now. I just thought that being married to my best friend was the safe and secure way to go, especially after witnessing my parents' horrible relationship."

"I get that," he said. "But you shouldn't settle either," he pointed out.

"I know," she agreed. "I've realized that more and more as I've fallen for you. So, your turn. Where do things stand for you?"

Charles considered his words carefully before he responded. "I've felt trapped in my marriage for years, pretty much since the beginning," he said honestly. A fact of which Tori was already aware. "You know my situation. I just don't know how to untangle myself from it. I'd be risking everything if I did and, to be honest, it scares the shit out of me. I do know, though, that I want to be with you. I've never in my life felt like this about anyone," he said, baring his soul and laying it all on the table.

"I feel the same way," she confessed. "So that leads us back to the original question. What the holy fuck are we going to do about this mess? I've never wanted to be anyone's mistress or summer bit on the side, Charles. I have too much respect for myself for that. My parents had a miserable marriage and my dad fucked around on her so much. I *do not* want to be that person," she said with conviction.

"And I'd never ask you to be. *I* have too much respect for you for that."

"For now, I just don't want to think about all of it," she

said. "I just want us to live in this little sheltered cocoon we're in and not think about the real world for awhile. I want to enjoy what we have for the time we have, no matter how limited it might be, and we can figure the rest out later. Can we just leave it at that for now?"

"Yes, we can," he said, agreeing to table the matter for now as he took her in his arms and began kissing her tenderly.

They stayed like that for some time and things began to heat up between them, until Tori eventually pulled away. "I'm sorry, Charles, I've got a lot to process right now and I don't want to do anything that I'll regret," she apologized.

"Don't be sorry," he reassured her. "I don't want you to feel any pressure from me whatsoever to take this to a physical level. I'll admit that I want you more than I've ever wanted anything in my life, but if you decide you don't want to go there, I'll respect that and not push you."

"Can I ask you a question?"

"Of course, anything."

"How often have you been unfaithful?" she asked hesitantly. She did not ask *if* he had been unfaithful. She knew it was unrealistic to expect that a man as attractive as he was would never have found some way to fulfill his physical needs for all these years.

He paused, uncomfortable answering this question, but he wanted to be completely transparent with her. "I won't lie to you and say I haven't been," he began, feeling uneasy. "But it's been on very rare occasions. I never do anything when I'm at home, but occasionally when I've been out of town for conducting gigs, I've given in to it when some woman comes on to me. I've told you before that I don't believe in casual sex, and that is the absolute truth," he said emphatically. "I believe it should be a very intimate and meaningful experience between two people who love each other, but sometimes…" his voice faltered in embarrassment as he bowed his head to avert his gaze. He did not want to disappoint her in any way.

"It's okay, Charles," she reassured him. "You don't have to

explain. You're an attractive man, not a monk." Charles could have his choice of women, with just a snap of his fingers any time he wanted if he chose to act on it. The fact that he rarely ever did proved to her once again what a decent man he was.

Relieved, Charles exhaled his breath then, which he realized he had been holding while anticipating her reaction. She leaned over and kissed him to reassure him that she was okay with his answer.

"I really am too old for you, you know," he told her. 'That does concern me a bit."

"Don't you think I should be the one to decide that?" she asked. "It doesn't bother me in the least. To be completely honest, I've always been attracted to older men. So, why does it bother you? Do I make you feel old, Charles?"

"No my love, quite the contrary. You make me feel young. But think about it. You just turned twenty-five and I'll be forty-one next month. That's nearly sixteen years. So when you're fifty, I'll be sixty-six, and when you're seventy, I'll be eighty-six. It might not bother you now, but it's going to matter then. I mean, you're closer in age to my son than you are to me, which, I'm not gonna lie, is a complete mind-fuck for me. But, at least I'm not old enough to be your father, so that's some consolation, I guess."

"Charles, there are no guarantees in this life. You could die of a heart attack at fifty, or I could get snuffed out by a bus the next time I get off this boat. I'd like us to be two old people still madly in love in forty years, but we just have to cherish every moment we have and hope for the best," she lectured. "I mean, Chanel's father died leaving her mother a widow at thirty-nine, to raise three kids by herself. So I don't want to hear that argument any more. Got it?" she said forcefully.

"Yes ma'am," he said. "Boy you are really sexy when you get all worked up like that," he said, snuggling into her neck.

"Oh really?" she said playfully.

"Mm-hmm," he said, kissing her passionately, with all the desire that had been pent up for so long.

She left his room then and returned to her own. As soon as she opened the door, Chanel jumped up off her bed, dying to know what had happened. "So, tell me everything," she said. "I wasn't even sure if you'd be back tonight, to be honest."

Tori plopped down on her bed with a goofy, lovesick grin on her face. "He loves me," she sighed, like a teenager in love.

"I knew it! It's about freakin' time!" Chanel shouted. "So what now?"

"We have no fucking clue," she said, coming back to reality. "We're just going to enjoy our time together while we have it, and try to figure things out. Things were getting kind of hot between us, so I left before I did anything I'd regret," she confessed.

"Well, I'm really happy it's finally out in the open," Chanel said, and Tori agreed with her. She had never been so unsure of what her future held as she was at that moment, but the one thing she did know was that she loved Charles enough to find out.

For the next few days, Tori and Charles kept their budding relationship to themselves. The only people they talked to about it were their closest confidants: Chanel and Steven, but everyone who knew them could instantly see the change in their outward appearance. Their love for one another was obvious in the way they looked at each other and in their body language. Each night when they were finished working for the day, they found themselves in Charles' stateroom talking and kissing, feeling like teenagers, but Tori would always halt things when they started getting too heavy.

"I'm sorry Charles, I don't mean to be a tease, I really don't," she said, feeling badly.

"I told you before, and I meant it," he said. "How far we take this is entirely up to you. There's absolutely no pressure."

As much as she wanted him, she felt conflicted, and always forced herself to leave at the end of the night before they went too far. But one night, about a week after they first declared their feelings for one another, neither one of them could resist their desire for each other any longer, and Tori knew that she was not going to push Charles away that night as their passion enveloped them. "Make love to me," she whispered.

"Are you sure?" he asked hesitantly when he realized she was ready to give herself to him.

"I want this as much as you do," she confirmed decisively as she began unbuttoning his shirt, but just then Charles noticed she was trembling in his arms.

"Tori, you're shaking," he said, his voice full of concern. "Talk to me my love. What's going on? Sweetheart, if you have any misgivings whatsoever, we don't have to..."

"No," she quickly reassured him, "I have absolutely no reservations. At least not about how badly I want to be with you, or how much I love you."

"Then what is it baby?" he questioned gently. "Whatever it is, you can tell me. I'm right here and I'm not going anywhere. You can talk to me about anything."

Tori hesitated before she admitted her fears to him. "It's just that, well, I've only ever been with one man before, and I'm afraid I'll seem so inexperienced to you. I feel like a virgin all over again. Plus, you know about all my hang-ups about my body. This isn't something I take lightly and I'm just... I'm really nervous," she confessed quietly.

Charles gathered her into his arms and kissed her. "Oh my darling, you have nothing to be nervous about. You're beautiful, inside and out. I love you with my entire being and there is not a thing that could change that. I don't take this lightly either. Not *at all*," he emphasized. "There's nothing I want more than to make love to you and show you every day just how much you mean to me," he said, his love for her radiating from his eyes.

Tori's apprehension quickly turned to a feeling of complete inner peace, and she knew that in his arms was exactly where she belonged. She wanted to be his in every way, more than anything. She relaxed then, feeling safe in the circle of his embrace as he began to slowly undress her. He unfastened her lacy black bra, freeing the most beautiful breasts he had ever seen. He bent to take one of her full pink nipples in his mouth, feeling it harden under his tongue. When they had finished undressing each other, he swept her into his arms and carried her naked body over to the bed. For a moment, he just looked at her lying there, her hair fanned out like a golden halo on the pillow. "Sweet Jesus, you're beautiful," were the only words he could conjure as he admired the natural beauty of her perfectly proportioned body. She felt vulnerable being so exposed in front of him and became self-conscious as she watched him looking at her. She pulled the covers up over herself.

Charles smiled at the gesture and slid under the covers beside her. "Baby, I think it's so adorable how bashful you are about your body, but you have no reason to be. It's perfect," he whispered in her ear as he wrapped himself around her, fitting his body to hers. He held her so close that he felt as though they had become one. "Just relax and let me love you," he said, nibbling on her earlobe.

His hands began to caress her flawless silky skin and he cupped one of her breasts in his hand, rolling her nipple under his fingers like a pebble. His mouth moved from her ear to her neck and shoulders, and he turned her onto her back as he made his way down her exquisite body. He kissed her breasts all over and took her ripe nipples gently into his mouth, sucking them and teasing them with his tongue.

She let out a contented moan as her body tingled from his touch. As he fondled her breasts, he began to gently massage them with both hands as he continued to tantalize her nipples with his mouth. He squeezed her firm breasts close together to allow him to take both nipples in his mouth at once, flicking his tongue rapidly from one to the other as she cried out in euphoric delight.

He continued his journey down her body and kissed her slim, finely toned midsection, and when he reached her scar, she flinched and her body immediately tensed. "It's okay, baby, just relax." he said softly. "I want to make love to every single part of you." He kissed the entire length of the scar and ran his tongue over its edges. He moved down her torso, stroking her hips and bottom with his hands. He wanted to know every single groove of her body.

He parted her legs then, grazing her inner thighs with his lips, and finally inserting his tongue into the most private parts of her body, drinking in the taste of her and pleasing her by probing into all the right places. He expertly played her body like a harp, and every one of his senses were intoxicated by her. The sight of her delicate body overwhelmed him with desire, and the sound of the gentle crescendo of her satisfied moans and his name on her lips as she cried out in ecstasy were music to his ears. The feel of her soft creamy skin under his hands and lips drove him wild. He inhaled deeply, savoring her scent as it filled his olfactory senses, while the taste of her wetness as he expertly darted his tongue between her legs left him breathless. He brought her to the brink several times but always pulled his mouth away before she reached the point of no return. "Oh, no you don't," he said as he mounted her.

Her entire body was quivering with anticipation by then with a passion she had never experienced before. "Oh Charles, pleeease," she begged. "I can't wait any longer. I need you inside me," and as he slowly entered her, she cried out in complete abandonment. He moaned as he felt her surround him, and looked her directly in the eyes as they moved together. "I love you so much," he said as she arched her body toward him and wrapped her long slender legs around his waist, pulling him even deeper within her until he filled her completely and she no longer knew where she ended and he began. When they simultaneously reached their explosive climax, finally releasing months of pent-up sexual frustration and longing for one another, they lay breathless and panting in each other's arms.

"Are you okay?" he asked her softly.

"I'm better than okay," she sighed. "I've never experienced anything like that before in my life."

"No regrets?" he asked with concern.

"Not one," she said as she raked her fingers through the hairs on his chest.

"I've never felt anything like that before, either," he revealed, kissing her. "I've learned two very important things with you," he said. "First of all, I've learned that there is a big difference between having sex and making love. I'm forty years old, and no, this is not my first rodeo, but I've realized that I have never made love in my life, until now." He kissed her again and continued. "I've also realized that I've never *been* in love before either, until you." He looked at her lovingly, his face betraying everything he felt for her. He knew he was putting himself out there, baring his raw soul to her, but he wanted her to know all that she was to him.

Tori was overwhelmed by his words and his love as tears sprang to her eyes. She thought that what he had just said was the most beautiful thing anyone had ever said to her, and she knew there was no turning back now. She was his in every way: mind, body, heart, and soul. "When did you know?" she asked.

"What, that I was in love with you?" he asked, stroking her shoulder as he held her close.

"Yeah," she confirmed.

"Oh, I knew for awhile that I was feeling things for you. That day in my office with the batons was pretty intense," he answered. "But when I really knew without a doubt that it was much more was the day we walked in Central Park. I held you when you told me about your brother and all I wanted to do was take away all your hurt and love you for the rest of my life."

"That was it for me, too," she agreed. "I didn't want to let go of you that day."

"I had all I could do not to kiss you then," he confessed. "and also at the ball," he added.

"I actually thought for a minute that you were going to," she revealed. "I wanted you to so badly, both of those times."

"I almost did," he admitted. "I was wearing my heart on my sleeve that night. Andy and Steven both said they thought I was going to kiss you right there on the dance floor."

"Seriously?" she exclaimed. "What did Andy say?"

"He totally encouraged me to go for it. He said we're perfect for each other and I'd be a fool to let you get away. I was actually blown away by his candidness and insight. He's not stupid. He knows where things stand between his mother and me, and he thinks she's a horrible person."

"Wow," she said. "He implied it when he danced with me, too. He said that you were happier than he's ever seen you and that I was good for you."

"He's absolutely right. You're the best thing that's ever happened to me," he said. "I can't believe it's taken me this long to find the love of my life. I only wish I'd found you sooner."

"Well, to be fair, if you'd met me much earlier, I'd have been jail bait," she said with a giggle.

"Okay, true. Fair point," he conceded with a grin. "I guess the important thing is that I have you now, and I never want to let you go," he said, kissing her deeply. He was aroused and ready for her again, and began exploring her body once more.

"Not this time," she said. "This time it's my turn." She was hungry for his sensational body, after wanting him so desperately for so long. She rolled him over onto his back so that she was on top of him and began the process of exploring every inch of him.

She started with his earlobe and neck, as he had with her. She then caressed his arms and chest until her mouth found his already taut nipples, which grew harder as she teased them with her lips and tongue. He felt her hair cascade around his chest as she traced his well-defined abs with her fingers and later with her mouth, kissing every part of him tenderly as she moved down his body. When she finally reached his fully erect desire for her, she teased him sensually with her tongue, licking the massive length of him and kissing his hardness as she slowly caressed him. She never took him fully in her mouth, which aroused him even more than if she had. Instead, her lips were like butterfly wings, lightly brushing him erotically. He was getting close and she knew it. She straddled him and slowly lowered herself onto him, feeling him gently slide within her. He groaned as he started to thrust and reached his fingers up to tease her hard nipples, and when they once again reached their climax together, it was even more gripping for them both than the first time. She collapsed on top of him, breathless, and lingered there for another moment with him still inside her. She looked into his eyes and smiled lovingly when she saw that his cheeks were damp with tears. He encircled her tightly into his embrace as she softly kissed away his tears. When she finally rolled off of him, she was completely spent.

"I never knew an orgasm could be that powerful." she confessed. *Or that lovemaking could be so loving and gentle, yet urgent and intense at the same time*, she thought. Making love with Evan, while tender, was also predictable and lacking in passion, she realized now. She felt guilty then and purged thoughts of him from her mind.

"Me neither," Charles said, drawing her into his arms. "God you are so orgasmic." The sensation of her muscles contracting so powerfully around him when they made love filled him with an intensity of emotions for which he could find no words to adequately express.

He took her to the heights of ecstasy several more times that night until they eventually fell into a deep, contented sleep, wrapped in the circle of each other's love.

"Charles," Tori said in a groggy voice as she began to drift off to sleep.

"Yeah, baby, what is it?" he asked gently, kissing her forehead.

"I love you so freakin' much," she said drowsily.

"I love you too, my darling. More than you could possibly know," he said, wrapping his arms even more tightly around Tori's now sleeping form. For a few minutes he just lay there watching her sleep before drifting off himself with a broad smile across his face.

Tori awoke the next morning to the sensation of his mouth on her nipple. She moaned with pleasure as she stirred.

"Good morning, gorgeous," he said.

"Mmmm, now this is quite a way to wake up. I could get used to this," she murmured, stretching. "So this really wasn't a dream?"

"Not unless I'm having the same one," he said, continuing to feast on her nipple with his gifted mouth until they abandoned themselves to the sweet surrender of their lovemaking.

Afterward, he ordered breakfast from room service, and as soon as they finished eating it, they were back in bed, once again engulfed by passion.

"Charles, we really do have to get out of this bed," she said woefully in the late morning. "We have responsibilities." They were due in the lounge in a couple of hours.

"I know, I know, but I don't want to," he complained with a reluctant groan, as he began to rise from the bed.

Just then, a horrifying thought occurred to Tori and she sat bolt upright in the bed, looking completely mortified. "Oh my God, Charles," she said, panic stricken. "I just had a very disturbing thought!"

Alarmed, Charles folded her in his arms and said, "What is it? Tori, you're as white as a sheet," he observed.

"I just realized that we didn't talk about protection last night and you probably assumed that I'm on the pill, but I stopped taking it this summer because I really didn't see the need to take it while I was away, and, oh my God, I'm so sorry Charles. I should have said something, but I just didn't think about it. I feel so irresponsible, and..." she was panic-rambling and she felt sick.

Charles placed his finger on her lips to silence her. "Shh, baby, take a deep breath," he soothed, holding her close. "You don't have to worry about that my sweetheart," he said to reassure her.

"How can you possibly be so sure of that?" she asked, wide-eyed with terror.

"Because I had a vasectomy several years ago," he

revealed. "Not that Meredith and I have been intimate in years, but when she got pregnant, we had used protection, so I just didn't want to take any more chances ever again. I have Andrew and that's enough for me. I'd never do anything that risky with you my love. Not ever. I'm sorry I didn't mention it before. I could have totally avoided this terror for you if I had."

"Oh, thank God," she said, falling back onto the bed and trying to control her racing heart rate.

"Like I said, I'd never do anything risky like that with you," he reiterated. "Are you okay now?" he asked, still concerned.

"Yeah, it's all good," she said, gradually calming down as the adrenaline rush began to dissipate.

"So, how about we take a shower together?" he suggested.

"Do you really think there would actually be much showering going on if we get in there together?" she asked, laughing.

"Maybe not, but we can give it our best shot," he said, leading her to the bathroom.

He turned on the water and they lathered each other's bodies with a soapy sponge. He couldn't keep his hands off her and played with her nipples as she rinsed her hair. He bent to take her nipple in his mouth and she moaned, wanting him again. He gripped onto her bottom and raised her up so he could ease himself inside her. She wrapped her legs around his waist and they made love while the water cascaded over them.

He turned off the water and carried her, naked and dripping wet, to the bed and ravished her flawless body once more. They lay in each other's arms after, satisfied and exhausted as he raked his fingers through her soaking wet curls.

"So what's the secret to these curls of yours, anyway?" he asked.

"There really isn't one," she replied. "I just wash it, comb it, and what you see every day is how it dries naturally. Absolutely no maintenance whatsoever."

"Wow," he said. "That's amazing."

"For most of my life, I've thought that my hair and my eyes are my only redeeming physical attributes," she confessed.

"Well, I can say with great authority after last night, that that is definitely *not* the case," he said. "And I'm happy to prove that to you anytime you like," which he proceeded to do once again.

When they finally reluctantly got out of bed and got dressed, they only had an hour before their afternoon lounge set. "Oh, God, I'm going to have to do the walk of shame downstairs now. I hope there aren't too many people around. They're definitely going to talk now," she lamented.

"So let 'em. We love each other and I'd personally like to shout it from the top of the Empire State Building," he said, wrapping his arms around her, already starting to feel aroused again. "Be gone with you, or you'll end up in that bed again," he finally instructed.

Tori laughed. "See you in an hour," she said, kissing him one last time.

"I'm already counting the minutes," said Charles as she opened the door to leave.

"Me too," she said, closing the door behind her.

When Tori got back to her room to change and get ready for the lounge, Chanel was there and greeted her with a sly grin. "Well, welcome home," she said. "So, you didn't come home last night, so I'm assuming you and Charles... did the deed."

Tori's face turned a deep crimson. She had been expecting this.

"Oh, Tori, don't be embarrassed," Chanel said. "You and Charles love each other. It's a perfectly natural and beautiful thing."

Tori wasn't accustomed to discussing such private things with other women, but confirmed her friend's suspicions. "Chanel, I honestly never experienced anything like that before. I mean, he did things to me that I couldn't even have imagined. I felt like a virgin." And in many ways, she knew she had been. "But it's not just the sex, although that was mind-blowing. It's just... it's everything that he is, and all that we mean to each other." She was struggling to find the right words to describe everything she was feeling, but there were none that could adequately convey the depth of the bond that had already developed between them.

"I'm so happy for you," Chanel said sincerely. "I'm really rooting for you two." She walked over to Tori and gave her a hug. "You are really great together."

"Yeah, I couldn't agree with you more," said Tori, her heart full with the memory of that morning and the night before. "He told me that he has never been in love before until now, and that he's learned the difference between having sex and making love."

"Oh my God, I'd melt if a guy said that to me," said Chanel, dreamily.

"Yeah, that's pretty much what I did," responded Tori. "It brought me to tears."

"So, you have no regrets, then?" asked Chanel.

"No, not at all. I mean, I have regrets about what I'm doing to Evan, and I don't know if I'm going to be able to look him in the face now. But I really think Charles is the one great love of my life, and we just couldn't keep this from happening, no matter how hard we tried."

"I know you tried, but I've seen this brewing for so long. I knew you guys wouldn't be able to resist it forever."

"He even told me that his son gave him the green light to pursue a relationship with me," Tori told her.

"Get out!" Chanel exclaimed. "Are you serious?" she asked, astounded. "Even he saw it?"

"Yup, and Steven told him the same thing, and you also said as much to me. Seems like the only person who didn't see it was me. But then again, in my defense, I was fighting my own feelings for him at the time."

"So I guess I get my own room now," Chanel realized. "I mean, you know I love you, girl, but this kind of rocks for me, too," she said, laughing.

"Yeah, I guess you do," said Tori. "So anyway, please keep this to yourself. I don't want the rumor mill running rampant any more than I know it already will be."

"Oh, don't worry a thing about me. I got your back. My lips are sealed," she assured her. "Even if yours aren't," she teased, shooting her friend a wicked grin.

Tori blushed again and changed the subject. "Anyway, enough about my love life, let's talk about yours," Tori said, winking at her friend. She had seen Chanel hanging around with one of the ship's photographers lately and meant to ask her about it. "You've been spending quite a bit of time with Marcus lately, so what's with that?"

"We're enjoying each other's company," Chanel said shyly. Now it was her turn to be put on the hot seat. "I met him on the cruise last year and we've been friends. He's actually from Oregon, too. I mean, what are the odds of that? Anyway, we really like each other and we're just going to see where it goes. But, I gotta say, Tori, I *really* like him."

"Oh, Chanel, that's so great," Tori said with a broad smile. "He seems really nice. And he's hot, too," she added. "I mean, not as hot as Charles, but he's pretty easy on the eyes," she observed about the attractive young Latino photographer.

"He sure is," Chanel said with a grin.

"I can't wait to get to know him better," said Tori. "Bring him along more often when we're doing stuff."

"I will," Chanel promised, as Tori left to go to the lounge for her set with Charles.

In the meantime, Charles felt like a million bucks and could not hide his happiness as he ran into Steven in the hallway on his way to the lounge.

"Well, you're looking like a happy bloke," Steven remarked. "To what can I attribute this new spring in your step? Or do I even have to ask?" he said with a suggestive wink.

"A gentleman never tells," Charles said with a goofy grin. "Let's just say there's been another new development in my relationship with Tori since yesterday."

"Oh, I'm so happy for you, mate. For both of you," Steven gushed, clapping his friend on the back. "It's about time."

"Thanks my friend. I feel like a new man," Charles said and continued on his way to the lounge with a giant smile on his face.

Chapter 12

The following Monday, Tori could not face Evan after she and Charles had become lovers, so she texted him, cancelling their usual Monday visit, telling him she wasn't feeling well. He cancelled the week after, saying he had to do an interview for a story, and Tori was relieved that she would not have to face him for awhile. She took the opportunity to meet up with her father that week instead.

Meanwhile, Charles and Tori blossomed in their love for one another. The weeks after their feelings were finally out in the open felt like a honeymoon to them, and neither had ever been as deliriously happy in their entire lives. They were constantly together: working together in perfect harmony during the days and evenings, and spending long wonderful nights and mornings rediscovering each other's bodies. Their desire for one another was insatiable and they were often barely able to make it through performances before falling into bed each night, leaving a trail of clothes from the door of his room to the bed. Sometimes their clothing fell victim to their fits of passion, with the usual casualties including several of Charles' tux shirt buttons and a pair of cuff links.

"We really need to be kinder to your clothing," Tori joked as they lay nestled in each other's arms in bed one night.

"Luckily I have spares," he replied with a grin.

"Have I ever told you how friggin' sexy you are in suits?"

"No, I don't think you have."

"Fuck, I almost had an orgasm right there on the spot when I first saw you in your tux," she admitted. "And then there was that very first time I met up with you at Juilliard. You were wearing a suit that day and you were looking seriously hot."

"Hmm, good to know. I'll have to file that piece of information away for future reference," he noted. "But I get where you're coming from. True confession, I get a major hard-on whenever you sing that Meghan Trainor song you do at karaoke."

"'Made You Look,'" she said, reminding him of the title.

"Yeah, that's the one. Whenever you sing that line about having 'nothin' on,' all I can do is think about how badly I want to see that. And you're so flirty when you perform it. It just turns me on."

"Oh, really?" She was a little taken aback by his comment. Charles didn't usually say crude things like that. "Okay, I'll never think about that song the same way again," she said with a giggle. "So, no disappointments when you eventually did see me with nothin' on?" she asked playfully.

"Are you kidding me? Let's just say you definitely made me look," he said, making reference to the song's title.

"I'll never stop being amazed by that. I think my body is atrocious."

"Oh yes, you're absolutely *hideous*," Charles said, feigning repulsion. "I don't know how I ever manage to force myself to make passionate love to you every single day. I mean, *ugh*." He screwed up his face in mock disgust and they both burst out laughing.

"I love that song to pieces, but I always feel a little awkward singing it, because, as you know, I've never felt terribly confident about my body, and that song is all about being comfortable in your own skin."

"Well, sing it loud and proud, baby, because you have the body of a goddess," he said. Charles could not fathom how anyone could consider a body as flawless as hers to be anything less than perfect.

"Even with the scar?" she asked.

"Yes, even with the scar," he assured her. "Speaking of

that, I don't think it's as bad as you think it is."

"It's faded a bit. It was really angry looking for, like, the first year."

"If you really want to get something done about it, I don't think it would be too difficult. The right plastic surgeon could deal with that pretty well, I think. A good makeup artist could also do wonders with it if you're worried about having to expose it in performances."

"Okay, that's actually very encouraging," she said. "I have some stretch marks I'd love to deal with as well."

"How did you get stretch marks?" He hadn't seen any and God knew he had been all over her delectable body numerous times. "I've never noticed any."

"Well, they're there," she replied. "I was overweight as a kid. I lost a shit-ton of weight in high school, before I went to Carnegie Mellon. That's when the eating disorders started. Once I decided I wanted to go into theatre, I knew I had to lose the weight."

"Oh my love, I hate that you're so tortured by this all the time. I look at you and all I see is perfection, while all you see are your flaws. You're the woman I love and I wish you could see yourself as I do. I'd be happy if you never got rid of your scar or any of it," he confessed.

"Really, why?" she asked quizzically.

"Because it's part of you, and I love everything about you."

"Oh, that's sweet," she said as he traced her scar with his finger. She no longer felt self-conscious with him about it now.

"Well, it's how I feel," he said sincerely.

"Self-compassion was a major theme in my therapy, because basically, I have none. I'm a perfectionist who cannot deal with making mistakes, and I have so many insecurities. I'm constantly working on it, but I'm a work in progress, I guess. Honestly, I'm surprised you didn't run screaming from me as you started to find out more about me. Are you sure you want to get involved with me and all my baggage?" she asked him in all seriousness.

"There's not a doubt in my mind. It was precisely the opposite for me, actually. The more I learned about you, the harder I fell, because I realized more and more as I got to know you just how truly extraordinary you are," he said. "But you know, you worry *way* too much and allow things to take up far too much real estate in your brain. My advice to you, my sweetheart, would be to get out of your own head and stop overthinking everything so much. And this is not just coming from the man who loves you. I'm speaking as a musician, as your music director, and someone who has taken more trips around the sun than you have. Take it from me, there will always be something to beat yourself up over, and as a performer, you'll come to realize that you'll always have detractors: people who will either look down their noses at you and criticize you because they think they're better than you, or people who will be jealous of you because they know *you're* better than *them*. You've already encountered that type with Simone, and I'm sure you've come across it at Carnegie Mellon or in your various regional theatre experience at some point as well. So you might as well just live your life, do the best you can, and stop worrying so much or it will eat you alive. Worrying is like paying interest on a loan you haven't taken out yet."

"Ooh, I love that. More pearls of wisdom from your dad?"

"No actually, that one came from my mom."

"You're so wise, you know that? You always know how to talk me down and help me keep things in perspective. I love you for that. You're so lucky, Charles. You're so easygoing and even-keeled," she said enviously. "You probably have no hang-ups." He always exuded such an air of calm about him that she couldn't imagine anything rattling him.

"Says who?"

"Okay, name one," she challenged.

"Well, I'm claustrophobic, for one," he admitted.

"Really? I didn't know that."

"Oh yeah, I actually found it really bad when I played in orchestras. That's one of the things I love about conducting:

there's no one in my space. Same with teaching for that matter."

"Wow. Is that why you always stand at the back of the room near the exit whenever you come to karaoke?"

"Yes, that's exactly why," he answered. "Another thing is that I'm more than a little bit OCD about organization and things being in their place."

"Oh, now some things make more sense to me," she said.

"Like what?"

"Well, I noticed that every time I was in your office at Juilliard, it was always impeccably organized and tidy. And I've noticed the same thing about your space here," she observed. An organized man was every woman's dream. "Well, we're actually really compatible that way because I'm very much like that as well."

"Yes, I've noticed," said Charles. "Trust me, if you weren't, it would drive me absolutely nuts." Having her stay with him in his room had given him a glimpse into what it might be like to live with her, and he thought they would be very compatible. "So there you go, we all have our issues. Even me. And in answer to your question, yes, I'll take you, baggage and all," he declared, and made love to her again before they both fell into a peaceful sleep.

When they were finally able to come up for air long enough to tear themselves away from one another each morning, they immediately began to yearn for the day's activities to end when they would inevitably wind up in bed once again, succumbing to their unbridled passion. There were many days when they were unable to get through the day without racing to his stateroom for an afternoon matinee.

"Jesus Christ, you have no clue what you do to me. Even little things, like watching you lick an ice cream cone, turn me on," he said while they were eating ice cream on deck one afternoon. He began to feel the all-too-familiar stirring in his pants that he had become quite accustomed to dealing with over the last weeks. "I can think of a lot more interesting things you could be doing with that tongue right now," he said suggestively with a devilish grin. He leaned closer so his lips were touching her ear. "Can I interest you in a little... afternoon delight?" he whispered provocatively, a slow sexy smile spreading across his face.

Tori's cheeks reddened. "*Charles*," she said, giggling. "You're incorrigible. Seriously, are you horny *all* the time?"

"For you, yes," he admitted unapologetically. "Come on, you know you wanna," he said playfully, his eyes dancing.

"Yes, I wanna," she replied with a naughty smile, taking his hand as they dashed to his room to quench their desire.

When they reached his room he looked at what she was wearing and his mouth quirked into a wicked grin. "I don't know if I can make love to you while you're wearing a Bambi t-shirt. I already feel like I'm robbing the cradle as it is," he said, his eyes twinkling mischievously.

She pulled the t-shirt off over her head then, flinging it across the room. "There," she said, "problem solved." Charles unfastened her bra and buried his face in her glorious breasts, his concerns forgotten.

"So, what was that you were saying about interesting things I could be doing with my tongue?" she asked seductively, as she fell to her knees and took his full erection in her mouth, demonstrating her superior skills with her tongue. This was an act she had never felt compelled to engage in before, until him.

"Oh Jesus," he whispered as he took her head and pulled her closer, thrusting himself deeper into her mouth. She expertly worked her tongue, teeth and lips on him until he finally cried out as he erupted into her mouth, making him feel dizzy. When he finally regained his senses, he took her to the bed and made love to her.

"You know, we really should start seeing other people," she proclaimed afterward.

"*What?*" he said, horrified, his eyebrow arching.

Tori burst out laughing. "Oh my God, the expression on your face right now is priceless," she said. "What I mean is that we hardly ever hang out with other people anymore. I've really neglected Chanel, and when's the last time we spent any time with Steven? I mean, don't get me wrong, I'm definitely *not* complaining about what we've been doing to fill our time, but honestly, Charles, is there something wrong with us? I've never been this sexual in my life," she said as they held each other. He had ignited a fire within her that could not be extinguished.

"Neither have I, actually," he said. "But if wanting you every second of every day is wrong, I don't wanna be right. Besides, it's all your fault. I can't help it if I get frisky every time I see you."

"*Frisky?*" Tori said, howling with laughter. "Oh my God, Charles, what are you, eighty? I mean seriously, 1950 called. They want their word back."

Charles' face turned scarlet with embarrassment. "Oh fuck," he said laughing. "Don't remind me of how old I am." He wrestled her playfully until she was underneath him, pinned her to the bed and started tickling her, causing her to writhe in uncontrollable laughter. "Do you surrender?" he asked.

"Yes, *yes!*" she squealed, unable to catch her breath. He stopped tickling her and they collapsed on the bed in peals of laughter.

Once they settled down, they lay intertwined in each other's arms, peaceful and contented. Charles picked up one of her curls and twirled it around his finger. "Looks like my fortune actually came true," he said, lightly stroking her hair.

Tori looked at him blankly. "What?" she asked, confused.

"My fortune cookie from the night we saw the show with Andy," he reminded her.

"Oh yeah, so what did it say?"

"It said, 'A new relationship will blossom. You will be blessed.' And I am. And let me just say for the record that I am also *very* blessed in bed." They laughed, remembering their conversation over the fortune cookies that night. "I have absolutely no complaints in that department."

"You won't hear any from me either," she concurred.

"Well, I'm glad to hear that. So, I assume you're not one

of those women who prefers chocolate to sex," he said with a devious grin.

"Oh, *hell* no!" Tori exclaimed. "Although before you, I probably would have said yes to that. But now I realize that those women are most certainly sleeping with the wrong men." She also knew that she had been one of them, until now. "I told you once that you are a very multi-talented man, and you most definitely are, Dr. Ryan. In more ways than one." Charles was a very considerate and selfless lover, always making sure to please her before fulfilling his own needs. He was an artist in his lovemaking, her body his canvas. She marvelled at how well he knew his way around her body and delighted in the multitude of ways he found to satisfy her. It was usually after her second orgasm before he even entered her each night, and by the time he finally did, she was begging for him. He was masterful at drawing out her orgasms longer than she ever thought possible.

"Oh my God, you spoil me in bed," she said, shuddering under his tongue as she climaxed for the second time. "I never knew an orgasm could last so long."

He closed his lips around her and sucked the wetness that exploded from her into his mouth as she continued to tremble, the taste of her more intoxicating than any alcohol. "I just want to love you the way you deserve to be loved."

"Your mouth is talented in more ways than just playing the trumpet," she said, breathless. "And you're not just a maestro in front of an orchestra." She reached down between his legs then and fondled his growing erection, feeling his arousal throb with every stroke of her fingers until he was rock hard. Then he proceeded to demonstrate his multiple talents to her several more times that day.

Charles awakened a sexual side of Tori that she never knew she possessed, and she was discovering experiences in his bed that were entirely new to her. They had both discovered countless ways of pleasuring one another and she became far more adventurous sexually than she ever imagined she could be. They could not get enough of each other and Tori lost all of her inhibitions with him, no longer shy about her nakedness or self-conscious about her body. She could be unabashedly herself with him and became more comfortable in her own skin. Her self-confidence bloomed, which showed in her performances as well. She beamed now whenever she sang "A Wonderful Guy," one of her solos in the revue show, exchanging knowing glances with Charles whenever she preformed it, as the song took on new meaning.

Charles even managed to finally convince Tori to accompany him to the swimming pool. "I'm going to go to the pool," he announced one morning as they were getting up. "Please come with me Tori," he pleaded with her.

"Oh, I don't know, Charles," she said dubiously.

"For me," he insisted. "You'll be sexy as hell in a bathing suit and I want you to go with me. I don't want to pressure you, but I know it'll be fun. Do you have a swimsuit with you?"

"Yes, I did bring one," she admitted hesitantly, "but I don't know why I did, because I never had any intention of using it."

"Please put it on for me, my love," he requested softly. "I really want to see you in it."

"Okay fine," she relented, and a moment later, she emerged from the bathroom in a one-piece suit in multiple shades of purple that moulded the curves of her splendid body to perfection. Charles' jaw dropped as he looked at her, and he felt himself growing hard as he walked toward her.

"Oh my God, why the hell are you so self-conscious?" he said in awe. "You're so goddamned sexy. And in case you're wondering just how sexy," he began, taking her hand and placing it over his stiff groin, "*that's* how sexy. You take my breath away every single time I look at you, do you know that?"

Tori blushed, kissing him as she wrapped her arms around his neck. He peeled the suit off of her and made love to her. Afterward, when they finally made it to the pool, they had a wonderful time together, playing and frolicking in the water. Charles gathered her into his arms and kissed her.

"I'm so glad you decided to do this with me," he said.

"How do you feel?"

"Amazing," she answered, "thanks to you."

"You look incredible. I mean it, Tori. You're a beautiful woman. I've been watching the men around here since we arrived, and every guy from seventeen to seventy has stopped and turned their heads when they caught sight of you. But I'm the lucky one who gets to take you home with me and make love to you." And that's exactly what he did a few minutes later. When they reached his room, he once again peeled the wet bathing suit from her body and they made love again. Then they took a shower and began the rest of their day.

As fulfilling as their physical relationship was, their emotional connection was even stronger. They were perfectly attuned to one another's thoughts and could finish each other's sentences. They were two parts of one whole and both felt incomplete without the other.

They did not publicly flaunt their relationship, but also knew it was the worst kept secret on board. Everyone could see how much they loved one another, and couldn't help but notice that they were glowing all the time now and were demonstrative in their affection for each other in subtle ways. However, neither of them spoke about the thing they dreaded most, which was the end of the cruise season. They couldn't even bear thinking of having to go back to reality. She took off her engagement ring and he also removed his wedding band, which only served as reminders of something they did not want to face.

Their blossoming relationship did not go unnoticed by Simone, either. One night after a show, Simone angrily accosted Tori and launched into a verbal attack.

"I knew it all along," she spat in accusation. "I knew you were sleeping with him."

Tori took a deep breath. "Please Simone, don't do this," she pleaded. "You have come so far in the last couple of months. It's done my heart good to see the changes in you and to watch you build relationships with the rest of us." She wanted to be honest with this young woman whom she now considered a friend. "This relationship between Charles and me is new. I swear to you that we were not involved before now. We've been fighting our feelings for some time, but we were not involved back when the parts were decided. I barely knew him then. You have to believe me."

Simone softened, sensing Tori's sincerity. "I'm sorry," she apologized. "I guess old habits die hard." They both laughed. "It's obvious to everyone how much you love each other and I'm happy for you," she said and meant it. "But he *is* married."

"Oh, I know it," said Tori, "and I'm engaged. It definitely brings a whole new level to 'it's complicated,' but we're trying not to think about it right now. I know the day of reckoning is going to come, but I just can't face it. All I know is that I love him with my whole heart. As for what happens next, your guess is as good as mine."

"I don't envy you," Simone said, "but I'm hoping it works out for you two. I really do consider you a friend now, Tori, and I want to thank you again for everything. I have you to thank for helping me realize where I was headed."

"I consider you a friend, too," said Tori warmly. "And you're giving me far too much credit. It was in you all along. You just needed someone to help you find it."

"Charles told me you stopped him from firing me. I'm very grateful to you for that. With the way I treated you, I wouldn't have blamed you if you had encouraged him to do it."

"I just saw something better in you. I could see that you were being ruled by insecurity rather than a mean spirit. I thought you deserved another chance."

"Well, you nailed that," Simone admitted. "I felt really threatened by you. I mean, you're beautiful and bubbly, and insanely talented. You're the whole package and everybody loves you. You've just got it all so... together."

Tori laughed at the irony of that. "Oh Simone, if you only knew half of what I go through in order to perform every day, it would blow your mind."

"Really?" Simone asked in confusion. "Like what?"

"Oh, I have crippling performance anxiety," she confessed. "It's actually really debilitating sometimes."

"Are you *serious*?" said Simone, shocked. "I never would have said that about you in a million years."

"Well, there are very few people in my life who know about it. Charles is one of them. He saw it immediately when we started rehearsing together in New York. He's been wonderful with me and so encouraging. He's really helped build my confidence."

"Wow," said Simone. "You certainly do a great job dealing with it, because nobody would ever know you're going through all that when they see you perform."

"Well, it just goes to show that things are not always what they seem. You never know what's going on with someone from what you see on the surface," Tori pointed out.

"Yeah, no kidding. You just appeared so confident to me and so well put together. I was envious, and then you got the lead and I took out my insecurities on you."

"You have no reason to feel that way, Simone," Tori reassured her. "You're amazing. I envy your dancing prowess. I have to work really hard on that part of my performance. I love to act, and singing is my strongest skill, but dancing, not so much. But you... you're a true triple threat," she complimented her sincerely.

"Wow, thank you. That's really high praise and I'm kind of blown away," said Simone. "So anyway, just ignore my little outburst earlier. I'm really sorry. Are we okay?"

"Absolutely," Tori reassured her. "No worries whatsoever," she said with a smile. "We all have our moments."

One evening in late July when they returned to Charles' room after finishing a show, Tori opened the door to find a large box tied with a big bow on top sitting on the bed.

"What's this?" she asked, curious.

"Open it and find out." Charles urged with a twinkle in his

eye.

"What's the occasion?" she mused.

"Just consider it a belated birthday gift," he answered.

"Oh, Charles, you made it the best birthday of my life. You don't need to do anything else." She untied the ribbon and removed the lid from the box, and when she parted the tissue paper, she gasped when she saw what was inside. "Oh my God, my dress!" she exclaimed, her eyes wide, overwhelmed to see the gown that she had worn to the ball on her birthday.

"I spoke to Steven about it before that night was over," he said. "He agreed to let me buy it. It took a little while for Kayla to deal with getting it cleaned and packaged, but better late than never, I guess."

"Charles, I can't accept this. It's too much."

"I couldn't bear for you not to have it. I can't see anyone else wearing it but you. You were stunning that night. You turned every head in the place," he said with love in his eyes. "Especially mine."

"We weren't even together when you offered to buy this. Charles, I don't know what to say," she gushed.

"I don't want you to forget that night, ever," he said tenderly. "I know I won't."

"Kayla was okay with parting with it?" she asked. "I know she's really proud of this one."

"Yes, she was actually over the moon that it would be yours," he assured her.

They made love then and when they lay in each other's arms afterward, Charles noticed a somber expression fall over Tori's face, just for a second.

"Hey, penny for your thoughts. Where did you go just then?" he asked with concern. "Your face just clouded over for a sec."

Tori exhaled and finally confessed what was the matter. "Tomorrow is Monday and I'm seeing Evan for the first time since, well, us."

Charles sobered. "Oh," he replied and hesitated then,

unsure of what to say. "I'm sure you're feeling pretty apprehensive about that," he finally said, stating the obvious.

"My stomach is in knots," she affirmed. "I don't know if I'll even be able to look at him, let alone carry on a conversation."

He drew her closer and kissed her on the top of her head. "I'm sorry love. As much as I love you, and the fact that I'm happier than I've been in my entire life, I wish you didn't have to be put in this position."

"I love you, Charles and I'd never change any of what we've done. I just regret what I'm doing to him. I don't know where I'm going with this, and with him. At the end of the day, I want to be with you, but I'll be hurting my best friend and I'll probably lose him forever. That kills me," she said, her eyes brimming with tears. "And I don't even know where things will stand with you when this is over."

"The one thing I can tell you is that I will love you until the day I die," he said and they made love again.

She slept fitfully that night and when she awoke, she had a text from Evan. *Working from home today. Can you meet me at the apartment?* it said. She texted back that she would be there. She wanted to go home anyway to drop off some things she no longer needed and pick up some new outfits for singing in the lounge.

Evan ran to greet her lovingly as soon as she arrived. "Hey baby, I missed you so much," he said, embracing her tightly.

"I missed you, too," she said, smiling up at him affectionately, realizing that part of her really had.

"I made us some lunch," he said and she followed him into the kitchen. She had missed their quiet compatible time together. They ate lunch and caught up with each other's news. She, obviously omitting the biggest news in her own life.

She went to their bedroom then and put away some of the things she brought back and picked out some new outfits to take to the ship with her. She was happy for the few moments alone as she caught her breath and tried to slow her racing heart. There had never been any secrets between her and Evan, and she was unaccustomed to deceiving him.

Evan came into the room then and wrapped his arms around her from behind. He began to kiss her neck as his hands roamed under her shirt, finding her breasts. She could feel him growing harder against her backside. *Oh, God, no,* she thought. She hadn't anticipated this.

"Oh, honey, I'm so sorry," she said, thinking on the fly, "but it's that time of the month," she lied. She knew a lot of women had sex while on their period, but she was most definitely not one of them, so she knew the excuse would not arouse suspicion in Evan.

"Damn!" Evan exclaimed. "I just miss you baby." He held her and kissed her gently.

"I know, it's just bad timing right now." The lie tasted bitter on her tongue.

He noticed her missing engagement ring then. "Hey, where's your ring?" he asked with alarm, worried it had gotten lost.

Fuck! Tori thought, searching her brain for a probable explanation. "Oh, I have to take it off for the shows and I just forgot to put it back on, that's all. Don't worry, it's in a safe place." Another lie, but he seemed to believe her.

They talked for awhile longer until it was time for her to go back before the ship set sail again.

When Charles saw her after she returned, she looked sad and subdued. "So, judging by your expression, I'm guessing it's safe to assume that you had a difficult day," he deduced.

A shadow passed over Tori's face. "It definitely wasn't easy." she answered, frowning. "He tried to make love, but I put him off. I told him I was on my period."

Charles was relieved to hear it. He grimaced at the thought of her in another man's bed.

"Oh, and I also forgot to put my engagement ring back on. He picked up on that, too."

"How did you explain that?"

"I told him that I have to take it off for the shows and I just forgot to put it back on," she replied.

"Do you think he suspected anything?"

"No, I don't think so. He's usually really attuned to me, but I think he bought it. I feel like such a traitor. He doesn't deserve this. And when did I become such a good liar?" she asked, riddled with guilt. She started to cry then. It had been a rude dose of reality for her that day.

Charles took her in his arms and held her. "I love you," was all he could think of to say to comfort her in that moment. He wished he could wave a magic wand and make this all go away for her, and he felt so helpless, knowing he couldn't. All he could do was try his best to console her and reassure her of his love.

"Just make love to me," she requested in a whisper, and for awhile, there was only him, and all was right with the world as she forgot about everything else that was looming large in her future.

Chapter 13

The first week of August was upon them and it was a week Tori and Chanel had been looking forward to all season, as they grew more excited to welcome Tori's aunt Helen and Chanel's mother aboard. On the night before they were to board, Tori voiced her concern to Charles about her aunt finding out about their relationship.

"We'll be more discreet this week," he said. "Maybe she won't pick up on it."

"I don't know," she said dubiously. "My aunt and I are very close and I feel like she'll just know."

"How do you think she would react if she did find out?" he asked.

"Actually, I think she'd be supportive. I just don't want to disappoint her. I know she'd frown on it if she knew I was having an affair with a married man."

"Oh, sweetheart, I hope she would understand. I mean, I don't know her, but from the way you've talked about her, she seems like the kind of person who would not be judgmental." Charles actually felt a little nervous about meeting her. She would be the first member of Tori's family he would meet and he wanted it to go smoothly.

When the two ladies boarded the next day, there was much joy and hugs all around. Chanel's mother was still overcome by Helen's generosity in offering her such a wonderful gift. The girls gave them a full tour of the ship once they were settled in their staterooms and both women were overwhelmed by the sheer size and splendor of the *Aurora*.

"I'm going to be lost every day," Helen exclaimed with a giggle.

"Oh, don't worry," said Tori, "I was lost for the first week I was on board. Chanel or Charles had to walk me everywhere until I finally got my bearings."

Helen and Brenda were excited to explore everything, but most of all, they couldn't wait to see their girls at work in performances. They went to karaoke every time Tori and Chanel were hosting it, and they never missed Tori and Charles in the lounges, either.

Tori introduced Charles to her aunt the first time Helen saw them perform in the lounge. "Aunt Helen, this is Charles Ryan, our music director here on board."

"It's nice to finally meet you, Charles," Helen said graciously. "So you're the person she had all those extra rehearsals with while she was in New York staying with me?"

"Yes, ma'am," he confirmed. "That would be me."

"Well, it certainly paid off," Helen complimented them. "You two make beautiful music together."

Yes, Charles thought, *in more ways than one*. He winked at Tori and gave her a knowing glance, with an impish gleam in his eye and a devilish grin spreading across his face. She shot him a warning glare in response.

They introduced Helen and Brenda to Steven and Marcus, and on most evenings, they would all gather together at the end of the night for a drink after everyone was finished work for the day, before they all turned in for the night. A fun rapport developed between the members of the group and they all had a great time together. The relationship between Chanel and Marcus was getting more serious and Brenda liked him right away. She was happy to see that her daughter had found someone who looked like a good match for her.

When Brenda and Helen finally saw the stage shows, they were brimming with pride and thought Tori and Chanel were the most talented people on the stage.

"Oh, my baby girl, I'm so proud of you I could burst,"

Brenda beamed at her daughter on the night of the first show. "I never thought I'd ever get to see you dong this, but thanks to my dear friend, I can." She turned to Helen then and said sincerely, "I still don't know how I can possibly thank you enough for this, Helen."

"Seeing you like this is all the thanks I need," Helen replied. "Plus, I brought you along for selfish reasons, too. You've become such a good friend to me and I didn't want to hang out on the cruise all by myself. I'm having such a great time with you." The two women were like schoolgirls, taking in all the ship's activities. Tori even convinced them to sing at karaoke one night and the ladies sang a Donna Summer tune together.

Tori asked Charles to sing a duet with her for her opening number that night, and as they sang "Only Us" from *Dear Evan Hansen*, they gazed into each other's eyes and both thought about how fitting the lyrics of the song actually were for their own situation.

Tori and Chanel joined Helen and Brenda on all of the ports of call, and Helen had booked some onshore excursions for them all in each place, which Tori and Chanel had never been able to afford. They all especially enjoyed their visit to a sled dog camp in Juneau.

About halfway through the cruise, Tori and Helen were sitting on deck having lunch together when Helen broached a sensitive topic with her niece. "So Victoria," she began gingerly, "what's going on with you?"

"How do you mean?" asked Tori. "I'm fine. I'm actually really enjoying doing this cruise thing. It suits me."

"That's not what I mean. I can see you're thriving. You look more radiant than I've ever seen you. But I don't think it's all about the work. Talk to me sweetie," she implored. "What exactly is going on between you and Charles Ryan?" she asked, not mincing words about Tori's involvement with the handsome maestro.

Tori was quiet for a long moment, mulling over her words carefully before deciding on her reply. "What makes you think there's anything going on? Yes, Charles and I have gotten close, but..."

"Oh, come on Victoria, I'm not buying that. Be honest with me," Helen coaxed. "It's written all over both of you, and you can cut the sexual energy between the two of you with a knife. Besides, I noticed that there's hardly any of your things left in your room, and Brenda told me that she has spent some nights in your room with Chanel because apparently, you never stay there anymore."

Well damn, Tori thought, *I guess we weren't as discreet as we thought*. "Okay fine," she finally admitted to her favorite aunt what Helen had already surmised. "Charles and I are together, and I love him with my whole heart. We make each other insanely happy."

"But Victoria, I hear he's married," Helen said, although she had not seen a ring on his finger. She had also noticed that Tori wasn't wearing her engagement ring either. Another slip on their part.

"He is, but it's not a marriage. It's a miserable situation," Tori informed her.

"That's what they all say," Helen wisely pointed out, always the voice of reason.

"No, Aunt Helen, it really is true. He told me about it long before we got involved. Plus, I know his son and he even encouraged his father to pursue a relationship with me. Trust me, I didn't go looking for this. We both fought it for so long, but I knew I loved him before we finished in New York, and so did he. We didn't admit it to each other or give into our feelings until early July. I know you're probably very disappointed in me and that's the last thing I ever wanted," she said sadly, averting her eyes in order to avoid the disapproving stare she feared she would see looking back at her on Helen's face.

Helen took Tori's hand across the table and squeezed it tightly. "I could never be disappointed in you, Victoria," she said gently. "I know life is what happens when you're busy making other plans, and that shit happens, so there's no judgment here.

I'm just concerned that you're setting yourself up for a world of hurt by getting involved with him," she said with genuine concern.

Tori looked at her aunt with a grateful smile. "Well, I can play Monday-Morning-Quarterback 'til I'm blue in the face, but it's really not productive at this point," she said in resignation. "Besides, I wouldn't change it, anyway. Being with him is the best thing that's ever happened to me."

"So what now?" Helen inquired. "What happens after this is over and you have to go home to Evan?"

"Honestly, we've been trying not to think about it and just enjoy what we have for as long as we have it. We want to be together, but his situation is really complicated and he feels trapped in his marriage. Every time he brings up divorce, she threatens him with financial ruin and tells him her father will destroy his career. She also threatens him with not seeing his son. And then there's Evan and me. He's my best friend, Aunt Helen, and I wouldn't hurt him for all the tea in China. If Charles can't figure out a resolution to his marriage, I don't see why I would leave Evan. We're good together, and he treats me like gold. Maybe he never has to even know about this," Tori contemplated.

Helen carefully considered what Tori had said. "Secrets in a relationship always have a way of coming out, honey, and if you know you don't love Evan in that way, it's not fair to either of you to settle, just to take the safe route. Yes, you'd no doubt have a good life with him, but is that enough?" she mused.

Tori sighed. "I know you're right. What Charles and I have is incredible. It's loving and gentle and passionate all at the same time. I've never known anything like this, and I didn't realize what was missing in my relationship with Evan until I finally found it with Charles. He's such a good man, Aunt Helen, and he's tried to do the honorable thing by his marriage and his son, but he deserves so much better than that."

"Well, this certainly is quite a debacle isn't it," Helen said, feeling sympathy for her niece. "Darling, please keep in close contact with me. You'll need someone to talk to and I want to be there for you through this," Helen said, her immense love for Tori evident in her voice and all over her face.

"Thanks, Aunt Helen," Tori said, hugging her tightly. "I'm going to need all the support I can get." Helen decided that she would have a little chat with Charles Ryan for herself if the opportunity presented itself.

Tori told Charles that night about her conversation with Helen that day. "So, Aunt Helen knows," she said.

"Okay, so what did she have to say?" he asked tentatively.

"Like I thought, there was no judgment at all. She's just worried I'll get hurt," Tori answered. "And if I'm being honest, so am I."

"Well, I can't blame her for that. She's concerned about you and I'd expect nothing less." He changed the subject then. "By the way, I think there might be another blossoming romance on board right now," he said, grinning.

"Oh really. Inquiring minds want to know. Do tell."

"Well, I saw your aunt on deck today looking a little cozy with Steven."

"Whaaaat?" Tori said with a smile. "I didn't see *that* coming."

"Just reporting what I saw," said Charles with a wink. "They didn't see me, but I definitely saw them."

"Well, well, well, isn't that interesting." She actually loved the idea of her aunt and Steven together. She liked him a lot and had noticed them spending some time together, but had never considered that it might have turned romantic. "They'd be good together, I think. What's his story anyway?" she asked.

"He's divorced and has a grown daughter. It's really hard to maintain a relationship with the kind of life he leads. He's on cruise ships half the year, if not more. But he's based out of New York, so it might just work out for them. I know he's considering retirement in the next few years, anyway, so the timing might just be right for them."

"Wow," said Tori. "I guess love really is in the air on this ship."

Helen's opportunity to corner Charles did present itself the next day when she happened upon Charles sitting alone at the piano in the lounge, preparing for his upcoming set with Tori.

"Good afternoon, Charles," she said cordially in greeting.

"Hello Helen, good afternoon to you. Nice to see you," said Charles, feeling somewhat apprehensive about where this conversation might be headed.

"Where's Victoria?" she asked. "It seems you two are always joined at the hip," she observed.

"I assume she's getting ready for this," he replied.

"Good, I was hoping I'd get a chance to chat with you alone." Charles felt his stomach lurch directly into his chest. *Yes*, he thought, *she's going there.*

"I'm sure I know what you want to talk to me about, Helen," he said stiffly.

"So, while I think this is a conversation you should be having with her father, I have to ask you, exactly what are your intentions toward my niece, Mr. Ryan?" Helen asked, not beating around the bush.

"I can tell you that I love her more than my own life and I've never felt this way before. I can also tell you that I want to spend the rest of my life with her," Charles answered, his love for Tori obvious in his voice. He was putting it all out there, but he wanted to be fully transparent with her.

"But I understand it's more complicated than that, yes?"

"You would be correct in that assessment," Charles affirmed. "We both definitely have some things to work out."

"And just how likely do you think you are to resolve your situation with your marriage?" she asked him, being as direct as she could be with him.

"It's my first priority when I return to New York," he said, continuing to be completely upfront with her.

"Well, here's the thing," she began. "I'm fiercely protective of my niece. She's like a daughter to me and I don't want to see her hurt. Although I fear it may be too late for that if you are unable to resolve things on your end. But what I am asking of you, Charles, is that if you can't extricate yourself from your mess of a life, please do the right thing and set her free. It will destroy her, but she may eventually be able to move on, and she deserves that. It would be far easier than stringing her along, only to break her heart later," she reasoned.

Charles knew she was right. "Yes," he said, "I will make you that promise." He had been put on notice and he knew it.

"Thank you. So we understand each other, then?" Charles nodded. "You seem like an honorable man," Helen continued, "and it's obvious how much you and my niece love one another. I'm hoping with all my heart that it works out for you both," she said and meant it. "Oh, and I'd appreciate it if you didn't tell Victoria about this conversation. I don't want her to think that I'm trying to meddle in her life, because that is not at all my intention here."

Charles nodded again as Tori walked into the room.

"What's going on here?" Tori asked, looking from one to the other, concerned about what Helen might have said to him.

"Oh, nothing dear," Helen said. "Just having a little chat with Charles while we waited for you to get here." Helen left then and took a seat in the lounge with Brenda and Chanel, who had just arrived.

"Okay, what was that all about?" Tori urgently whispered to Charles when Helen was out of earshot.

"Nothing," Charles said, attempting to sound nonchalant. "Just making small talk."

"Are you sure?" she asked, still concerned. She thought they both had looked far too serious when she arrived than two people just making small talk.

"Absolutely, it's all good," he said with a forced smile, and they began their set.

The week passed far too quickly and, in the blink of an eye, the time had come to bid adieu to Helen and Brenda. On their last night, Tori finally got a chance to corner her aunt about Steven. "So," she said, "looks like I'm not the only one to find romance on this ship."

Helen blushed. "It would seem that way," she replied sheepishly.

"So, now it's your turn to 'fess up. What's the story on you and Steven?"

"I like him so much," Helen gushed. "I haven't dated anyone since your uncle died. It's new, but we're going to keep in touch and see where it goes. I feel like a young girl again."

"That's wonderful!" Tori said. "I've really liked him since the day I first met him. He's nice and really funny, and I think you're good for each other," Tori concluded, giving her blessing to the budding relationship. "Please keep me posted on this."

"I will," Helen promised. "Like I said, we're just taking it slow and we'll see what happens. And Victoria, I meant what I said, please keep talking to me about all this stuff with Charles. I'll want to know what's happening."

"I promise I will, and thanks for being so supportive," Tori said, hugging her. "So what are your plans for when you leave tomorrow?"

"I'm actually staying in Seattle for a few days to spend some time with your father before I head home," she said.

"Please, Aunt Helen, don't say anything to Dad about all this," Tori begged her.

"Oh, you know I won't say a word. I'll take it to my grave if I have to," Helen reassured her, and Tori knew she could trust her.

"Thank you," said Tori with relief.

The next day, they hugged the ladies goodbye and life aboard the *Aurora* went on as usual.

Chapter 14

The time after Helen and Brenda left went by very quickly. They celebrated Charles' forty-first birthday on August fifteenth, and he laughed when he opened his present from her: several sets of new tux buttons and a beautiful pair of cuff links.

"There's no possible way I can make your birthday as special as you made mine, but I thought the least I could do was replace the buttons and cuff links we destroyed," she said.

"Well, I definitely don't need to make a birthday wish," said Charles, "because my wish already came true. But I can think of something you can do to make my day special," he said with a seductive grin, burrowing his face into the curve of her neck and leaving a trail of kisses as he made his way to her earlobe.

"Well, you get that every day," she joked.

Charles looked her directly in the eyes and grew serious. "Yes, I do, and every day it's a gift. Every day you give me the gift of your body, your soul and your love, and there's no greater gift you could ever give me. Tori, you *are* my gift," he said lovingly.

"Well, would you like to unwrap your gift now?" she asked suggestively.

"You don't have to ask me twice," he said, and with that, he took her in his arms, carried her to the bed and made love to her for the rest of the evening.

"I was just thinking," she said, lying in his arms later, "about how many of those songs that we picked out for the lounge right at the beginning turned out to foreshadow what was about to happen with us. It's like it was serendipitous that we chose them. I mean, look at that line from 'Anyone Can Whistle' that talks about learning to let go. That is a perfect description of what you've done for me, Charles. You helped me learn to let go, lower my guard and learn to be free, just like the song says. You've changed my life in so many ways, my love."

"And you've changed mine," he said and kissed her, long and slow. "But, I know what you mean about the songs. I feel the same way about the ones that I do. Whenever I sing 'Not While I'm Around' and 'Love Changes Everything,' I'm singing them to you. Same with 'Being Alive.' But the one that hits me the most has to be 'You're Still You.' I sing that from the bottom of my soul," he confessed, "just for you."

"I picked so many of those selections that I did at karaoke especially for you, too. 'Break My Heart,' and 'Clumsy.' Lots of them."

"Yeah, same here. And then it was a song you did at karaoke that eventually brought us together," he said, referring to "That's How You Know."

"I still can't believe you did all those things. That was probably the sweetest thing a guy could do. When I figured it out, I nearly passed out."

"I was of two minds about that," he confessed. "Part of me hoped you'd never put two-and-two together, while the other part of me wanted you to. I knew that if you did, it would reveal how I felt and I honestly didn't know if that would be a good thing or not."

"So how do you feel about that now?" she asked.

"I've never been this deliriously happy in my entire life. Tori, you are the sun, moon and stars in my world," he said, gazing into her big beautiful eyes. Falling in love with her had made him feel more alive than he had in years, and he realized even more acutely what had been missing in his life.

"And you are mine," she echoed, and they made love again. Afterward, she let out a contented sigh as she lay encircled in his arms, her head resting on his chest as she drifted off to sleep to the beating of his heart.

The end of August came and Andy returned for his second week aboard with them. After he boarded and got himself settled, he knocked on his father's room door and was pleasantly surprised when Tori answered.

"Andy!" she cried with delight when she saw him.

"Hey, Son," Charles said, coming over to embrace him. "Come on in. We can't wait to hear all about your summer."

Andy came in and sat down on the couch. He told them he'd had a great time at theatre camp and Tori asked with interest about what show they had done.

"*Guys and Dolls*," he replied.

"Oh, fun!" Tori enthused. "What part did you play?"

"Nathan Detroit," he replied proudly.

"Oh my God, I wish I could have seen it!" Tori gushed. "I'll bet you were awesome."

"I hope so," Andy replied modestly. "People seemed to like it, anyway. We got a lot of positive feedback."

"I played Miss Adelaide in that show once during summer stock when I was in college," Tori told him. "It was probably one of the most fun shows I've ever done."

Just then, Tori and Andy broke into a rendition of "Sue Me," which is performed in the show by Nathan and Adelaide. They broke up laughing when they were done, and Charles applauded. "I think you guys are ready for the next Broadway revival of that," he joked.

"Oh, it's such a great show. Frank Loesser was a genius," said Tori, referring to the show's legendary composer.

"So, what's happening now?" Charles asked. "What do you two want to do?" It was still mid-afternoon and the ship was about to set sail. Charles and Tori did not have to be at the lounge on Monday afternoons while passengers were boarding for the next cruise, but they did have to go that evening, and she had karaoke after that. "We've got a few hours until we have to do the lounge."

"I'm starving," said Andy. "Let's go grab a snack on deck," he suggested.

"I'm up for that," Charles agreed.

"Actually, I gotta go," Tori said. "I've got an appointment to get my hair trimmed." Mondays were a favorite day for staff to take advantage of the spa and salon on board, as it was their slowest day, due to the cruise change-over.

"Okay, we'll see you in a little while, then," Charles said, kissing her on the cheek.

While Charles and Andy were eating a light lunch on deck, Andy smiled at his father. "So, it's not hard to tell that things have changed in your relationship with Tori," he said.

Knowing there was no point in denying it, Charles replied, "I guess you could say that, yeah." He was glowing and couldn't hide his happiness from his son.

"Well, hallelujah!" Andy cried gleefully. "It's about time. So when did this happen?"

"Actually only a few days after you left at the beginning of July," Charles confirmed. "It just got too difficult for us both to keep fighting it anymore."

"Well, this just makes my whole summer," Andy said, delighted.

"Son, I'm not proud of being unfaithful to your mother. That's not who I am," Charles said with genuine remorse.

"Dad, look, I told you earlier this summer that she doesn't deserve your loyalty. It's obvious how insanely happy you are with Tori and I couldn't be happier."

"It doesn't make it right," said Charles ruefully.

"Look, I agree with you. I didn't grow up with you as my father without learning a strict moral code. But Dad, it's about time you were happy. So what are you going to do now?"

"I really don't know, Son," Charles said honestly. "I'm trying not to think about it, but I know the time is coming up pretty quickly when I'm going to have no choice but to face this."

"You need to get out of this farce of a marriage with Mom and marry that girl. That's my two cents," Andy said bluntly.

"That's what I want more than anything. But it's more complicated than that, and the last thing a parent should ever do is burden their children with their problems. You already know far more than is proper for you to know."

"Don't sweat it, Dad," Andy said. "After all, I did tell you two months ago to go for it," he reminded Charles.

Charles smiled. "Yes you did," he said, "and you were right. She's the best thing that's ever happened to me. Aside from you, that is," he added. He hugged his son and they left to go see if Tori was finished with her hair appointment.

Charles and Tori had another great week with Andy, and in a flash, it was over and time for him to head home. But this time when Charles left him at the airport, he knew he would be seeing him again in a couple of short weeks. However, as happy as that made him, it was also a rude reminder that his time with Tori would be coming to an end sooner than he cared to admit.

During their last two cruises, a pall settled over Charles and Tori as the prospect of their uncertain future weighed heavily on their hearts. Things got tense between them and they were both irritable and often short-tempered with each other, as they tried to come to terms with the fact that their fairy tale summer was coming to an end and they would inevitably have to face reality very soon. They made love more often than they ever had, which neither one of them would have even thought possible, and clung to one another with a desperation they could not put into words.

Everything in the last week was bittersweet and the last time they did the stage shows was very emotional for Tori. It brought tears to her eyes when she and Chanel sang their duet together in the revue show for the final time, which was "For Good" from *Wicked*, the lyrics about friendship resonating deeply with both of them. And when the full company closed the show with "Seasons of Love" from *Rent*, Tori could barely hold it together. She savored her last week of fun at karaoke, and she found the thought of not performing with Charles again in the lounges to be unbearable.

On their last night on the *Aurora* before docking in Seattle the next day for the final time, Tori was gathering up all of her things that had migrated up to Charles' room over the previous two months, so that she could take them back to her room to begin the arduous task of packing. She and Charles both felt as if someone had died, and looked morose, as though they were in a deep state of mourning, which effectively they were.

"So, we've known all along that this day was coming," she said. "We've just been evading the issue for months, but we can't run away from it any longer."

"I know," he said ruefully, wrapping his arms around her.

"So what the hell happens now?" she asked.

"I don't know. I just know I want to be with you every single day for the rest of my life. But beyond that, I have no idea how we get there," he lamented.

"What do you plan to do about Meredith?" she asked, fearing his answer.

"I've been thinking a lot about that," he said. "I'm going to tell her I want a divorce, but I know what she'll do. She'll do what she always does and remind me that she has me by the balls and that it would not be in my best interest to pursue that, which takes me right back to square one. I don't know what choice I have. I'm as trapped as I've always been," he said, feeling defeated and frustrated that he could not see a way out of his predicament.

"There's always a choice, Charles," she said evenly, a little more testily than she had intended. "If I am indeed the great love of your life, and you want to be with me as much as you say, then there's a choice. But you're the one who has to make it," she stated matter-of-factly.

"I'm not the only one in a situation here, in case you've forgotten. You're fucking engaged and you don't want to deal with that either," he shot back at her, his voice sharp.

Tori's body went rigid. "Yes, I'm having issues breaking my best friend's heart and losing him for the rest of my life.

THAT'S HOW YOU KNOW

Sorry if that's so fucking difficult for you to grasp," she retorted, exasperated. "Charles, we've only ever lived together in this little sheltered cocoon, where we have none of the responsibilities of real life. I've never even seen where you live, for Christ's sake. What if we risk everything to be together and find out we're an absolute disaster in the real world and completely incompatible?"

"Well, we know we're compatible between the sheets," he said with a seductive grin in an attempt to defuse the tension, his eyes flickering suggestively toward the bed.

Tori rounded on him, furious. "Fuck, Charles, I'm being serious here," she rebuked him, narrowing her eyes and meeting his gaze squarely.

"I know, baby, I'm sorry. I deserved that," he apologized. He moved closer to her then and reached out his hand to touch her shoulder. But she flinched, refusing to be placated, and recoiled from his touch for the first time ever in their relationship. She was angry with him and was making it perfectly clear through her body language that she wanted him to keep his distance. The space between them felt like an ocean and Tori wondered if it could ever be crossed again. Every muscle in her body wanted to throw herself into his arms, but she remained motionless, her anger bolting her body rigidly in place.

"I honestly don't think we have anything to worry about," Charles said, trying to reassure her and alleviate her doubts. "We're so well-matched in every way, not just in the sack, and I think we'd be perfectly fine. Besides wasn't it you who told me that there are no guarantees in this life, and sometimes you just have to take a leap and hope for the best?"

She did remember saying that, and was not happy to hear her own words being used against her now. "Look," she said irritably, "be that as it may, this keeps coming back to you and whether you're willing to do what you have to do to get out of your marriage. If your financial security and your career are more important to you than us, then I'm not willing to risk losing Evan, either."

"So are you saying that if I were free, you'd break it off with him?"

"Yes, Charles, that's exactly what I'm saying," she said definitively. "And I'll probably lose the best friend I've ever had. But that's you now, Charles. *You* are my best friend. You are the other half that makes me whole. So yes, I'm willing to do what I have to for us. The question is, are you?" she pressed.

He hesitated for a spit second, his pain evident in his beautiful hazel eyes.

"Well, I guess that's my answer isn't it?" she said as tears fell from her eyes. "When you figure out your shit, Charles, let me know," she demanded. "But until then, I will stay with Evan, provided I can live with myself for hiding this from him, and I'll marry him next August if you haven't managed to work it out," she said stubbornly. "So the ball, as they say, is entirely in your court." She didn't want to give him an ultimatum, but she didn't see any other way around it.

"So you're just willing to settle then, even now that you know the difference after what we've shared?"

"Oh, that's fucking rich coming from you," Tori yelled, combative. "Isn't that exactly what you're doing? You're settling for a shit personal life to protect your finances and your career. What's the difference?"

"The difference is that I made my bed and I've forced myself to lie in it. But you, you're a beautiful young woman and could still prevent yourself from making a huge mistake. You've got your whole life ahead of you and could still be with someone you love eventually, even if it's not me." The thought of her being with anyone else made him ill, but he knew he owed it to her to point out the error in her judgment.

"Charles, I don't want to be with anyone but you. If I can't have you, then I might as well be with a man that I adore, and who would give me a wonderful life and treat me well. If that's settling, then I guess that's what I'll do."

"Tori, I'm scared, goddammit. I love you so fucking much

and I'm just so scared of losing you forever," he wailed, his anguish etched on his face. "I can't bear the thought of you in another man's bed, or loving anyone but me," he added as tears threatened to spill from his eyes.

"Then make your decision and let me know when you do," she challenged him. "Until then, I will do my best to move on with my life... without you," she spat with a sense of finality.

Her words hit him like a slap in the face. "Wow, that's harsh. Why don't you tell me how you really feel," he said sarcastically. The hurt that was so raw on her face was unbearable to Charles and he averted his eyes to avoid her fierce stare. "So you're basically saying I need to grow a pair?" he finally asked.

"You can interpret it however you like, Charles," said Tori, her eyes blazing. "Look, I need some air and some space. I haven't even started packing yet and it's already nearly midnight, so just give me the space I need right now. Please, Charles," she pleaded.

"Okay, I'll respect that," he acquiesced, barely able to speak through the lump in his throat. "But will I see you tomorrow before we leave?"

"I'll see how I feel," she answered, and he died a little bit inside as he watched her walk out of his room, and possibly his life, forever. He sat on the bed they had shared for the last two months and wept.

Tori went for a walk around the ship then. It was pretty much deserted at that late hour, so she allowed herself to linger in all of her favorite places, savoring the memories she and Charles had made there together. She sat in the lounge where they had performed together so many times, and finally allowed the tears to overtake her. Steven walked by then and stopped when he saw the state she was in. He sat beside her and put his arms around her. "Hey, hey, what's going on here?" he asked in a soothing voice. "You can't be that sad to leave us, now can you?"

"Oh Steven," she said, a ravaged look in her eyes, "everything is such a giant fucking mess. Charles and I just had a fight. We knew this day was coming, but it's just so real now," she said, sobbing into his shoulder.

"I know, I know. Charles has been dreading this, too. But I can tell you this. He loves you with everything he has, and I know you will find your way back to each other. Of that I have no doubt whatsoever. I've never seen a love like you two have in my life."

"But does he love me enough to risk it all to be with me? That's the question," Tori responded, her voice trembling.

"I've known Charles for several years now, and one thing I do know is that he's never felt for anyone in his life the way he does for you. He's told me a million times. So I trust that he'll work it all out, and by the time this all gets started again for next season, you'll be back in each other's arms where you belong. You have to believe that, Tori," he implored.

"I'm trying," she said through her tears. "Anyway, I have to go. I haven't even started packing yet, so I still have a lot to do before this night is out."

"Let me walk you back to your room," Steven offered. She took his arm and let him lead her like a child back to her room. When they reached her door, she thanked him for being such a good friend, and went inside to find Chanel finishing her own packing. As soon as she saw Tori's tear-stained face, Chanel rushed over to her and put her arms around her friend. "Tori, oh my God, what's wrong?" she asked, alarmed.

Tori collapsed in her friend's arms as a fresh wave of tears overwhelmed her. "Charles and I had a huge fight," she managed to choke out.

"Come sit down and tell me everything," Chanel said, sitting beside her on Tori's bed.

Tori tearfully recounted the details of her conversation with Charles. "Oh, I'm so sorry," Chanel finally said after Tori was finished unloading her immense burden.

"I mean, if he's not willing to fight for us, I don't know what else there is to say," said Tori grimly. "I know he's scared, but so am I. I've already told him I'm willing to break Evan's heart and potentially lose my best friend for him, but not if he's not willing to get out of his marriage."

"Tori, I know in my heart that he's going to do the right thing. I've honestly never seen a man so in love in my life as he is with you."

"That's what Steven said. I just hope it's enough," Tori said, devastated. She sat there for a long time and Chanel held her friend in her arms and let her cry for as long as she needed.

Finally Tori got up and said, "If I don't start packing, I'm never getting out of here tomorrow. Anyway, enough about my mess, I want to know how things are going with you and Marcus. Where do things stand between you two?" she asked.

Chanel perked up at the mention of her beau. "Tori, I think he could be *the one*," she said, her face lighting up. "He's planning to move to Portland this fall to be closer to me. He thinks he could do well there as a freelance photographer, but it means quitting a decent job and a sure thing where he is." Marcus lived in Salem, Oregon and worked as a photographer at a local newspaper during the seasons when he wasn't working on the cruise ship. "It's a big step, but we're ready for it, and I've never been happier."

"Chanel, that's wonderful!" Tori said sincerely. This news had definitely brightened her night. "I'm so freakin' happy for you I could burst. You deserve this."

"You deserve happiness with Charles, too, and I want that for you more than anything," said Chanel.

Tori's mood sobered once again at her friend's comment. "Me too," she said as she continued packing. She went over to her closet and pulled the box from the top shelf, which contained the dress Charles had given her. She opened the lid and gently ran her fingers over the soft fabric as a torrent of fresh tears engulfed her.

Chanel stood beside her and put her arms around her. "You'll wear that again for him for something really special. I can feel it. You have to believe in him, Tori," Chanel urged.

"I'm trying to," she sobbed.

By the time Tori finished all her packing, Chanel had drifted off to sleep. Knowing there was very little chance of her getting any rest that night, Tori sat down at the desk, took out a sheet of her favorite stationary and tasked herself with writing a letter to Charles, pouring out everything she felt for him, her fears, and her hopes for their future together. She hoped she would get the chance to give it to him before he left the next day. She found that writing the letter was actually quite therapeutic and allowed her to get a lot off her chest. When she finished, she went to bed and fell into a restless sleep as she hugged the teddy bear Charles had given her so many months ago when she had been ill.

Meanwhile, Charles wasn't faring much better in his own room. This was the first night he had spent without Tori since they first made love, and he couldn't believe that they weren't spending their last night together in each other's arms. He was sitting miserably on his couch when he heard a knock on his door. He jumped up and rushed to answer it, hoping with every cell in his body that Tori had come back to spend the night with him. His face fell when he opened the door to find Steven standing there.

"Sorry mate," Steven said apologetically, seeing the devastation on Charles' face. "I know I'm not the person you were hoping to see, but I wanted to check on you to see if you're okay. I just saw Tori crying in the lounge. I just walked her back to her room, so I knew she wasn't with you. Charles, she's absolutely gutted."

"I know how she feels," Charles said in agony. Steven could tell he had been crying as well.

"She told me about your quarrel."

"It's not like we didn't know this day was coming," Charles said. "We've been avoiding facing the situation, but the time has come when we have no other choice."

"So what are you going to do now?" Steven inquired.

"Fucked if I know," Charles admitted. "She told me the ball is in my court. She said she's willing to leave her fiancé, but that she wouldn't do it if I can't get my shit together. She said that if we can't be together, she'd marry him because he's her best friend and she does love him. She just realizes now that it's not the kind of love that we have. I know what I have to do, but I'm terrified of what I stand to lose in the process."

"You have much more to lose if you don't," Steven pointed out. "'With great risk comes great reward,'" he said, quoting Thomas Jefferson. "And she's worth fighting for, Charles."

"I know she is," Charles confirmed. "Helen told me that if I can't work things out at home, I should do the right thing and set her free. I know she's right," he said, mournfully. "I just can't bear the thought of it."

"I do agree with that," Steven said, "But I also know the kind of man you are, Charles, and I know you're going to do whatever it takes to be with her."

"Unless I'm too much of a goddamned coward to follow through," Charles said, giving voice to his self-doubt.

"I don't believe that for a second," Steven said, patting his friend on the back in reassurance. "I'm here for you any time you need me, day or night. All you have to do is ring me up. Doesn't matter when. I'm in New York during the autumn months, so I won't be far if you need anything."

"Thanks, Steve, you're the best friend a guy could ask for, and I appreciate all your support," Charles said, embracing his friend.

Steven left then and Charles attempted, unsuccessfully, to get some sleep.

The next day dawned sunny and gorgeous as the *Aurora* docked in Seattle for the final time, but the splendor of the day did not match Tori's mood. The ship was busy as everyone, both passengers and crew, bustled about as they debarked. As expected, Tori got very little sleep and looked tired and distraught as she got ready for the difficult day ahead.

When Chanel was ready to leave, she embraced Tori for a long moment. "I want you to take care of yourself, alright," she said to her friend.

"I'm going to miss you so much. You're the best girlfriend I've ever had and I love you to pieces," Tori said, crying again. She felt like that's all she had done since she and Charles argued the night before.

"Hey, I'm not that far away. Call me anytime. I don't care what time it is. And besides, we're going to see each other. I'll take a trip to Seattle at some point to visit you and you can come to Portland whenever you want. We'll always be besties. 'For good,'" she said, quoting the lyrics to their duet from *Wicked* that they had performed together all summer in the revue.

After Chanel left and most of the others had also cleared out, Tori sat on her bed thinking about how much her life had changed since starting this journey back in March. She hadn't anticipated any of it, and certainly hadn't gone into it expecting to fall desperately in love with this man, who turned her entire world upside down. She lingered in her room for as long as she could, not wanting to face what awaited her when she finally returned home.

She wanted to give Charles the letter she had written the night before and hoped he had not debarked yet. She called the front desk to ask if he had already left and was told that he had not. She grabbed the letter and was about to open the door when there was a knock on it. She opened it to find a dishevelled Charles standing in front of her, looking as though he had had as horrendous a night as she had.

"Oh, thank God you're still here," he said, relief washing over his face. "I was afraid I was too late and I couldn't bear the thought of you leaving without hearing me tell you how much I love you. I realized last night when you left that I hadn't said 'I love you' and I never want you to leave my presence ever again, even for a moment, without that being the last thing you hear out of my mouth." He knew he was rambling, but couldn't stop the barrage of words spewing from his lips. There were tears freely falling onto his face, but he didn't care. He just urgently wanted her to know where he stood.

Tori took him into her arms and started kissing away his tears as they mingled with her own. They stood there, kissing passionately for several minutes. "I love you, Charles. You are all I want, and you need to know that," said Tori, her heart consumed with the love she felt for him, and her voice filled with all the anguish she was feeling in that moment.

"Last night was the hardest night of my entire life," he admitted. "I got absolutely no sleep and all I wanted was to spend our last night together, making love to you."

"It was the hardest night of my life, too," she said. "Charles, can you please make love to me now, one last time?" she requested softly.

"I can't think of anything I'd rather do," he said as he began to undress her.

Their lovemaking was bittersweet as they basked in every part of each other's bodies, as though they were trying to etch every inch of one another into their memory in anticipation of their upcoming separation, not knowing if or when they would see each other again. They were gentle and slow with one another, and came together with a force that mirrored the intensity of the desperation they both felt at that moment.

"Looks like we survived our first real argument," he said as they held each other afterward.

"Yeah, I guess we did. I have to say that the making up after is amazing," she said.

"So do you still have no regrets about us?" he asked. "Would you have thought twice about getting involved with me, knowing what you know now, in order to avoid this heartache?"

"No, absolutely not," she said adamantly, standing by what she had told him months before. "If this turns out to be all we have, I'll cherish it for the rest of my life. Maybe we're like the butterfly when it emerges from its cocoon," she said, returning to the cocoon analogy she had used before. "The butterfly emerges, amazingly beautiful, but only lives for a short time. Maybe that's us, and we're the butterfly, beautiful for a short time but not meant to last," she said as tears spilled from her eyes once again.

He took her angelic face, marred by her tears, in his hands and kissed her deeply. "Don't give up on us yet, my love," he said with tenderness in his eyes. "I'll find a way to work this out. In the meantime, don't be alarmed if you don't hear from me for awhile. I don't want to risk Meredith finding out about us. If she gets wind of who you are, she'll try to take you down with me and I won't have her destroying your life, too. So, just know every day how much I love you, and have faith that I'm dealing with things on my end."

She nodded, understanding his reasoning, but it did not make it any easier for her to deal with the grim reality of this forthcoming separation. "I get that," she said simply.

He looked at the time then and sighed. "I have to go. I've got a plane to catch." Tearing himself away from her naked body was the hardest thing he'd ever done. "I love you with my life. Always remember that," he said, kissing her for the last time.

She remembered the letter she had written him then and gave it to him when he finished getting dressed. "I wrote you this last night. There's nothing in there you don't already know, but I wanted you to have something to remind you every day of how much I love you." He took the letter and tucked it into the inside pocket of his jacket, intending to read it on the plane.

He hated the thought of leaving her, and they both looked forlorn as he closed the door behind him. Tori got dressed after he left, wondering how she was going to go home and try to go back to living her normal life again. She knew she would not be able to avoid Evan's advances now and didn't know if she would be able to let him make love to her that day, while she could still so vividly feel Charles' hands and mouth on her skin and smell his scent in her hair. Could she even look Evan in the face now? She sat on her bed and sobbed. This was a nightmare from which she desperately wanted to awaken.

Meanwhile, as Charles was boarding his plane, he was already missing her. When he got settled in his seat and the plane took off, he took the letter she had written in her immaculate handwriting out of his pocket and read it.

My Darling Charles:

I can't believe I'm sitting here writing you this letter instead of spending our last night together in your arms. I think, subconsciously, I figured that picking a fight with you would make it easier to say goodbye to you tomorrow. Well, it didn't work. All it did was deprive us of our last opportunity to make beautiful love to each other before we are forced to part, and I am so sorry for that.

How can I even begin to tell you how you've changed my life in these last six months? You've shown me love I didn't know could even exist, and it has changed me immeasurably for the better. You've brought out a side of me I didn't think possible, and I know now that you are the one great love of my life. When I first gave myself to you physically, I became entirely yours in every single way, and I want you to know that making love with you is the most beautiful thing I have ever experienced in my entire life. For me It is far more than just the melding of our bodies; it also represents the fusion of our two souls, joining together as one. I need you to go away from here knowing that there is only you for me and you are all I ever want in this life. The thought of continuing on without you now is unbearable for me, but it is my unwavering belief that our love will transcend all the obstacles in our path. I guess I wanted to write you this letter so that you could keep it with you for those times when you need reminding that you are my universe, and that I never want to live in a world that doesn't involve having you by my side every day for the rest of my life. Be well, my love, and know that I will not be whole again until I am back in your arms.

Forever yours,
Tori

Charles reread the letter several times with tears welling

up in his eyes, and knew he would read it many more times over the coming months. He knew exactly what he had to do. He had a full-scale war to wage with Meredith and he just hoped he wouldn't lose everything he had worked so hard for in the process. But he also knew his future with Tori was worth fighting for and he could no longer imagine his world without her.

Part 3

After the Cruise

Chapter 15 – Tori

Tori's stepmother picked her up at the terminal after she debarked from the *Aurora* and dropped her home after they had a quick lunch together to catch up. Tori was relieved to find her cozy apartment empty when she opened the door. Evan was still at work and she welcomed the time alone to wrap her head around her current reality. It felt as though the entire stable foundation she had built with Evan over so many years - a lifetime - could be in danger of crumbling, and that thought sat heavy on her heart.

She unpacked and took a shower, hating to wash the residual traces of Charles and their lovemaking of that morning from her body. Her tears mingled with the water cascading over her body as she stood there, bereft at the thought of living her life without Charles in it.

She began prepping food for dinner and realized she had actually missed cooking during the months she was away. She thought of the day by the fire pit at the park in Juneau when Charles told her he loved to cook and may have become a chef if he had not decided on music as a career. Was this what it was going to be like for her now? Was she destined to think of him every minute? Would everything she did somehow remind her of him?

She was making spaghetti sauce when Evan walked through the door. "Hey baby, you home?" he called to her as he entered.

"In the kitchen," she called back.

He entered the kitchen and pulled her into a loving

embrace, kissing her. "It smells really great in here," he said. "Boy, it's nice to finally come home to smell food cooking. It's been way too long."

"I know. I actually missed cooking while I was away," she said.

They chatted with their usual ease while she finished making dinner, and after they ate and the dishes were done, she called her father to touch base with him. She got a text from Chanel saying she got home safe and sound, and then she and Evan cuddled up on the couch to watch a few episodes of their favorite show. It was getting late by then and she was feeling tired, so they decided to go to bed. Tori's heart began to race as she thought of what would surely come next. She knew she could not put Evan off forever, and just as she had expected, as soon as they entered the bedroom, he took her in his arms and began kissing her passionately.

"Please don't tell me you're on your period again," he said with a quirky grin. She adored his clean-cut boyish good looks and deep brown eyes.

She wasn't, but for a second considered lying to him. "No, I'm not," she said, deciding to be honest about it. He unbuttoned her blouse then and unfastened her bra, teasing her nipples with his fingertips. When they finished undressing each other, he led her to the bed and they made love with the usual tender and gentle familiarity of two people who had loved one another for so long. But Tori realized now, more than ever, that it lacked the kind of passion she had found in Charles' arms. They held each other afterward and Evan noticed that Tori was unusually quiet. He was used to talking with her during the time after their lovemaking.

"You're really quiet, honey. Are you okay?" he asked gently.

"Yeah, I'm fine. It just feels a little weird being back to my normal life. It's kind of disorienting after being in a totally different world for so long, you know." She really hadn't been in her normal routine since she left for New York in late March.

"It'll probably take a few days for me to get my land legs back and start feeling settled again, that's all." *It wasn't a total lie*, she thought.

"That makes sense," said Evan. He fell asleep soon after and she turned away from his embrace as silent tears slid from her eyes onto her pillow. She felt like she had just been unfaithful to Charles and didn't know if she could continue to do that for long.

The next morning, after Evan went to work, she called her mother to check in. She had kept in contact with her while she was in New York, but not as much while she was on the cruise. Her mother was thrilled to hear from her and wanted to know all about Tori's summer. Tori told her everything about the cruise and how much she loved the experience, but said nothing of Charles and their affair.

After talking with her mother she ventured out to check in at the 5th Avenue Theatre to find out if everything was still on track for the December and February shows she was slated to be in that season. They confirmed that everything was still going ahead as planned. She would be playing a featured role in the December production of Irving Berlin's *Holiday Inn*, but would be playing the lead in February in Bacharach and David's *Promises, Promises*. That would be a fun show, which was slated to run through Valentine's, and she was delighted to learn that the male lead who would be playing opposite her in that was someone she had worked with many times before and absolutely adored. She also set up a schedule to return to her part-time administrative duties that she usually did for them during the season.

After leaving the 5th, she ran a few more errands and headed home. She and Evan cooked dinner together that night and he seemed distracted. Now it was her turn to ask him if anything was amiss.

"No, no, it's all good. Just a little tired is all," he answered vaguely. They watched some more episodes of their show again that night and she was relieved when he did not try to make love to her when they went to bed.

Life settled back into its usual routine throughout October, and in some ways, her summer with Charles felt like an out-of-body experience or a dream. She missed him so much it hurt, and she thought of him constantly, wondering how things were going on his end. She talked to her aunt Helen and to Chanel frequently, and they were both a great comfort to her. It was reassuring to have people in whom she could confide and who knew what was going on with her.

She noticed that a slight distance had developed between her and Evan and they did not make love as often as they used to. By late October, she knew she could no longer continue pretending that the relationship was any more than a platonic friendship for her, and she knew they needed to have a serious talk about their future before she got any more entangled in wedding preparations for the following summer. She realized it wasn't fair to either of them to continue in a relationship that was a lie.

It was the weekend before Halloween when she finally got the courage to address the subject with him. They were getting ready for bed after getting home from a Halloween party, where they had dressed as Jack and Sally from *The Nightmare Before Christmas*. "Evan, there's something really important that I think we need to talk about," she tenuously broached as she sat on the bed, folding her costume.

Evan heard the instability in her voice and climbed into bed, concerned about what was on her mind. "Okay, what's up?" he asked gingerly.

Tori took a deep breath, not knowing exactly how to begin this difficult confession she knew she had to make. "So," she began and paused before she spoke again. "Um, Evan, something happened during the summer while I was on the cruise." She hesitated, trying to will herself to continue.

Evan could easily see the discomfort this was causing her. "Go on," he prodded her gently, a perplexed expression on his face.

She knew the only way to get through this was to just spit it out. "I met a man during rehearsals in New York, and we fell madly in love with each other. Neither one of us wanted to give in to it, but eventually, we just couldn't fight it anymore. I came back here with every intention of putting it behind me and moving on with you and our life, but I love him, Evan, and I realized it's not fair to either of us to continue like this." She was openly crying now. "I don't even know if we're going to be able to be together, if I'm being totally honest. He has a lot to work out before that can happen, but either way, I couldn't go on, knowing that my love for you wasn't more than friendship. I didn't fully realize that until I experienced the kind of love I feel for him. All I've been able to think about is that I don't want to lose you. You're still my best friend, Evan, and the thought of hurting you tears me apart. I can't bear to live my life without you in it, but I know that that might not be possible now." She paused and looked at Evan, trying to gauge his reaction, but he remained stone-faced.

"We've been through so much together," she continued. "You were there through James' death and my eating disorders, my years in therapy, my appendix debacle and my recovery from that. We even lost our virginity to each other. It just seemed natural for us to take our relationship to that next level. I think everyone simply expected that to happen, including us. I just can't forget all that and go on without you."

Evan was silent for a long time. "Please say something," she begged him, crying harder now.

Evan knew it was time to tell her something that he had been keeping from her as well. He finally spoke after mulling over his words for awhile. "So, if we're making confessions about last summer here," he began, "I have something to tell you, too." He drew in a deep breath and let it out slowly. "I met someone during the summer as well, and we also love each other. I've been struggling with the same dilemma as you have. I've realized that we were not meant to be more than best friends, and I've been sick over the thought of losing you."

"Oh my God," she blurted out, stupefied. This was the last thing she ever expected to hear from him, but then again, it was probably the last thing Evan had expected to hear from her as well. "So where do things stand with you two now? Who is she? Is it someone I know?"

Evan braced himself for his next confession and to speak words that he had never said out loud to her, or anyone else for that matter. "Well, that's another thing, and this is really difficult for me to tell you, and I hope it doesn't totally mess you up, but the person I fell for is not a woman. His name is Ben. Tori, I'm gay." His voice faltered to a whisper and she was unsure whether she had heard him correctly.

All the color drained from Tori's face and her body went rigid as she tried to process what he had just said to her. She looked at him, utterly gobsmacked, with her mouth hanging open in disbelief. "Wait, what?" were the only words her brain could manage to generate. "I didn't hear that right. I couldn't have." How could she have known this man for their entire lives and been as intimate as they were without her knowing something that important about him?

"I know this is a lot and I can only imagine what's going through your head right now," he said, averting his eyes from her bewildered stare. "He's a trainer at the gym I go to and we just clicked."

Tori could not keep up with the rush of questions invading her mind. "How long have you known that you're gay?" She could barely make herself say the words.

"Since I was twelve or thirteen. It really scared me and I didn't want to admit it to myself. I vowed to make a relationship with a girl work, and who better than with my best friend. But Tori, I want to be perfectly clear that I never, ever used you to keep who I am in the closet. I went into our relationship with all the best intentions. I wanted us to be happy, and I think we have been. I'm still crazy about you and you're the most important person in my life. I'd die for you without a second thought," he said, hoping with everything in him that he could make her understand.

"How many relationships have you had with men since we've been together?" she asked, unable to believe that she was having this conversation with him.

"Only one other before this one," he told her honestly. "I had a short-lived relationship with a guy when you were at Carnegie Mellon. Again, I was scared of the truth and that's when I asked you to marry me. I'm sorry Tori, I'm so, *so* sorry. I know this is a lot to take in," he said, openly crying himself now. "I couldn't come out. Not with my parents as ultra-conservative as they are. I know how they feel about homosexuality, and I knew they'd disown me. But now, I'm realizing that it's my life and I have to live it as my true authentic self."

"So where do things stand with this man now?"

"He pretty much told me at the end of the summer that until I'm ready to be open about who I am, we're done. We haven't been together since you got home." Tori thought it was interesting that Evan had been given a similar ultimatum to the one she had given Charles about getting out of his marriage.

Tori cringed as her next question began to formulate in her mind. "Were you ever with him in our bed?" she asked, feeling bile rise up in her throat as she awaited his answer.

"No, no, not *ever*," he said, shaking his head emphatically. "I'd never do that. We always went to his place," he reassured her. Tori was relived to hear that.

"I thought I knew everything about you," she said, mortified, after taking a moment to let it all sink in.

"And you do," said Evan. "You do know every single thing about me, except for this one thing."

"Well, it's kind of a big fucking thing, Evan!" she retorted, still in disbelief of all he had confessed to her that night.

"I know, and It's killed me to keep it from you." As hard as this was, he felt the weight of a giant boulder lifted from his shoulders.

"How could I sleep with a gay man for all of these years

and not know it?" The thought was unfathomable to her.

"It's really not uncommon. Lots of gay men are married for years and have kids and their wives never know," he pointed out.

She knew that was true, but never imagined it would be her. "Yes, I know, but every time I hear about a situation like that, I've always asked myself how the hell the wife couldn't know something that intimate about her husband," she said, baffled.

"Don't beat yourself up about that," said Evan. "Gay men can usually have sex with a woman without any problems. It's just not where their passions lie. Please know that making love with you was always a beautiful experience for me because I do love you so much. It was always a genuine expression of my love for you," he told her honestly, and he had to admit to himself that there was a part of him that would miss the physical intimacy of their relationship.

Tori's head was still reeling. "I have to take some time to process this, Evan. This is just a huge mind-fuck for me. I'm sure you can understand that," she finally said. "But I want you to know that I love you and I completely accept who you are. I just wish I had known about it years ago."

"I know. I agree that it was an error in judgment on my part," he acknowledged, running his hand though his clean-cut light brown hair. "But I was only a kid and I was so scared. I still am. I hope you can forgive me, and I hope even more that you'll be with me though all this. I'm going to need my best friend more than ever now. But I understand if you can't."

Tori wrapped her arms around him and they stayed like that, crying for a long time before she spoke again. "I'm not going anywhere, Evan. You can count on me to be by your side through everything in our lives, no matter what," she said with conviction, looking him directly in the eyes. The more she thought about it, as the reality of their situation sunk in, the more she believed that this could turn out to be the best outcome for them. They were now free of their current romantic relationship, which both of them now knew had been the wrong path for them, but they could keep their friendship intact as they moved forward to face whatever life threw at them.

"Do you really mean that?" he asked, thinking it was more than he could ever have hoped for.

"Yes, I mean that," she confirmed. "You can't get rid of me. You're my best friend and that's not going to change." He took her face in his hands and gently kissed her on the mouth. It was a long, tender, loving kiss and as they broke apart, they each knew it would be the last time they ever shared a moment quite like that again.

"I love you," he said, as he had so many times throughout their life together, but this time he meant it in its truest form. Not in a romantic or sexual way, but with all the love and gratitude he felt for how lucky he was to have her in his life.

They got into their bed then, for what they knew would be the last time, and just held each other. They talked some more about where they were headed moving forward.

"The more I think about it," said Tori, "the more I think that we don't need to change our living arrangements anytime soon," she said decisively, which surprised him.

"Really?" he asked, raising his brow as he contemplated what she said. "It surprises me that you'd say that."

"Well, think about it. We have two bedrooms and we're still the best of friends, so why upset the apple cart at this point?" Evan used the second bedroom as an office, but they did have a pull-out sofa bed in there that they used if someone was visiting. It could work well for the time being. "Have you thought about telling your parents?" She knew this would be a difficult question for him to answer.

"I'm going to have to sooner or later if I want to be with Ben. He's out and proud and doesn't want to be with someone who isn't there yet. I'm terrified as fuck to tell them, and I think I'll wait until after the new year to do it. The holidays are coming up and I don't want to rock the boat. I'll tell Ben that you know now and that I'll tell my parents in good time, and hopefully he'll take me back. I really love him, Tori. I've never felt this way before," he confessed.

"That's how it is with me and Charles," she said.

"Wait, is that Charles Ryan, the music director that you were singing with in the lounges?"

"The very same," she confirmed. "There's almost sixteen years between us, and he was really concerned about that at first, but we just fit like a glove. We're perfect together."

"You said he had some issues to work out. What's the story?" asked Evan.

"He's married to a woman he detests and they have a fifteen-year-old son. Every time he talks about divorcing her, she threatens him with a litany of things and says she'll ruin him if he leaves. She's too accustomed to a comfortable lifestyle now and wants to keep it that way. It's just so fucking complicated. So when we parted, I gave him a similar ultimatum to the one that Ben gave you. I told him I would not be anyone's mistress and I'd marry you if he couldn't get things sorted out. So, now I just wait and see what he does. I'm absolutely sick about it, and I miss him terribly." She laid it all out for him, wanting to be completely honest about where things stood for her. "But I just couldn't go on pretending with you, and knowing how much I'd be hurting you by keeping this secret. I love you too much for that. You deserve to be with someone who can love you fully in every way, and I know I'm not that person."

"I want the same thing for you, and if he hurts you, he'll have to answer to me," Evan said protectively.

She cuddled into him then and they fell into a deep sleep in each other's arms.

In the days and weeks that followed, Tori and Evan continued to live together, both realizing that, aside from the sleeping arrangements, nothing else had really changed between them. He and Ben were now back together and in mid-November, Tori met him for the first time. She expected it to be very awkward, and was nervous about it, but as soon as she met him, she loved him and knew he was a perfect match for Evan. She was very happy for them and could see that what they had was the real deal.

"So," she said to Ben on that first meeting, "he's my best friend and if you hurt him, know that I'll be coming for you," she said, putting him on notice. She was only half joking and he knew it as they all laughed together at what she had said.

"Yes ma'am, I totally understand that. But I don't think you have anything to worry about," he said, giving Evan a quick kiss. She found it strange to see Evan in this light, but it was obvious how happy he was, and she was glad he was finally being true to himself in his lifestyle and relationship.

In mid-November, she gave Steven a call to find out if they could use her again the next summer on the cruise. "Tori, how are you?" he greeted her warmly from his end of the line.

"I'm surviving," she said. That was about the best word she could find to describe it.

"So how are things?" he asked. "Have you heard from Charles at all?"

"No, and he told me I wouldn't while he was working things out. Have you?"

"No, not since we left the *Aurora*. I've been meaning to check in with him, though." She had hoped he might have some information for her, but no such luck.

"Aunt Helen told me she sees you quite a bit," said Tori. "She's happier than I've seen her in years." A fact that made Tori very happy.

"Well, that makes both of us," Steven said then. "She's a wonderful woman." Tori could hear the elation in his voice.

"That's so great. I love the hell out of the both of you, so I'm so glad you found each other," said Tori sincerely. "Look, I was calling you to find out the status of next year's Alaskan cruise. Have you started finalizing the entertainment yet?"

"Yes, we've started on that," he confirmed. "We've been running auditions again this fall and trying to gauge who's coming back from previous years."

"Do you have room for me again next year?" she asked

hopefully.

"Of course we do!" he answered, excited she was considering rejoining them again next season. "But I thought you weren't available next year."

"Yeah, change of plans," was all she said about it.

"Oh," he said, but decided not to pry and question her further. "Well, you're in if you want it. You're one of the best to ever grace our stage," he said, "and our lives," he added.

"Oh, Steven, what a sweet thing to say. I feel the same way. I loved getting to know everyone last year. Has Charles signed on for next year as well?" she asked, tentatively.

"Yes, he absolutely has," Steven confirmed.

"Well, I'd appreciate it if you didn't say anything to him about my coming back," she said. "I'd rather wait and just deal with him in person when I see him there in March."

"Okay, that's fine, I won't say anything," Steven promised. He understood why she would make such a request. "I really hope he's worked everything out by then and you two can just be happy together." Steven wished that for both of them, more than they knew.

"Thanks Steven. I'm excited to do this again, even if I'm nervous as hell about Charles and where things will stand with us," said Tori honestly.

"I hope you're doing okay, Tori. I've been thinking about you and Charles quite a bit. It broke my heart the way you two left things."

"Mine, too. And it's been ripping my heart out every day since," she admitted, and Steven could hear the anguish in her voice.

"Well, I, for one, am thrilled to have you back next season," Steven said before they said goodbye to each other.

Tori was fully absorbed in rehearsals in November for *Holiday Inn* and she welcomed the distraction from thoughts of Charles, which occupied her mind whenever she wasn't immersed in something else. She felt a dull ache in her heart all the time now, and longed to be in his arms, and in his bed.

She and Evan celebrated Thanksgiving with Evan's parents and neither one of them noticed any difference in Tori and Evan's behavior towards each other whatsoever, because essentially, there *was* no change in them. They were still exactly as they had always been. They went to Tori's father and stepmother's that evening after having dinner with Evan's parents, and they were also none the wiser.

November gave way to December and Evan and Ben were going strong, but it concerned Evan to see Tori falling into an intense sadness as she pined for Charles. By then, Evan had learned all the details about her relationship with him, and his heart bled for her. She had even shown him the gorgeous gown that she had worn to the ball, and that Charles had so generously given her. She showed him the photos they had taken that night and a few selfies she had of them on her phone as well.

"Damn, he's hot!" Evan exclaimed when he saw the photos, and Tori laughed.

"Yes, he certainly is, and every woman on the damn ship knew it," said Tori. "I've never seen anyone get hit on as much as he does."

"Fuck, I'd hit on him," Evan joked.

"Sorry baby, but he doesn't bat for your team," Tori said, chuckling. She could always count on Evan to make her laugh, even when she was at her most miserable. She loved the fact that she and Evan could be so open about his being gay, to the point where he could feel comfortable joking with her about how desirable he thought Charles was. To say she never anticipated this in her wildest dreams was an understatement. She giggled as a thought occurred to her.

"What?" Evan asked. "What was that about just then?"

"I was just thinking how bizarre it is that I'm standing here, discussing the hotness of my lover with my gay ex-fiancé, whom I fucked around on with said lover, while my ex-fiancé was fucking around on me with his gay lover. I mean, how batshit crazy is that? What the hell is this, *Days of Our Lives*?"

Evan guffawed at that. "Okay, when you put it like that,

it's pretty fucked up," he agreed and they both collapsed in a fit of hysterical laughter.

Performances of *Holiday inn* went phenomenally well and were well received by audiences. One evening when the house lights came up during their bows, Tori could have sworn she saw Charles in the audience. She mentioned it to Evan when she got home that night after the show.

"I think I'm completely losing my shit," she said. "I swear to Jesus I saw Charles in the audience tonight. Not only am I missing him so much it hurts, but now I'm seeing him everywhere, too. I must be going crazy," she lamented miserably.

"You're not going crazy," Evan reassured her, folding her into his arms in a comforting hug. "You're grieving."

"I hope you're right," she said doubtfully.

In mid-December, a package arrived for her at the theater. She opened it to find two beautifully wrapped gifts from Charles. The first was a gorgeous bangle bracelet with an inscription engraved on the inside that said *My Heart is Yours Forever, Charles*. She gasped when she opened the second gift to find a pristine first edition of *To Kill a Mockingbird*, which she had told him months ago was her favorite book. He had not forgotten. She had always wished for a first edition of that book. It was the first contact she had had from him since the day they parted, and tears welled up in her eyes as she put on the bracelet and hugged the book close to her chest. She took a chance on sending him a quick text, simply saying, *Thank you. I love you.*

Evan was blown away by the gift when she got home and showed it to him. "He must really love you," he said. "I want so badly for this to work out for you." It broke his heart to see her in such deep grief.

Christmas came without much of Tori's usual fanfare. She adored Christmas, but didn't have the energy to put her customary gusto into it that year. There was no denying the feeling of gloom that fell over the holiday for her as she wished she were spending her first Christmas with Charles. This time, she and Evan had Christmas dinner at her father's, as they had spent Thanksgiving with Evan's parents, and they went to Evan's parents' on Christmas Eve.

Evan shocked her with the most amazing Christmas gift. He gave her a stunning necklace and pair of earrings that perfectly matched the gown that Charles had given her from the cruise. "I know you'll wear that dress with him again someday, and now you'll have something from me as well to complete the ensemble." She loved the thought of wearing something from both of the most important men in her life as part of the same outfit. She surprised him with two full VIP ticket packages, complete with Meet & Greet, for his favorite band for their upcoming concert in Seattle the following summer. She had also learned that Ben was a major fan of the band as well, so the gift was a hit with them both.

Chanel came for a visit during the week between Christmas and New Year's, and Tori planned to go back to Portland with her in the new year to visit for a few days before she started rehearsals for *Promises, Promises*. When Chanel arrived, they greeted each other with screams and giant hugs. They had been talking regularly over the last few months, so they were up to speed on each other's news, but they had not visited in person and had missed one another a great deal.

Tori introduced Chanel to Evan and she liked him immediately. "Oh my God, Tori, Evan is such a doll," she said later when they were alone lounging on Tori's bed on the night Chanel arrived. "I can totally understand why you were so torn up over hurting him."

"I know, he totally is a doll," Tori agreed. "Honestly, I was floored when he told me that he's gay, but the more I thought about it, the more I realized it was the best thing that could have happened as far as our friendship is concerned. I get to keep my best friend, and that's the most important thing to me."

"Still no word from Charles?" Chanel asked.

"Nope, aside from the Christmas gift, it's been radio silence on that front. But he did tell me as much when I saw him for the last time. He doesn't want to take any chances on his wife finding out about me and trying to make my life hell. I can understand that. It's just hard," she said mournfully.

Chanel could see the toll it was taking on Tori. Occasionally she would catch a fleeting glimpse of the effervescent girl she had known on the *Aurora*. Yet even when she seemed to be having a good time, there was a profound sadness about her now beneath her brave face, and the usual spark was missing from her eyes. Chanel also noticed that she had lost weight and her features looked drawn.

They spent a quiet New Year's Eve at Tori and Evan's. Ben came over and they made popcorn and some appetizers, and watched the ball drop. At one point, while flipping through the channels, they landed on PBS to check out the *Christmas from Carnegie Hall* special, when Chanel cried out, "Tori, it's Charles on TV!"

Tori came running into the living room from the kitchen, where she was taking some jalapeno poppers out of the oven. Her jaw dropped and she stood, frozen, riveted to the TV screen. There was the man she loved, conducting an orchestra on freakin' PBS! She couldn't take her eyes off him and was completely transfixed as she watched. She hadn't laid eyes on him for over three months, and she ached looking at him on her screen now. Seeing him brought tears to her eyes and drove home how much she wanted her arms around him and his lips on hers. They watched the remainder of the special and she recorded the repeat of it on her PVR, so she could see him any time she wanted. She was completely unaware of what was happening around her or any conversation the others might be having. There was only him, and she was mesmerized watching him do what he did best.

They turned back to Ryan Seacrest and the Times Square coverage just before the ball dropped, and as the countdown commenced, she wondered what the new year would bring for her and Charles.

Chapter 16 – Charles

It was late when Charles let himself into his modern Upper West Side apartment after a long difficult day travelling from Seattle to New York. He sat in the dark for a long time, feeling numb as he contemplated where his life was headed. He finally went to bed to deal with the first of many agonizing nights he would spend now without Tori by his side. It already felt like an eternity since he had made love to her that morning for the last time. As he lay there thinking of her, he felt sick to his stomach as it occurred to him that, at that very moment, she could possibly be making love to another man. He tried to banish the thought from his mind, knowing that if he allowed himself to dwell on it for long, it would most certainly drive him mad. He wept as he finally fell into a restless sleep.

He woke early after a fitful night, still dealing with some jet lag. He was cooking breakfast when Andy entered the kitchen. "Dad, you're home!" he exclaimed with delight. "I thought you must be when I woke up to the smell of food cooking." His mother certainly did not share his father's passion for the culinary arts. He looked at his dad then and said, "Holy shit, you look like hell."

"Well, thanks Son. Good to know," Charles said dryly with an exhausted grin.

"Sorry Dad," Andy apologized. "Tough day yesterday?" He knew how difficult it must have been for his father to say goodbye to Tori.

"In more ways than one," Charles confirmed.

Meredith walked into the room then, fully dressed in a stylish beige professional pantsuit, her long straight black hair pulled back in a stark bun at the nape of her neck. "Oh, you're home," she said, acknowledging Charles' presence with absolutely no warmth whatsoever. "Fuck, you look like shit."

"Yeah, so I've heard. Good morning to you, too, Meredith. Thanks for the warm welcome," he muttered sarcastically.

She grabbed an orange from the fridge and poured herself a cup of coffee. She had never been one for eating early in the morning. She left soon afterward to begin a full day of meetings with her interior design clients, and Andy departed for school shortly thereafter.

After clearing away from breakfast, Charles just sat for awhile on the uncomfortable couch in his living room. He loved his apartment but hated what Meredith had done with it. There was no question about her talents as an interior decorator, he'd give her credit for that, but he had always found the apartment to be cold and lacking in the welcoming, cozy atmosphere he had always preferred in a home. He looked around, wondering what Tori would do with it. He knew it would be something radically different and would reflect her warm, upbeat personality.

Thinking of her made him ache all over. The sheer physical withdrawal from her caused him pain as he remembered their long nights of lovemaking. They had made love every day since their first time in the middle of July, except for the days during Tori's cycle. But even then, they shared a bed, and cuddled while talking long into the night, until they finally fell asleep in each other's arms. He was already yearning to feel her touch, see her radiant smile, and hear her melodic voice. He could not even contemplate how he was going to cope with a long separation from her.

Thankfully, his work would provide a welcome distraction and consume his thoughts with something other than her, even if only for awhile. He would have to fly to Chicago in just a few days to conduct a concert there, barely giving him enough time to adjust to being home.

He left the apartment soon after and decided to go to Juilliard to check in. Even though he did not teach in the fall semester, he still spent a fair amount of time in the haven of his office, actually feeling more comfortable there than he did in his own home. He sat at his desk, remembering all the hours he had spent there rehearsing with Tori before they left for Alaska. Everything reminded him of her now. He couldn't even turn on the radio without hearing a song he knew she loved, or one that she had sung at karaoke.

He shelved the music books that he and Tori had used so often on the cruise. He took the Andrew Lloyd Webber collection, placed it on the piano, and sang a heart-wrenching rendition of "'Til I Hear You Sing," from *Love Never Dies*. He felt every word from the bottom of his soul, the lyrics perfectly summing up the agony he was feeling at that moment. When he finished the song, he put his head down on the piano and sobbed.

He went to Chicago and did the concert there, and when he returned to New York, he knew he had to start putting things into motion to begin the process of getting his life in order.

When he entered the apartment after returning from Chicago, Meredith was actually home, looking at fabric swatches for a client's furniture upholstery. There was no warm greeting between them, but then again, there never was.

"How was Chicago?" she asked without much interest. She had never cared much about what he did for a living.

"Fine," was all he said in reply. He decided there was no time like the present to address the elephant in the room that he knew he had to bring up eventually. He took a deep breath and plowed ahead. "Meredith, I want a divorce," he announced, matter-of-factly.

Meredith sighed as if already bored with the conversation. "Oh Charles, not this again," she said as if speaking to a toddler. "Every few years you bring this up and I have to remind you of all you stand to lose if you pursue this."

"Meredith, we're obviously not happy in this situation, and we can barely be civil to each other. Why continue to live like this? You must want more for yourself than this."

"I have a comfortable life, I come and go as I please, and my career is on a good path," she pointed out. "As for you, I really don't care how you feel about it."

"Why do you take such delight in making me suffer, Meredith?" he asked.

"Because I can," she answered simply. "It's the least I can do after you fucked up my life for so many years."

"You know what, Meredith, the last time I checked, it takes two people to get knocked up. You played a part in that, too, but you've always been unwilling to accept your role in it. You could have gone into our marriage with an entirely different attitude and tried to embrace it and our son, but you refused to do that."

"Come on, Charles, we both know we were never much more to one another than a casual booty call when we were bored." He knew she wasn't wrong about that, and it was one of the reasons he did not believe in casual sex. He had seen all too well the ramifications of it.

"It didn't have to be like that. I tried to make some semblance of a marriage out of it, but you weren't having any of it. You resented me, and Andy. I've given you a cushy life and all you can do is treat me like I'm the fucking enemy," he chastised. "You really are a first-class bitch, you know that Meredith?" he spat.

"Well, I'm nothing if not first-class," she retorted with a sadistic grin. "Look, we both know you'll never go ahead with this. You're too much of a coward to risk it. So let's just forget this conversation, once again, and move on."

"Not this time," he said with determination as he walked out of the apartment to take a walk and calm his nerves.

The next week he had to fly to Los Angeles to guest conduct the LA Philharmonic, an experience he would ordinarily have relished, but he was merely going through the motions now without Tori. It was the second week of October when he returned and the next day, he called his lawyer to begin putting divorce proceedings into motion. He was scared shitless about what would come next, but he knew he now had something far more important to fight for.

"I'm not gonna lie to you, Charles," his long-time lawyer, Seth Horowitz, said to him after listening to Charles pour out the details of his predicament, "it's going to be messy." He had known for years now just how mean-spirited Meredith was toward her husband. "She's not going to take any of this lying down, but neither should you. Honestly, if you ask my personal opinion, it's long overdue. So do you finally want to move forward with this?"

"Yes, I do," Charles answered affirmatively, his heart pounding in his chest as he thought about the Pandora's box he was about to open. But he knew he would rather live like a pauper with Tori by his side than leave things the way they were. There had never before been greater impetus for him to take action. "It scares the fuck out of me, but it has to happen."

"Okay, I'll draw up the papers and she'll be served with them within a week or so," Seth confirmed. Charles knew he had to brace himself for the shit to hit the fan once that happened, but found he no longer cared what potential ruination faced him. He knew now that life without the woman he loved would be a far worse fate than whatever fresh hell Meredith could dish out.

"Okay, thanks Seth," he replied, "Let me know what you need from me." They hung up then, and all Charles wanted to do at that moment was hold Tori in his arms.

Meredith received the divorce papers a week later as Seth assured him she would, and shit did indeed hit the fan. She stormed into the living room as Charles sat studying a score for an upcoming concert.

"You fucking bastard," she shouted, railing against Charles in full attack mode. "What the fuck do you think you're doing?"

Charles looked up from his score, meeting Meredith's fierce gaze squarely and preparing himself for the wrath that would inevitably ensue. "I'm finally growing a pair, Meredith and ending this sham of a marriage, once and for all," he said evenly, appearing far more composed than he felt.

"Like shit you are. Do I need to remind you of..."

"Nope, you don't," he said, cutting her off. "I've heard it all before, many times. But here's the thing, Meredith," he challenged her, "I no longer give a single fuck what you do to me. This has gone on long enough. Andy is not a child anymore and can make up his own mind where he stands on this, and as for everything else, I just don't care anymore," he said, stripping her of her power over him. "That ship has finally sailed. No actually, the ship sunk a long time ago. I'm just sorry that I lost so many years of my life by allowing myself to go down with it."

Meredith decided to play her trump card then. "Does this have anything to do with the little piece of ass you hooked up with on the cruise ship this summer?" she asked sharply.

Charles' mouth dropped open in shock. He hadn't seen this coming at all and stayed silent as he tried to process what she had said.

"Ah, so there it is," she said, taking in his expression. "You see Charles, what you don't know is that a good friend of mine was on one of those cruises in August. You don't know her, but she certainly knew who you were. She saw you in a very intimate moment with your little sex kitten and told me all about it. So, when you got home and threatened divorce yet again, I took the liberty of snooping around your room a bit. Imagine my delight when I found this," she said, tossing a manila envelope at him. He knew what was inside even before he opened it. It contained the photos taken on the ship of him with Tori and Andy at the ball, as well as the letter Tori had written to him before they left, which he knew would be quite damning. He kept it in a locked drawer in his room, and looked at its contents almost every day. He had read the letter so many times, he knew it by heart.

"I assume you know what this is?" she hissed at him, her cold dark eyes blazing as she watched him open it. His face turned ashen and he was unable to utter a single word as he examined the contents. She snatched it back after he had returned the items to the envelope.

"Give that back to me," he demanded. It was the last thing he had of Tori and he cherished it.

"She seems quite young for you, Charles, and it would seem she was part of your show company on board. Wow! I wonder how that would look: the music director hooking up with the young ingénue under his charge. Rather inappropriate, don't you think, especially considering you could technically be considered her boss. She doesn't look any older than your students at Juilliard, Charles, and I'm sure that a prestigious school like that would not take too kindly to doubts surfacing about one of its most respected professors messing around with young girls."

Charles knew as he listened to her how bad this could look if the right spin was put on it. He also knew that Meredith had absolutely no scruples and would jump at the chance to expose his affair with Tori in order to get what she wanted. Most of all, he realized that he needed to protect Tori from Meredith at any cost, even if it meant he would lose her forever.

"So Charles, it seems you have two choices," Meredith continued. "Either you drop this divorce bullshit, or you continue with it and I expose all of this, which would not bode well for you. You could even lose your job over it. Sexual harassment is not taken lightly these days and I'm sure Juilliard wouldn't want a potential scandal on their hands if there was even a shred of doubt brought forward about your conduct. I don't even need my father to destroy you," she said with a smirk. "You just handed me everything that I need on a silver platter all by yourself. So you just think about it now and let me know your decision. Either way, I win," she gloated. "Oh, and you can keep this," she said, throwing the envelope back at him. "I have copies," she said smugly, and walked out of the room, victorious.

Meredith left the apartment a few minutes later and Charles could not have cared less about where she was going. All he could think about was Tori and how hopeless it all seemed now. Charles poured himself a stiff drink and just sat, stupefied, over all that had just happened. His heart was beating in overdrive as he sat there with his head in his hands and cried. This was the state Andy found him in a few minutes later when he arrived home.

"Oh my God, Dad, what the hell is going on?" Andy asked with alarm when he saw the condition his father was in. "Dad, are you... *drinking*?" he asked in astonishment when he spotted the drink in Charles' hand.

"Yup," said Charles, looking as utterly devastated as he felt.

"Okay, now I *know* something big is up. You hardly *ever* drink," Andy observed.

Charles looked at his son, all the torture in his heart evident in his eyes. "Your mother found out about Tori and me," he told him honestly, "and now she's threatening to make it public. Not only can she hold infidelity over my head, but now she can make it look like sexual harassment and try to destroy my career."

"Bitch!" Andy exclaimed, and for once Charles didn't even try to reprimand him for it. "What are you going to do now?" he asked.

"I don't know. I'm still trying to digest it all. I know the last thing I want to do is subject Tori to whatever your mother could try to do to her. I will *not* let her go down with me," he said emphatically, "even if it means we can't be together. As for me, I don't give a damn anymore what she does to me."

Andy could see that his father was completely broken, and he did the only thing he could do for him: he put his arms around Charles and let him cry on his shoulder. For the first time in his life, Andy felt like the parent, desperately trying to comfort a distraught child.

"Dad, you can't give up and let her win," Andy said finally. He knew Charles had filed for divorce, and Andy was thrilled that he had, at long last, gotten the courage to take that huge step to free himself from Meredith's clutches. "You and Tori belong together. You have to keep fighting for it," he urged. "Dad,

I know that one of the biggest reasons you've stayed all these years is because of me. I know I was an accident, and you did the honorable thing, and I'm grateful to you for that. You never treated me like I was a mistake, but Mom did. You stayed to give me a shot at a good life and a stable home, but I'm not a kid anymore. It's only a couple of years and I'll be considered an adult, and then neither one of us will have to worry about her anymore. I'm old enough now to make my own decisions, and I'll tell any judge in this state exactly what my mother is and where I want to be. So don't let any of that sway your actions now."

Charles was overwhelmed by his son's maturity. "You may have been unplanned, Andy, but you were no accident," he said, looking into the face of his son, which was a younger mirror image of his own. Charles had never doubted Andy's paternity. All he had to do was look at him to know he was his. "You have been the joy of my life since I laid eyes on you the minute you were born," Charles continued, "and however my marriage to your mother turned out, I've never regretted you for a second of my life. I'd do anything for you. You need to know that."

"I *do* know that, Dad. You've proven it every day for the last sixteen years," Andy said with all the love he had for his father. "But now it's your turn. You can't take this lying down. You and Tori are made for each other, and life is too short for you not to be together."

"I know we are. I've never been so miserable in my life as I have been since I got home in September," Charles admitted.

"I know, and I've been worried as hell about you," said Andy. Charles felt strongly that a parent should never burden their kids with their problems, and he regretted that Andy was in the middle of it and was worrying about him. "I know this sucks, Dad, but no matter how bad it gets, you can't start doing *this*," he said holding up Charles' drink in his hand. "The last thing you need right now is to start a drinking habit on top of it all," he reasoned, stating the obvious.

"I know, I know, you're right," Charles agreed. "God, when

did my sixteen-year-old son become the voice of reason in my life?" he said with a grin.

Andy returned his grin. "So here's what I think," he said. "I think you need to dish it out as well as she does. I know she's screwing around on you. She doesn't even really try to hide it when you're away. Sometimes she doesn't even come home until very late at night." Charles never had any doubt that this was true, and was sure Andy was correct in his assessment. Charles just didn't care one way or another what she did.

"So what I think you should do is hire a private investigator and get proof of it," Andy suggested. "Turnabout is fair play, Dad, and if you could get the goods on her, it might help your case."

Charles thought about this for a moment and had to admit that he had not considered that angle before. But then again, the stakes had never been this high before either. He looked at his son, seeing him in a new light. Andy really wasn't a child anymore. He had grown up and was now a smart, sensitive and insightful young man. He had just turned sixteen and was so much wiser than his years. "You might have a point there, Son," he said. "Let me give this some thought."

Over the next few days, Charles did give some thought to Andy's suggestion and decided to call Seth Horowitz for some advice. He considered Seth a friend in addition to being his personal attorney. He brought Seth up to date on Meredith's latest tirade and his relationship with Tori, and asked his honest opinion as to whether he should drop the divorce.

"Jesus, Charles, she really is a piece of work, isn't she?" Seth said after listening to the details Charles gave him.

"That's the understatement of the century," Charles replied to his friend's accurate assessment of his wife.

"Honestly, if I were you, and I'm not," Seth began, "I'd call her bluff and let it ride. There's a major backlog in the courts right now, so this is not going to see the inside of a courtroom for months. I think I'd bide my time for a bit," Seth advised.

"But what if she follows through on her threat to expose it

to Juilliard?" he pondered.

"I don't think she'll do that. I think she'll play her hand close to her chest for now. She'll want maximum outcome for the information she has, so I think she'll wait for her day in court for that in order to ensure herself a handsome payout in the divorce," Seth speculated logically. "I know you'll be shitting bricks every single day until then, but it might just pay off."

Charles considered this for a moment and realized his lawyer had a point. "Another gargantuan understatement," he said finally.

"You love this girl, Charles?" Seth asked him then.

"I'd lay down my life for her without a second thought," Charles told him.

"Then fight to the death for her," Seth said, wishing for his friend to be happy for once. "Life is too short."

"That's what Andy said."

"Smart kid."

"Don't I know it," Charles said, smiling for the first time in days, and then he remembered the other thing he wanted to ask Seth about. "By the way, my son actually suggested I hire a PI to follow Meredith and see what I can find out about what she's up to. Andy thinks she's fucking around, and I've never doubted that she is, so maybe it wouldn't be a bad idea. I don't suppose you know a guy?"

"Your kid might just be on to something there, my friend," said Seth. "And yes, I actually *do* know a guy. Best in the business. I don't know how he gets the information he does, but if there's anything to be found out, he'll find it." Seth gave Charles the contact information for the PI. "Keep me posted on this, okay?" he said. "In the meantime, as I said, I'd let it ride for now. Wait and see what the PI finds out. You've got time before you end up in court."

"I will, and thanks, Seth, for everything," Charles said gratefully.

Charles called the PI, Chris Hernandez, as soon as he hung up the phone from talking to Seth. He explained the situation to him and told him he wanted his wife followed.

"Not a problem," said the PI. "If she's up to anything, I'll find out." Charles gave him all the particulars about Meredith, and prayed to whatever gods were out there that he would be able to help him. It could be his last hope. The gloves were off now, and if Meredith wanted to fight dirty, she would soon find out that he could play that game as well.

In the middle of November, Charles was delighted to get a call from his old friend, Tom Parsons.

"Yo, Chuck," Tom said warmly from the other end of the telephone. Tom and Jerry were the only people he knew who could call him Chuck and get away with it. But he figured that if they were stuck with being referred to as Tom and Jerry all the time, he could handle them calling him Chuck. They had done that since college.

"Tom, wassup?" Charles said.

"Oh, we're so busy right now with this new musical in development," Tom said. They also still had another one going strong on Broadway as well. It was the one Charles had taken Tori and Andy to see back in the spring. "Anyway, that's what I wanted to talk to you about," Tom continued. "Have you given any more thought to coming on to this project with us?"

"Yes, I have actually, and I think it might just work out this time," he replied. "Tell me more about it."

"Well, it's a modern take on the classic Sleeping Beauty story. That's one that hasn't really been tackled yet. I mean, *Cinderella* has been done. Overdone, really. *Beauty and the Beast* was hugely successful on Broadway, and *Aladdin* has been running for years. But I think *Sleeping Beauty* would go over well with families and even adults as well, for that matter. Jerry and I are composing all the new music, but we're also keeping the classic stuff from the animated film in there as well." That was par for the course for any stage adaptation of a musical film.

Charles immediately thought of Tori. "Do you have anyone in mind for the princess, yet?" he asked.

"No, not really," Tom answered. "Why do you ask?"

"Because I think I know the perfect girl for you. She sings like a dream and she definitely has the right look for it," said Charles. "What's the vocal range for the role?"

"She'll need to have a good range," Tom answered. "It's actually one of our biggest concerns about the show. The girl who did the part in our early readings is lovely, but she just doesn't have the depth for it, and she knows it. She'll do the workshops, but she's not pursuing it for Broadway. We'll definitely be auditioning for that role. Finding the right girl is going to be tough, and if we can't find her, we'll have to make some changes musically."

"I know my girl would be perfect for it. She's incredibly versatile and can sing any style. She's great for operatic stuff, but then she has the softest, sweetest princess voice you ever heard. She can also belt with the best of 'em and has an insane range on both the lower and upper end. She really is quite extraordinary."

"Wow, impressive." Tom could hear the obvious pride in Charles' voice in the way he spoke of her and couldn't help but wonder exactly what the nature of his relationship was with this obviously exceptional young woman. But he did not want to pry and left it at that. He figured his friend would confide in him if and when he felt moved to do so. "Alright, well, we'll make sure to keep you posted about when auditions will be held. Tell her to come try out for it. We'd love to see her." Tom was definitely interested.

"Yeah, I definitely will," Charles said, making a mental note to follow up on it. "So, what's the timeline?" he asked then.

"Well, Jerry and I have finished the music and lyrics. Jerry is also writing the book and still has some work to do to finish that up, but that won't impact you at all. We're hoping to workshop it in the spring, audition for the roles in the early fall, and hopefully our out-of-town tryout will be next Christmas or early in the new year. We're working with the 5th Avenue Theatre in Seattle on that, so hopefully it will be happening there." Charles knew the 5th had hosted out-of-town's for Broadway shows in the past and found it interesting that it would premiere there, in Tori's neck of the woods.

As he continued to get more details from Tom, Charles realized it would be a huge undertaking for him, as the show would boast the largest orchestra that Broadway had seen in many years. It was an ambitious project and Tom and Jerry had big expectations for it. Charles was up to the challenge, but knew he would have to start on it immediately if he was going to finish putting together orchestrations for a fairly large orchestra on time. He said as much to Tom, who promised to get music to him right away so he could get started on the endeavor.

"So, what else is new?" Tom asked when they finished talking about the musical.

"Don't even fucking ask," Charles said. "My life is a colossal shitstorm right now."

"Why, what's gong on?" his friend asked with concern.

"I'm finally divorcing Meredith," Charles announced. "And it's not gonna be pretty."

"Holy shit, finally!" Tom blurted out. "What brought that on?" Tom was astounded to learn that this was finally happening.

"Short version, I fell in love and it's worth fighting for," Charles revealed.

"No way!" said Tom. "Do tell."

Charles filled him in on the events of the previous summer and Tom could tell how much he loved Tori and wanted to be with her.

"If I can get out of this marriage somewhat intact, I'll marry her in a heartbeat," Charles confessed. "She's engaged and that complicates things further. So she has some stuff to work out now, too. She's actually the girl I have in mind for your princess."

"Wow, this is big news. I'm rooting for you, buddy. Nobody deserves to finally be happy more than you do."

"Thanks man, that means a lot."

Also in mid-November, about a month after Meredith was

served with the divorce papers, Charles received a call from Seth Horowitz. "Well we finally got her response," he said without preamble. "She's contesting the divorce."

"Well, there's a fuckin' surprise," Charles muttered cynically under his breath.

"Yeah, so no surprise there," Seth agreed. "We were expecting this."

"So where do we go from here?" asked Charles.

"I think this one is going all the way to trial, to be honest, Charles," Seth said candidly. "We know Meredith is not going to settle on anything and now she has dirt to hold over you, so it's going to be a shit show and a half in my opinion. Not to mention costly."

Charles was not at all surprised by Seth's revelation. He had been expecting it as well, which is why he hadn't pursued it in the past.

"Her demands are outrageous," Seth declared. "There's no way any judge will give her everything she wants."

"Honestly, Seth, all I care about is Andy, and I'd like to keep the apartment. It's close to Juilliard and Andy's school. It's his home, and I don't want him uprooted."

"That's definitely understandable, but if you want the apartment, it'll cost you. You're going to lose a hell of a lot somewhere else. You'll probably have to liquidate some of your other assets and cash in a lot of your investments."

"I just hope she doesn't go after Andy just to fuck with me," Charles said. "She barely acknowledges his existence as it is, so there's no way she actually wants him to live with her."

"She'll use him as leverage, I'm sure. The thing that won't work in your favor is that she has photos of you and Miss Stewart with Andy on the cruise ship. She could claim that Andy knew about the affair, and that would fall under the category of inappropriate behavior in front of a child, which is something the court will take into account."

"Fuck!" cried Charles in frustration. "I mean, full disclosure, Andy did know about us. But Tori and I weren't even together when those particular photos were taken."

"Doesn't matter in the long run. You two look very much involved in those photos. The fact is, Andy knew about it, and Meredith has solid proof of the affair from the very revealing letter Miss Stewart wrote to you. However, what *will* work in your favor is Andy's age. He's old enough to speak for himself and a judge will definitely take that into consideration."

"Will Andy have to testify in court?" Charles asked. That was the last thing he wanted Andy to have to deal with.

"The judge would probably interview him in closed chambers. That's how it usually works when kids who are still minors are involved," Seth reassured him.

Thank God for that, Charles thought. "Okay, well, keep me updated on any new developments you become aware of," he said. "We'll have to meet soon anyway to go over her list of demands and respond to them, I'm sure."

"We will, indeed," Seth confirmed. "Should be a real barrel of monkeys."

'Yup, I can hardly wait," said Charles sarcastically.

During Thanksgiving week, Charles had to go to Boston for a concert and to guest lecture at Berklee. Andy had been invited on a ski trip by his best friend's family for the season opening weekend at a resort about two hours from New York City, so Charles didn't feel as badly as he usually did about going away this time.

On the day before he left for Boston, he confronted Meredith about her response to the divorce. "So I see you're contesting the divorce," he said, getting straight to the point.

"Yes, and I see you didn't drop it, despite my recommendation that you do so."

"This is happening, Meredith. I'm not going to let you bully me anymore."

"Your choice, your consequences," she said flippantly. "I've decided to be charitable here, Charles. I'll give you until the new year to reconsider your position on this and come to your senses. But if you don't drop it before this goes to court, I'm going to Juilliard to expose this whole sordid affair, and you can let the chips fall where they may."

Charles was actually relieved to hear that he could bide his time for awhile, and hoped his PI would come up with something before then. "Understood," was all he said in response.

After he got back from Boston, Charles received an urgent message from another conductor he was acquainted with in the city, asking if he would be available to conduct this year's *Christmas from Carnegie Hall* special for PBS. The regular conductor for the annual program had gotten into a car accident, and while he was going to be fine, would be out of commission for awhile, leaving him unable to do it this year. This was a huge opportunity for Charles and he immediately accepted, even though it was incredibly short notice. The special would tape on December sixth, and broadcast on PBS several times over the holiday season. It would be amazing exposure for him, and he loved the music being performed this year: the John Rutter *Gloria*, as well as several other Christmas pieces by Rutter, for which the composer was so well known. It would involve a full orchestra, as well as a large choir, which was right up Charles' alley. However, due to the short notice, he would only have a little over a week to prepare and would have to run several rehearsals during that time as well.

The PBS show went better than Charles could have hoped, and he was busy throughout December with all the special holiday presentations he was involved with. As for Christmas itself, he would be taking Andy on their usual ski trip over the holidays after spending Christmas day in New Haven with his parents. He felt badly that Andy had never had a traditional Christmas in his life, but the state of Charles and Meredith's relationship was just not conducive to a warm and fuzzy family Christmas. As for Meredith, he didn't know what she was doing and frankly, didn't give a damn.

Charles had only one task to do as far as Christmas was

concerned. He had something special in mind that he wanted to send to Tori. He scoured every rare book seller in New York City until he finally found what he was looking for: a first edition of *To Kill a Mockingbird*, which he remembered was her favorite book. He also got her a beautiful bangle bracelet with a message inscribed on it. He packed the gift and couriered it to the 5th Avenue Theatre, to avoid any chance that it would raise suspicion should it fall into Evan's hands at home. She sent him a text when she received it, which simply said, *Thank you, I love you.*

During the fall, auditions for the cruise line had begun once again for the next season. Charles wasn't able to make all of the dates, but he did go to some of them, including Seattle in December, immediately following the taping of the PBS special. He sat on his flight thinking that this was where he first saw Tori, just one short year ago. In some ways, it felt like yesterday, while in others, it felt like a lifetime ago. He wanted to contact her with every fiber of his body while he was there, but knew he had to play it safe and not do anything that could bite him in the ass while Meredith was on the warpath. He did get himself a ticket to see her in *Holiday Inn*, however, and as he sat riveted in his seat, enthralled by her, he ached all over to go to the stage door afterward and take her in his arms and tell her how much he loved her.

When he got home from Seattle, he received a call from the PI, Chris Hernandez, with an update. "So what have you got for me?" Charles asked, trying not to get his hopes up.

"Well, you were right about your wife having an affair," he began, getting directly to the point. "She's involved with a man by the name of Aaron Leonard."

Charles recognized the name immediately. "That's her father's personal assistant," he said.

"That would be correct," Chris confirmed. "She meets him at his address regularly and they went on a quick holiday to the Bahamas over Thanksgiving, and they're booked to go back there again over Christmas." That had been the week he was in

Boston and Andy was skiing with his friend. "They stayed at a five-star resort, and a very high-priced one at that, sparing no expense while they were there," Chris continued. "I've got tons of incriminating photos for you of them there."

"How the hell did they get the money for that?" Charles wanted to know. "There's no way Leonard makes that kind of money at his job, and Meredith doesn't have access to it from me." Charles was meticulous in his record keeping on all financial matters and kept track of every penny. Meredith enjoyed spending money, but Charles kept close track of exactly where it went. And while she did well at her interior decorating business, it was not lucrative, certainly not to the degree that would allow her the cash flow for the kind of extravagant spending as she and her lover had been engaging in.

"Well, that's the million dollar question now, isn't it?" said Chris. "Honestly Charles, this reeks of fraud. In cases like this, they usually skim money unnoticed from a close family member when they've been put in a position of trust by that family member. My guess is her father. She's his daughter and Leonard is his assistant, so it would make sense. They would both probably have easy access to his accounts. But look, that's my next step here. You might want to keep this info under your hat for now until I can get you something more concrete on the financial side. If you can prove fraud, then you've got something solid. As for adultery, that won't do much for you. You've both got one another on that, so it puts you at a bit of a stalemate. Plus, the courts really don't care much about adultery, unless there are some extenuating circumstances around it. They only care that the partnership is dissolving, not how it got there. They're more concerned with the division of assets and property, custody of children, things like that. So we need to find something bigger for it to be really useful to you. You don't want to bring a knife to a gunfight, Charles, so just leave it to me, and I'll be in touch."

"Thank you so much," Charles said before they hung up. If there was a God, perhaps Chris would find something for him before Meredith could do any more harm. Time was of the essence now.

He went skiing with Andy over the holidays, as planned. Steven called him on Christmas Eve to check in and wish him a merry Christmas. Charles filled him in on the latest developments about his impending divorce, and Steven was glad to hear his friend was finally taking some action on it. He didn't tell Charles about his conversation with Tori, as per her request, nor did he tell him about Tori's broken engagement. He had heard the details about that from Helen, but Tori had also asked her aunt and Steven to keep quiet about it where Charles was concerned. As difficult as their imposed gag order was for both of them, they had agreed to keep their mouths shut about all of it and not interfere on either side. Charles also requested that Steven and Helen not mention what was going on with him to Tori, either.

"I just want this to be fully resolved before I get her involved. I don't want to take any chances with this. There's too much at stake," Charles told Steven, and Steven fully understood his reasoning.

"So how are things going with you and Helen?" Charles asked, changing the subject to a happier topic.

"Incredibly well." Steven sounded very happy to him, and Charles could see Steven's trademark grin even over the phone. "I've been looking for a woman like her all my life," he confided.

"That's so amazing." Charles was truly happy for his friend and Tori's aunt. "I hope things work out in the end for all of us," he said.

They talked for another little while, wished each other a merry Christmas and happy new year, and promised to touch base again after the holidays.

Charles and Andy rang in the new year at the ski resort and it was a very fun and festive night, with people all around them in a celebratory mood. But as Charles welcomed the new year, he was consumed with fears about what was in store when he returned home. He wondered what Tori was doing that night and longed to share a kiss with her on the stroke of midnight more than anything.

Chapter 17 – Tori

After the new year, Tori went back to Oregon with Chanel for a few days before rehearsals got underway for *Promises, Promises*. Chanel was no longer living at her mother's place. As planned, Marcus had moved from Salem to Portland in the fall and he and Chanel moved in together just before Christmas. Marcus was doing very well for himself as a freelance photographer, and Chanel was doing similar things as Tori was in Seattle - performing in plays and musicals in Portland's theatre scene. Tori was delighted to see how happy Chanel and Marcus were. It looked good on both of them, and Tori was very fond of Marcus. He and Chanel were a perfect match.

While in Portland, she and Chanel went to the Oregon Zoo, and did a bit of shopping. Tori was most enthusiastic about visiting the legendary Powell's Books, where she found a couple of autographed volumes by her favorite authors. Powell's was an excellent place to find such treasures, as many authors stopped there for book signings.

"So, who have you kept in touch with from the cruise gang?" Tori asked Chanel over a coffee and some gelato after they left the bookstore.

"Oh, a bunch of them," Chanel answered, catching Tori up on the news from the people she had met the previous year. "How about you? Have you kept in touch with anyone?"

"Yeah, you know, you're not going to believe this in a million years, and I can't even believe I'm saying it, but I talk to Simone all the time."

"Yeah, you're right about that one. Oh boy, did you ever

let her have it that day. You basically ripped her a new asshole," Chanel reminisced with a smile. "I'm as surprised as you are about that."

Tori had learned a lot about Simone since they had mended fences the previous summer and came to realize that she really valued the other young woman's friendship.

"How much does she know about you and Charles?" asked Chanel.

"Actually, quite a bit of it. She's been very supportive and really wants us to find our way back to each other."

"Well, I think that makes every one of us who saw you together last summer. I really can't believe you haven't heard a word from him about what's going on from his end, though."

"I'm not," Tori confessed. "He was very clear with me about that the last time I saw him. He doesn't want to drag me into his clusterfuck, and he knows how vindictive his wife is. And, to be fair, I totally understand his reasoning. I'm just aching to hold him again and hear his voice. If he gets himself out of this mess, I know I'd marry him in a heartbeat if he asked."

"Oh, I know he'll be asking," said Chanel with absolute certainty. "And I, for one, cannot wait to dance at your wedding." Chanel was relentless in her unwavering hope for Tori and Charles' future together.

"Well, you'll be one of the first to know. I'll want you to be my Maid of Honor."

"You can count on it," Chanel confirmed and hugged her friend.

When Tori returned from Portland, she was immediately thrown head-first into rehearsals, but there was another more pressing concern in her life at that point as well. Evan was finally ready to come out to his parents and he was sweating bullets about it. She asked him if he wanted her to be there with him when he broke the news to them, or if he would rather do it alone.

"I'd really like you to be there, if that's okay with you?" he asked.

"Of course I'm okay with it," she reassured him. "There's nowhere I'd rather be than holding your hand through all of this."

On the night he planned to tell them, Evan and Tori were scheduled to have dinner with his parents at their home. They still lived in the same house they had lived in for Evan's whole life, on the street Tori had also grown up on, and where she had met Evan so many years ago. Tori had always loved Gary and Joy Bateman. They were like second parents to her, and during the time of her own parents' split, she had needed them more than ever. But she was aware of their conservative views on things and wondered as much as Evan did about how they would react to his monumental announcement.

"Evan, you look like you're about to be led to your own execution," Tori said as they were about to leave for his parents' house.

"That's exactly how I feel," he lamented. "I'm just hanging on by a thread here, barely holding my shit together. Oh, God, how am I going to do this?"

"Hey, Evan, look at me," Tori said as she lovingly placed her hands on his face, turning his head so she could look him directly in the eyes. "Whatever happens tonight, remember that the one thing you never have to doubt is my love for you, and that I'll be here for you when it's over, regardless of the outcome. I'll be right there beside you throughout the whole thing. You've always been my anchor, Evan. Now it's my turn to be yours."

Evan nodded and pulled her into a tight embrace, unable to find adequate words to express his gratitude for her. "I love you," he finally said, his voice shaking.

"Right back at ya," she said with a smile.

Evan was quieter than usual throughout dinner and ate very little. After dinner, they all moved into the living room, and Evan was visibly uncomfortable.

"What's wrong, Evan?" his mother broached finally. "You hardly ate anything at dinner and you seem very distracted."

Evan's discomfort quickly morphed into full-blown panic

as he reached for Tori's hand. She laced her fingers through his and squeezed, reassuring him that she was there for him. He inhaled deeply and exhaled slowly. "Well, Mom, Dad, I actually have something very important to discuss with you, and, honestly, I don't know how you're going to feel about it," he began.

His parents shared a concerned look. "Is everything okay between you two?" his father asked with worry. "Are there any issues with the wedding?"

"Well, I guess you could say that, " Evan said, squeezing Tori's hand even harder. He was sweating profusely now and she could feel how damp his palm was. "Things are actually great with us," he reassured them, "but we're no longer getting married," he announced.

"What?" Gary and Joy said in unison. "What's going on?" his mother asked.

Evan braced himself for what he knew would be a shock to them, and would potentially change his relationship with them forever.

"Is there someone else?" Gary asked.

Evan swallowed hard. His mouth was as dry as the Sahara desert, and he took a sip of water. His heart was beating out of his chest by then. "Yes, there is," he said finally. "But it's not what you think," he proclaimed.

"Wait, I'm not following here. How could it not be what we think?" his mother asked, perplexed. "Either there's someone else, or there isn't," she stated simply.

Evan looked at Tori for moral support and she put her arm around him. He took a gulp of air before he continued. "Because," he said and hesitated, knowing that his next words, once spoken, could never be taken back again. "Because..." he stammered, "I'm gay," he finally choked out, his voice unsteady. "The other person is a man, and I'm very much in love with him." *There, it was out*, he thought as he exhaled the breath he had been holding.

The silence in the room was deafening as his parents took

in what they had just heard, both looking completely mortified. "No, this can't be right," his father finally said, his mouth agape as the color drained from his face. "There's no way. You two have been together all your lives. It's obvious how much you love each other."

"Yes, we do love each other, Dad. That's not up for debate. Tori is the most important person in my life. But it doesn't go beyond best friends, and we both know now that it really never did." Now that it was out, he wanted them to know everything. "I've known this since I was in middle school, but I was too afraid of telling anyone. So I started dating my best friend in high school, hoping that," he paused, considering his next words, "I don't know, hoping that I could change, or make it work with a girl. I knew how you'd feel about it, and I just couldn't live with disappointing you." Evan started to cry then and Tori put her arm around him again.

"How could you do this to her, Evan?" Joy asked her son in an accusatory tone of voice. Then, she turned her attention to Tori. "I mean, how can you even be here right now, supporting him?" she asked, baffled.

"Because he's my best friend and I don't love him any less than I ever have," she defended. "In fact, I think I love him more." She was being completely honest with them.

"But after he used you all of these years," Gary said, "how could you feel that way?"

"Because he didn't use me, Gary," she said, looking back and forth between both of Evan's parents. "I want to be very clear about this," she continued. "Evan's love for me has always been the purest form of love, and I feel the same way. He was scared and thought that starting a romantic relationship with his best friend was the best way he could think of to possibly make it work with a woman. Yes, I wish I had known earlier, but I completely understand that, and I don't hold it against him or feel used in the least."

"Well, you're a better woman than I would be in this situation," Joy confessed, wringing her hands.

Tori wanted them to know everything, even her part in it, and felt she owed it to them, and to Evan, to be completely transparent. "Full disclosure," she began. "It was actually me who broke our engagement before Evan even told me he's gay."

"What?" they said, once again in shocked unison, with identical dazed expressions on their faces.

"I met a man last year when I was working on the Alaskan cruises, and I fell desperately in love with him. I honestly came home and tried to put him behind me, but I just couldn't, and I knew it wasn't fair to Evan to continue with our engagement when I realized I only loved him as a friend."

"Well, at least one of you was mature enough to be honest," Gary shot accusingly at his son.

"Evan told me he's gay on that very night when I broke our engagement and confessed to him that I'd had an affair," Tori said. "And I knew it was probably the best thing that could have happened for our friendship. We were both afraid of breaking our engagement and possibly losing the other one in the process. Now we're still best friends, and even closer than ever."

There was silence then for a long moment, which felt like an eternity to Evan, while his parents took it all in. "Please say something," Evan finally said, imploring them to answer. "I won't be able to bear it if you can't accept this."

"Evan, you're my son and I'll love you no matter what," his mother finally said. "But I don't know how to reconcile this with my own beliefs. I've always felt that a homosexual lifestyle is a choice, and I just don't know how I feel right now."

"Well, Mom, I can tell you that I'm proof positive that it's not a choice. I tried so hard for so many years to fight this and change myself. But at the end of the day, I was hurting myself and Tori. She deserves to be with someone who can love her in every way, and frankly, so do I," he declared. He looked at his father, then, who hadn't said anything in a long while. "Dad," he ventured to ask his father an important question and wasn't sure if he would be able to handle the answer. "What are you thinking right now?"

His father ran his hand through his full head of graying hair. "I'm going to need some time with this, Son. I feel the same way as your mother does about that lifestyle. But I also want you to know that I love you. I just don't know how easy it's going to be for me to accept this."

Evan realized that, after dropping a bomb like this on his parents, he could not ask for more than that from them at this point. It had actually gone better than he had expected it to. "I really hope you can, and at some point, when you're ready, I'd like for you to meet Ben and see for yourselves what kind of relationship we share."

"I'm definitely not ready for that at this point," his father said honestly, and his mother nodded her agreement. "But give us some time, and we'll see how it goes."

"That's all I can ask," Evan said. "I just want you to know how much I love you. You've been amazing parents, and please also know that this has nothing to do with you or how you raised me. It's just who I am, and I need to finally live my life being true to myself."

He and Tori each hugged both of Evan's parents before they left. They all cried and promised to work things out, no matter how difficult it might be for Gary and Joy to come to terms with all of it.

"Well, that actually went better than I expected," Evan said on their way home.

"They'll come around, Evan, I know they will," Tori said to encourage him, and she sincerely meant what she'd said. "They're good people, and anyone who raised you to be as loving and compassionate as you are will come to realize that they just want their son to be happy, no matter how that looks."

"I hope you're right," Evan said, feeling exhausted once they got back to their apartment. "Thank you for being there for me. I couldn't have gotten through it without you," he said, pulling her into his arms, with tears falling freely from his eyes.

"There's nowhere else I would rather have been than right by your side," she said, looking at him with love. "And I'll be by your side though everything, always."

"Tori," Evan began quietly, "I know this is probably a huge ask, but do you think that we... I mean, would you mind if I sleep with you tonight?" he requested. "Not in a sexual way," he hastened to clarify. "I just need to hold you, and be held by you, and just know you're there. Do you know what I mean? Am I making any sense here?"

Tori had never seen him as vulnerable as he was in that moment. She walked over to him and folded him into her arms. "Yes," she confirmed, "you're making all kinds of sense." They went to bed then and slept soundly, wrapped tightly in the security of each other's arms.

Over the next couple of weeks, they had similar conversations with her father and stepmom, and her mother and stepdad. Evan felt he owed it to her parents to be as honest as he had been with his own, and Tori stood by him, just as she had when he told his parents. She was equally honest with them about her relationship with Charles, taking full responsibility for her role in the dissolving of their engagement. While shocked, both of her parents and her step-parents were far more accepting and supportive of Evan right from the get-go than his parents had been. But Tori knew in her heart that they would come around.

Once the news had been broken to all their parents, Tori slid her engagement ring off her finger one night and placed it in Evan's hand. "I guess now that the news is out, I should give this back to you," she said sadly. She had continued to wear it so that it would not arouse suspicion if his parents noticed she wasn't wearing it anymore.

Evan's reaction was not what she'd anticipated. "No," he said decisively. "I want you to have it."

"But Evan..." she began.

Evan interrupted her. "No," he said again, more adamantly this time. "That ring is as much a symbol of my love for you as it ever was. That's what an engagement ring is all about, am I correct? It's a symbol of love and commitment

232   JULIE SIMMONS

between two people and a promise to be a part of each other's lives forever."

"Well, yes," Tori agreed.

"Well, there's nobody I love more, and I'll be committed to you for the rest of our lives, so please keep the ring as a reminder of that. I will never in my life have a reason to give another woman anything this significant again, so if you want to, you can wear it on your other hand or on a chain around your neck. Or if you end up with Charles and he's not cool with it, keep it somewhere safe where you can see it every day and know what you mean to me."

There were large tears running down her face as she considered the sentiment Evan had expressed. She took the ring from him and placed it on her right hand. "I love you," she said and hugged him tight.

"I love you, too," he said, kissing her on the top of her head.

In January, Tori received a message from Andy, asking her a couple of questions that had come up for him regarding entrance requirements to Carnegie Mellon. But mostly, he just wanted an excuse to check in with her. She was so happy to hear from him and answered his questions. *How is your father, doing?* She asked at the end of her message, desperate for any information about him that she could get.

Not great, came his response. *He's trying to keep busy with work, but he's just going through the motions. He's unhappy and has been broken since he got back in September. He loves you as much as ever and misses you desperately.* Andy wanted to say more about what was going on, but Charles had put the kibosh on that immediately and was still steadfast in his resolve not to get her caught up in all of it.

Tori had hoped for more information from Andy, but sensed he had been silenced by his father. She did not mention her broken engagement to him either. She looked at the bracelet Charles had given her for Christmas, which she wore every day, and cried.

February was a busy month for Tori with performances of *Promises, Promises,* which played to captive audiences for every performance. Evan's parents were slowly coming to an acceptance of their son's sexual orientation, and were beginning to feel ready to meet Ben. Both Evan and Ben were extremely nervous about it, but when it happened on Valentine's Day, it went better than anyone had anticipated. Gary and Joy couldn't help but take a liking to Ben when they met him, and could see that their son was happier, in a different way, than they had ever seen him before. Evan was very proud of the progress his parents had made in the short month that had elapsed since he came out to them.

At the end of February, Evan moved out of the apartment he shared with Tori and moved in with Ben, marking the end of an era for him and Tori. It felt strange to her to be living without him, and she often felt lonely, the solitude giving her more opportunity to think of Charles and long for him even more.

On Valentine's Day, she received flowers from him, which he once again sent to the 5th Avenue Theatre, with a card that simply said *I'm working on it. Don't give up on us. I love you, Charles.* She cried when she read it, and wondered if she should dare start hoping that there was a possibility they would eventually share a life together.

Before she left to return to New York for cruise show rehearsals again in the middle of March, Tori decided to give up the apartment, putting all her personal belongings in storage and giving Evan and Ben whatever they wanted of the kitchen supplies and linens. She could always stay with her father for awhile if she returned to Seattle in September, but she hoped with everything in her soul that she would be with Charles by then.

When she got off the plane at JFK to her aunt's excited embrace, she couldn't help but think of how much her life had changed since she landed there one short year ago.

Helen saw the toll that all of it was taking on Tori the

instant she saw her. "Oh honey," she said with concern, "you've lost weight and you don't look well." She knew why and felt terribly sorry for her niece. "How are you holding up, or should I even ask?"

Tears pooled up in Tori's eyes immediately. "Don't ask," she said, her pain evident in her voice as well as her appearance.

"You haven't heard from him?" Helen asked, but already knew the answer.

"Only the Christmas present and the flowers. Otherwise it's been crickets."

Helen struggled not to tell her what she knew. She knew far more from what Charles had communicated to Steven over the last six months, but was sworn to secrecy. It put her in a difficult position and it wasn't easy, but she decided to abide by her promise and said nothing. Tori would know everything in a few short days anyway, she reasoned.

"So, how are things with Steven?" Tori asked in the hopes of discussing a happier topic.

Helen's face lit up at the mention of him. "It's wonderful," she said, sounding like a young girl again. "I've been so happy. I only hope your uncle would approve."

"Oh, Aunt Helen, I know he would. You were the light of Uncle Alan's life, and even when I was little, I loved the obvious connection you two had. But I know he would have liked Steven and that he'd want you to be happy," she assured her aunt.

"Thank you, sweetie," said Helen with a smile. "You'll actually have the house in Queens to yourself a lot more this year. I've been spending more time at Steven's in the city lately," Helen said shyly. Although, knowing what she knew, she expected Tori wouldn't be spending any time in Queens, either.

"That's wonderful. I'm so happy for you two. I hope I'll get to spend some time with you, though. I'll have to tell Steven that he has to give you up at least some of the time," said Tori with a grin.

"Oh, you can count on it," Helen said, giving Tori another hug. "I don't want to miss out on spending as much time with you as I can."

Tori spent the weekend getting settled and realized that, after only the six weeks she'd spent there last year, New York was already starting to feel like home. It was filled with so many memories of Charles that it made her heart ache to remember the times they had shared there. She was becoming apprehensive about seeing him again on Monday when she arrived at the rehearsal space once again. She wondered what she would do if his marital status had not changed. Would she easily fall back into his bed for another season of love and unquenchable passion, or would she be able to resist him? She thought the odds of that were pretty low. The truth was, she loved him far too much to keep him at bay, and that love had not waned one single iota in the past six months since their heart-wrenching parting on the *Aurora.*

Her heart raced with trepidation as she approached the rehearsal space on Monday morning and pulled open the door, trying to prepare herself for whatever awaited her on the other side.

Chapter 18 – Charles

Charles returned to work at Juilliard straight away after the holidays were over. He was always happy to go back to teaching every January, a job he really enjoyed, but was even more grateful for it this year as it proved a necessary reprieve from the stress at home and his constant longing for Tori. He was also very busy with the orchestrations for Tom and Jerry's new musical and knew that if he was going to finish in time for an out-of-town tryout at the end of the year and Broadway next spring, he was going to have to work on it all throughout the cruises that year. But he was happy for the diversion, knowing that being on the *Aurora* again without Tori would be torture for him. The ship would be filled with so many reminders of her.

In the middle of January, Charles received a call from Chris Hernandez with an update on his progress in the investigation into Meredith's potentially fraudulent activities. Chris got straight to the point as soon as Charles picked up. "I think I may have hit the jackpot for you my friend," he said to Charles to open the conversation.

"Tell me," Charles said urgently, sitting forward in his chair and gripping tightly to the phone.

"Well, it's exactly as I suspected," Chris began. "It would seem that Meredith acts as a Power of Attorney for her father so she can look after some things while he travels frequently on business. She has signing authority on his accounts and so does his personal assistant, Aaron Leonard, with whom she is having an affair, as I reported to you previously. Her father's accounts require two signatures of the four listed as signing authorities, which are himself, his wife, Meredith and Aaron. So basically, Meredith and Aaron can together authorize whatever they want. Looking into the bank records, I've found a great deal of activity that would not necessarily look suspicious on first glance, but when you dig deeper, you can see that they've been skimming money off him for years. It's a classic scenario that we see far too often unfortunately, usually in cases of elder abuse. But it often happens in these cases as well, where a high-powered business person places someone they trust in charge of finances or other aspects of their lives, only to be defrauded by them."

Charles listened in disbelief at what Chris was telling him. He wasn't shocked that Meredith would possess such a nonexistent moral compass as to do something so egregious, but the fact that even she would do it to her own father defied all reason. It just proved even further to him that Meredith was devoid of even a modicum of decency.

"Do you have some hard proof for me?" Charles asked.

"You bet," confirmed Chris. "I'll send it to you right away, along with the photos of your wife and Aaron Leonard that I got in the fall."

"I don't know how you did it, but thank you so much." Charles had paid a pretty penny for his services, but it had been worth every cent.

"Well, the less you know about my methods, the better," Chris said. "Let's just say I have eyes everywhere, and leave it at that."

Charles called Seth after he hung up from Chris to fill him in.

"Excellent news, Charles," said Seth. "This couldn't come at a better time. I just got your deposition date. March fifteenth."

"'Beware the Ides of March,'" Charles said, quoting Shakespeare.

"Yeah, I thought the same thing," said Seth. "Have you had any contact with Victoria Stewart?" he asked.

"Nope, I've been overcautious about that. I told her in September that she probably wouldn't hear from me until I straightened this out. I don't want to take any risks of her getting dragged into this clusterfuck with Meredith."

"Probably a very good plan. That's why I asked, actually. It's what I would recommend. If it should come up during the proceedings, you can truthfully attest that you are not, in any way, involved with anyone at this time. Anyway, please forward me whatever Chris sends you so that I have it in your file for safekeeping."

"Yes, I definitely will," Charles confirmed.

Later that day, Charles received the photos as well as detailed bank activity that would incriminate his wife and her lover beyond the shadow of a doubt. Charles was smiling as he tucked the evidence into an envelope when Andy walked in.

"Wow, I haven't seen you smiling like that in months," Andy observed. "You look like the cat that swallowed the canary. What's up?"

"You don't need to know the details, but my PI just got back to me with some very useful information," Charles said evasively with a satisfied grin.

"Useful, as in, you can finally shut Mom up and get out of this mess?" asked Andy.

"Yeah, that kind of useful," Charles affirmed.

"Thank God!" Andy shouted. "So what's your next move?"

"I'm confronting your mother with this as soon as I can?"

"YES!!" cried Andy in delight. "Oh my God, Dad, this is friggin' *awesome*."

Charles chortled and said, "Honestly, I've never seen a kid so happy about his parents splitting up in my life."

Andy laughed at that, too. "So when are you going to tell Tori?"

"Not until this is completely over. I'm not taking any chances. Once we're done with depositions in the middle of March and your mother behaves herself, then I'll contact Tori, but not before."

"But Dad..." Andy began in protest.

"But nothing, Son. I'm so close now. I'm not doing

anything that could screw this up. There's far too much riding on this."

"Okay, fine. I actually just messaged her about a Carnegie Mellon question. She wanted to know how you are. What do you want me to tell her?"

"You can tell her I love her and I miss her, but on no uncertain terms are you to say anything about what's going on with your mother," Charles warned. "I mean it, Andy."

"Okay, okay, I won't," Andy reassured him. "But I can't wait for this to be over and for you two to finally be together."

"Me too," said Charles. "I just hope I'm not too late."

When Meredith had been notified of their deposition date, she challenged Charles once again about his decision to pursue the proceedings. "So I said I'd give you until the new year to stop all of this," she said. "Well, the jig is up, Charles. What's your answer?"

"I'm calling your bluff, Meredith," said Charles defiantly. "I'm not backing down."

Meredith looked at him with a truly astonished expression. "Okay then. I guess I'm going to expose your affair, and we'll see how Juilliard feels about it."

"No, actually you won't be doing that," Charles said confidently, throwing a large folder at her. This was an all-too-familiar scene to the one that had played out a few months before, with Meredith throwing a similar folder at him, which had given her the upper hand. Charles smiled now that the shoe was on the other foot, knowing he was now in full control.

Meredith opened the folder and Charles took great satisfaction in seeing her face drop and her complexion turn ghost-white as she examined its contents. Inside she found the incriminating photos of her in the Bahamas with her lover, as well as the proof Chris had sent Charles that confirmed the fraud she had committed against her own father.

"What's wrong, Meredith?" Charles smirked. "It seems you're speechless for the first time ever. I like it. It's a refreshing change," he said with a scowl.

Meredith remained silent, truly stunned as she watched her carefully laid plans crumble around her. Charles took a deep breath as he prepared to unleash his plethora of demands upon her. "So, here's how this is going to work," he began, finally able to call the shots. "You're going to behave like a human being for the first time in your miserable life and you're no longer going to contest this divorce. When we go for depositions in March, you're going to be agreeable about everything, and you're going to leave Andy out of it. I want full custody of him, and he wants nothing to do with you, anyway. I want this apartment. It's close to my work and Andy's school. I do not want him to suffer any disruptions from this. As far as the rest of my assets are concerned, I would never consider being anything less than fair to you, even though you don't deserve it, because, unlike you Meredith, I'm not a vengeful person. But I'm not gonna lie, retribution feels really fucking good right now. Oh, and another thing," he continued. "You need to come up with a way to get your father to keep his mouth shut about me. I'm sure you'll manage to do that, unless you want him to find out what his little princess has been doing to him all this time." Rumors of his father-in-law's slanderous accusations about him around the city had already gotten back to Charles and he needed to nip it in the bud immediately. "So do we have an understanding, here, *darling*?" he spat at her, his voice dripping with vitriol, and venom in his normally warm hazel eyes. "I don't think you want to fuck with me right now, Meredith, because I guarantee you that I *will* follow through."

Meredith just stared at him in horror. Charles ordinarily possessed a good-natured disposition and was slow to anger, but seeing the hatred in his face, she knew, on no uncertain terms, that he meant what he said and she should not underestimate him any further. "Yes," was all she said in response.

"So glad to hear it. Oh, and you can keep the folder, I have copies," he smiled, quoting the exact same words Meredith had used on him when she discovered his envelope containing the photos of him with Tori and the letter she had written him in September. "Doesn't feel so great when the tables are turned, now does it?" he said smugly and turned on his heel. "Oh, and one other thing," he said when he reached the doorway, "I want you the fuck out of my house as soon as possible."

Meredith just stood there, dumbfounded.

February went by rather uneventfully for Charles. Meredith moved out the day after their confrontation. He didn't know where she went and he didn't care. He assumed she had moved in with her lover. His house was more peaceful than he ever remembered it being and he spent more time there than he ever had before.

Charles sent flowers to Tori for Valentine's Day with a note saying he was working on his situation and urging her not to give up on them. He sent them to the 5th Avenue Theatre once again, as he had done with the Christmas present, in order to avoid the possibility of them being intercepted by Evan. He knew she was in a show during February at the 5th and got an idea, which he decided to run by Andy.

"So, Tori is in a show in Seattle throughout February, and I was thinking of flying over there for a weekend to see it. Do you want to go?"

"Hell yes!" Andy shouted with glee. "Have you *met* me?"

Charles chuckled and immediately booked the flights and bought the show tickets.

They flew to Seattle the next weekend and, once again, as he had done in December, Charles sat, enraptured by her as he watched the show. He thought she had undeniable chemistry with the leading man, which caused a pang of jealousy in the pit of his stomach. He urgently wanted to go to her afterward, and Andy encouraged him to, but Charles remained unwavering in his decision to wait until after the March deposition. There was far too much on the line to risk it this late in the game. Andy was also transfixed while watching her spectacular performance and wished they could go see her, but he understood his father's logic and stood by him on it.

The Ides of March dawned as gloomy and foreboding as its title suggested, but the day went smoothly for Charles during the deposition. As he had hoped, Meredith was on her best behavior and amicable to everything that was suggested, including her willingness to no longer contest the divorce. They managed to settle several things and would now avoid a full trial. They agreed to Charles keeping the apartment, but as he expected, in order to do that he had to dig deep into the rest of his assets and investments to make up for it. There was no doubt he was going to feel the pinch financially, but he no longer cared about any of that. All he wanted was Tori, and if it meant he had to live like a church mouse to have her, it was a fair sacrifice. Meredith also did not contest Charles' request for full custody of Andy. He left feeling a lifetime of weight lifted off his shoulders. Now he could finally go to Tori with his heart in his hands and hope she still wanted him. Rehearsals for the new cruise shows were beginning the following week and he needed to be there to get that underway, but he booked a flight to Seattle for the next weekend so he could go to her and ask her to be his wife as soon as the divorce was final.

Chapter 19

Charles approached the rehearsal space on Monday morning and reflected upon how much his life had changed in the year since he had first met Tori. He felt like he had aged ten years in the last six months, but there was a spring in his step now as he anticipated seeing her that weekend in Seattle. He was nervous about the outcome of that visit, and had not given her a heads-up about his arrival. All he had left to do was buy her a ring, and hope she would say yes to his proposal.

He opened the door and was not in any way prepared for the vision that met his eyes when he did. There stood the love of his life, in the flesh. "Tori! what are you doing here?" he asked, thunderstruck at the sight of her. "I thought that... What about...?" He was completely tongue-tied, unable to string two thoughts together as he stood looking at her, open-mouthed.

"I broke my engagement back in October," she explained. "I called Steven in November to ask if they could use me again this season. I made him promise not to tell you. I wanted to wait to see you in person to fill you in and find out where things stood with you." Now that he was standing there in front of her, she could barely keep herself from lunging into his arms. She looked at his ring finger and noticed his wedding band was gone.

"I'm getting divorced. It's been a messy process, but I'm free now and I'm all yours." He hesitated before he continued. "If you still want me that is." He looked at her with all his hopes resting on her next words.

She flew into his arms and they kissed passionately. "Are

you kidding?" she said with tears in her eyes. "That's all I've wanted for almost a year now."

Relief flooded his body as he held her in his arms and kissed her again.

"I noticed your wedding ring was gone," she said.

"Yes, and I want to replace it with a brand new one as soon as possible," he said with a twinkle in his eye, broaching the subject of marriage with her.

"Well, Dr. Ryan, is that a proposal?" she asked.

"You bet your sweet ass it is," he answered as a smile played around his sexy mouth. "I've just put in the worst six months of my life and I never want to do that ever again. Tori, I've waited my entire life for you, and I want to spend the rest of it *with* you. So what do you say? Will you make me the happiest man on earth and become my wife? Do you want to become Mrs. Charles Ryan anytime soon?"

"Yes, yes, yes. A million times YES!" she cried as he took her in his arms and spun her around. Her response was met with a round of applause and cheers from everyone in the room who had overheard.

Steven and Chanel were the first to run over to congratulate them, followed closely by Simone. "I'm sorry mate," said Steven. "I knew all of this, but I'd been sworn to secrecy. Same with your aunt Helen," he said, turning to Tori. "It killed us to be in the middle of both your secrets, but I had a feeling you'd be engaged by the end of this day. Congratulations," he said sincerely. Tori hugged him tight, and then hugged Chanel and Simone.

They started the introductions then with similar speeches as the year before. Charles could barely concentrate on what he had to say in his introduction to the group, and couldn't stop looking in her direction as he spoke. Both of them were anxious to talk when lunch time came. They had a lot of catching up to do.

They grabbed a quick sandwich and some latkes at a nearby Jewish deli that Tori remembered loving the year before.

They sat down and began to unravel the events of the past six months.

She told him about breaking the engagement with Evan, and finally knowing she couldn't go on living a lie with him. "So how are things with you two now?" Charles asked. He had noticed she now wore her engagement ring on her right hand and wondered what the story was.

"Charles, you won't believe me if I tell you," she said. "Part of me still doesn't believe it."

"What?" he asked, intrigued now.

"Evan is gay," she said bluntly. "He met a man last summer when you and I got together and they fell in love. He was worried about losing me as his best friend, same as I was."

"Wait, what?" Charles said in disbelief, his mouth hanging open.

"Those are the exact same words I used when he told me," said Tori.

"Are you fucking shitting me right now?" Charles blurted out, aghast.

"No I must certainly am not," she replied. "Charles, I couldn't make this up if I tried. I was completely blindsided. I didn't see it coming at all. He said he's known since middle school but was afraid to come out and be honest about who he was. So, in an effort to put everything he had into a relationship with a girl, he thought that dating his best friend was the best way to achieve that, and well, you know the rest. I just can't believe I had absolutely no inkling of it"

"Holy shit," Charles said, still trying to process it. "So how are you with all of that?" he probed.

"You know what, it's all good. Actually, it's even better than ever. It tuned out to be the best of both worlds. We're no longer romantically involved, but we're closer friends than ever. We even continued living together until he moved in with Ben at the end of February."

Charles arched an eyebrow at her revelation. "What?" he asked, looking perplexed.

"Well, we had two bedrooms and we were still the best of friends, so we didn't feel the need to change our living arrangements," she clarified. "Besides, he wasn't ready to come out to his parents until the new year, so we didn't see the point of upsetting the apple cart and arousing suspicion about why we had broken up."

"How did it go with his parents?"

"Actually, better than expected. He was really worried they'd pitch a major fit because they're super conservative, but they didn't. It's taken a little while for them to accept it but they're coming around. They've met Ben and they really like him, and so do I. They're a great match. I was there with Evan, holding his hand the entire time he told his parents. Honestly, this whole thing has brought us even closer. I tried to give him his ring back, but he wouldn't take it. He said he wanted me to keep it as a symbol of our love and commitment to each other, which is why I'm wearing it on my other hand."

"Wow," he said, contemplating how he felt about that.

"So, I guess what I need to know from you, Charles, is if you're okay with that. I mean, our relationship is far from conventional. We still say 'I love you' to each other all the time, and we even still cuddle on the couch when we're watching TV. So basically, the only thing that changed was our sleeping arrangement. Next to you, he is still the most important man in my life, and I don't see that changing. Not ever. But my relationship with Evan is not in any way a threat to you, or to us," she reassured him. "I just hope you can accept it and that it won't weird you out or anything."

Charles considered all she had said and realized that it would not be a problem for him. He was secure enough in their relationship to know that she had risked everything to be with him, and he knew that he was her one true love. "He's important to you, so that makes him important to me, too. I want to get to know him and make him a part of our life together," he said, and she beamed back at him as relief flooded her face.

"Oh God, I'm so glad to hear you say that," she said. She

had been nervous about having this conversation with him for fear he would feel awkward about the unbreakable bond she still shared with Evan. She giggled then as a memory crossed her mind.

"What?" he asked. "What was that about?"

Tori laughed. "When I showed Evan your picture, he said he thought you were hot, and when I told him you get hit on a lot, he said 'Fuck, I'd hit on him.' But don't worry, I told him you didn't bat for his team," she said, grinning.

Charles' face turned beet red. "Oh, maybe that's a detail I didn't need to know," he said, embarrassed. "I hope I don't think about that when I meet him."

"Sorry baby," she apologized with a chuckle. "Too much information?"

"Yeah, maybe so," he said, laughing. "But, I am curious about one thing, though. Why didn't you want me to know you broke your engagement?"

"I don't know, I guess..." she paused, trying to find the right words. "I guess I wanted you to come to this on your own, without being influenced by anything I had done. I wanted to know that if you fought for us, it was purely of your own volition."

Charles thought for a moment about what she said. "Okay, fair point. I guess I can understand the logic in that. It makes sense," he finally conceded.

"So now I want to know how things went down with you," said Tori.

He recapped all that had happened with Meredith: her finding out about them, his hiring the PI and finding out the incriminating evidence against her and how he used it to his advantage. "Let me tell you, Meredith was none too pleased when I turned the tables on her. Shit, you should have seen her face. I wish I'd taken a picture so I could relive it forever," Charles gloated. "It was one of the greatest moments of my entire life."

"Oh my God, I bet it was," Tori said, laughing.

"So anyway, it's essentially over now, as of last week. All

that's really left is to wait for the formalities to become final. I booked a flight to Seattle for this weekend to go see you and ask you to marry me. All I had left to do was buy the ring, which I'm going to do as soon as possible," he promised.

Tori smiled. "There's no rush," she said.

"Nope, I'm not wasting any time," he replied. "I want to put a ring on this as soon as I can."

"How soon do you want to get married?" she asked him.

"Oh, six months ago," he said, and Tori laughed.

"I'm not kidding. I would have married you on that very day when we docked in Seattle for the last time," he said, kissing her before they made their way back to rehearsal. "I don't want to wait long. I can't wait to become your husband. We'll figure all that out while we're on the cruise this summer," he suggested.

"Sounds good to me. And I can't wait to become your wife," said Tori, running her fingers through his hair and noticing a more significant dusting of gray throughout. "You have a little more gray in there," she observed.

"I know. After all I've been through, I'm not surprised," he said.

"It's sexy as hell."

"Really?"

"Oh Yeah, really," she whispered seductively in his ear.

"Jesus, I can't wait to get you into bed and have my way with you," he said, pulling her close to him, and as he held her, he noticed she felt even smaller in his arms than usual. "You've lost weight," he commented with concern. "You're not doing anything stupid again, I hope."

"Oh no, not at all. It's just what happens when a girl is pining for the man she loves."

They went back to the rehearsal for the afternoon and when Tori was finally finished with the last dance practice for the day, Charles came up behind her and enveloped her in his arms. "I think I've waited long enough to get my future wife somewhere a little more private," he whispered in his most irresistible sexy voice, his breath hot in her ear. She could feel him growing stiff against her backside.

"Charles," she said with a giggle. "Can I at least get a shower first? I'm all sweaty from dance practice."

"Mmmm, I can't think of anything sexier at this point," he said, sweeping her hair aside and nuzzling the nape of her neck. "Besides, you're going to be a whole lot sweatier by the time I'm done with you." She couldn't wait to be in his bed again. "But go, get a shower then. I've waited this long to ravish your body, I guess I can wait a while longer."

When she was ready, they went back to his place, and as soon as the door closed behind them, they began to eagerly tear each other's clothes off. "Wait, Charles," she said. "Where's Andy right now?"

"Oh don't worry about that," he said. "He's at a rehearsal at school for the spring musical. He won't be home until sometime after nine. His best friend also lives in this building, so they always travel back and forth together."

They made their way directly to the bedroom then, and neither one of them could wait for each other any longer. As soon as their clothes were off, they tumbled into bed and Charles plunged himself deep within her with an urgency like none they had experienced before. They both came quickly, their bodies writhing in the throes of passion, and lay gasping for breath afterward.

"Well, that was intense," Tori said, panting.

"I'm sorry, baby," said Charles apologetically.

"What on earth do you have to be sorry about?" she inquired quizzically.

"I've never been that rough with you before," he said with remorse.

"In case you hadn't noticed," she said, "I was a willing participant."

"Well, now that that's out of our system, I can go back to loving you properly," he replied. And for the next two hours he made her body sing in ecstasy as they gently rediscovered each other's bodies, not wanting to leave a single inch unexplored.

Finally, they lay holding each other, completely spent and bathed in sweat.

"Well, I guess you were right when you said I'd be sweatier by the time you were done with me," Tori said with a grin.

"I tried to warn you," he replied.

"Yes you did," she said with a giggle. "Oh Charles there are no words to tell you how much I missed you," she professed. "I'd have given anything for just a moment with you, to see your face, hear your voice and your laugh, or to get just a glimpse of that adorable quirky grin of yours that makes me melt every single time. It literally caused me physical pain to be apart from you."

"I know the feeling," he said as he gathered her in his arms. "But I do have a confession to make, though," he admitted, growing very serious.

"What?" Tori asked with alarm, anticipating something she did not want to hear. Had he found solace in another woman's arms while they were apart?

"I went to Seattle and I saw you in *Holiday Inn* and *Promises, Promises*," he admitted. "You were outstanding."

"You did WHAT?" she asked, unable to believe what he had just said. She was shocked, yet relieved that it was not what she had initially feared. Then she remembered the night she thought she had seen him in the audience, and it all made sense. "Wait, so it *was* you I saw at *Holiday Inn* that night? I thought I was completely losing my mind. I convinced myself it must have been someone who looked like you."

"Yeah, I guess it was me. I locked eyes with you during your bows and wondered if you saw me." he replied. "I just couldn't resist it. I was there for cruise auditions in December, so that worked out nicely, but Andy and I made a special trip in February for *Promises, Promises*. I couldn't help it. I just had to see you, even if I couldn't hold you in my arms. Although, I nearly came to the stage door after to surprise you. It was all I could do to force myself not to."

"Oh my God, I can't believe you did that. I wish you had

come to see me."

"Like I said, I wanted to more than I can tell you, but Meredith was on the rampage and I still didn't want to chance anything. When I found out that she knew about us, I got overcautious. I didn't want to risk her dragging you into this. It was also the recommendation of my lawyer that I avoid any contact with you," he explained.

"I understand that," she said. It had been a difficult time for both of them, but worth everything they had gone through to finally be together. Now they had the rest of their lives ahead of them, and Tori knew, without a doubt, that he was her destiny.

She looked around his bedroom then, finally noticing her surroundings. "It feels strange making love somewhere other than on the ship," she commented.

"Oh, there are so many places I want to make love to you," he said in a sexy whisper.

"Oh yeah, like where?" she asked. "And do *not* say an airplane. I won't join the Mile High Club, not even for you," she said, laughing. "I would do anything for love, but..."

"You won't do that," Charles finished. They both laughed at the reference to the famous Meat Loaf song.

"Exactly," she confirmed.

"No, not an airplane," he said chuckling. "Airplanes send my claustrophobia into overdrive at the best of times," he confessed. "I want to make love to you on a deserted beach at twilight by a fire, or in front of a fireplace in a mountain cabin in the winter, skinny dipping in the ocean in Hawaii. And in a honeymoon suite with rose petals over the bed and lots of candles flickering all around, just to name a few."

"Well, make a list, my love," she said. "We have the rest of our lives to check all of them off, and I'll do my best to fulfill your every fantasy."

"All of my fantasies involve you," he said as he began kissing his way down her body.

They regretfully hauled themselves out of bed then as

Andy would be home soon. "I'm starving," Charles said. "I guess we worked up an appetite. Do you feel like an omelette?"

"Actually, yes, that sounds wonderful," she answered, realizing that she felt ravenous for the first time in six months.

They reluctantly got dressed and moved into the kitchen where he began preparing their food. "Is mushroom, spinach and cheese good for your omelette?" he asked.

"Yeah, that's perfect," she answered.

Charles placed his hands on her face and gazed into her eyes. "No," he said, "*you're* perfect. Perfect for me. You're my everything, Tori."

"And you're *my* everything," she echoed. "I love you, Charles, and I can't wait to start our life together." Charles kissed her gently, and then forced himself to pull away from her so he could go back to making their omelettes.

Tori looked around his apartment then, seeing it for the first time. "It's so weird," she said. "I've known you for a year and loved you for almost all of that time, and this is the first time I've seen your place." She surveyed the decor and, while it was artfully decorated, it did not suit her at all.

"I hate what Meredith did with it," he said. "It's not me at all. I mean, she's a talented decorator, I'll give her credit for that. But I'd like a home that's cozy and feels lived in. This is just so functional and cold, just like her. So, as soon as you want, I'd like for us to do a total overhaul on this place and make it ours. That is, if I ever have money again. I'm poor now, by the way," he said, grinning.

She walked over to him as he cooked and put her arms around him. "I could not care less," she said. "All I want is you. I don't care if we live in a cardboard box."

"Don't joke about that, it might happen," he said, and they laughed.

"You're still young enough to rebuild, Charles, I have no doubt you can recover from this," she said. "But as for redecorating this place, I can't wait to do that with you and make it our own. I can see lots of great things I can do around here for

Christmas. I hope you like Christmas decorations, because if I'm living here, be prepared for it to look like Christmas threw up all over this place," she said with a childlike smile.

Charles grinned. "I can't wait," he said enthusiastically.

Tori walked over to a shelf and picked up a family photo of a very stiff looking Charles and Meredith with a much younger Andy. Charles looked exactly the same, except for the lack of gray flecks throughout his hair. "I assume this is Meredith," she commented.

"Yup," Charles confirmed. "Andy was about ten there."

"Holy shit," Tori muttered under her breath.

"What?" Charles asked.

"Well, she just looks so... I don't know... *bitchy*," she observed. "I'd cast her as an evil queen in a heartbeat. She totally has the perfect look for it. Can she sing?"

Charles chuckled and considered her question for a moment before he answered. "You know, come to think of it, I can't even remember her so much as humming along with the radio. It always baffled me that I could end up with someone so completely devoid of an appreciation for music and theatre. We were just so mismatched in every way. Anyway, I'm planning to replace that photo with the one of the three of us at the ball on the *Aurora*."

Just then, the door opened and Andy walked in. Charles knew how excited he would be to see Tori. "In the kitchen," he called out to his son. "I have a surprise for you."

"It smells good in here," Andy said, walking into the kitchen. He spotted Tori then and quickly ran over to her to pull her into a warm embrace. "Tori!" he cried, "I can't believe you're here! What are you doing here?" he asked in shock. "Are you not engaged anymore?" he asked, unsettled over the potential answer.

"Yes, actually Andy, I am engaged right now," she said straight-faced.

Andy could not hide the disappointment from his crestfallen face, and Tori momentarily felt guilty for misleading him. "Oh," he said.

Tori smiled and turned to Charles with a question. "Do you want to tell him or should I?"

Charles looked at his son with a broad smile and a mischievous twinkle in his eyes. "She *is* engaged, Andy," he explained. "To me."

Andy couldn't contain himself as he picked Tori up off the floor and spun her around in much the same way Charles had earlier that day when she had accepted his proposal. "Are you serious?" he yelled. "Oh my God, finally! This is freakin' AMAZING!"

They ate their omelettes and Tori was impressed. "Oh wow, this is the best omelette I've ever had," she said.

"Dad's an awesome cook," said Andy. "He almost became a chef."

"I know, he told me that once," replied Tori. "Damn, you can cook for me anytime," she said to Charles.

"I can't wait to cook for you for the rest of my life," he said, leaning in for a kiss.

"I want that chicken and waffles you told me about," said Tori.

"Alright, you got it. How about I make it for you tomorrow night?" Charles suggested.

"You're on," she said. "I can hardly wait!"

"It's *soooo* good!" Andy weighed in enthusiastically.

After they finished eating and the dishes were cleared away, Andy said he was gong to turn in early. He had a busy day again the next day as rehearsals for the spring musical began ramping up. He hugged Tori and his father and congratulated them again. "I guess you're going to be my stepmother now," he said to Tori.

"Oh, yeah, I guess that's true," she realized. "I'll try not to be too much of a nightmare."

"I couldn't be happier," he said and headed to his room. As he passed his father's bedroom and looked in at the dishevelled bed, which Charles usually kept impeccably well made, Andy smiled to himself. "Go Dad," he murmured under his breath, and walked the rest of the way to his own bedroom.

"I really should call Aunt Helen," Tori realized then. "She might not even be there. She might be with Steven, but I don't want her to worry that I'm not home. I also want to call Evan to tell him our news."

"Okay, well, if I'm going to make fried chicken tomorrow, I have a few things to do to prep for it. I have to make a marinade. So I'll do that while you make your calls."

Helen picked up on the first ring. "Hello my darling," she said warmly. "I've been dying to talk to you all day. So, I assume you saw Charles today."

"Yes, I did," she replied, unable to keep the smile from her voice.

"Did you say yes?" her aunt asked, knowing Charles would most likely have asked her to marry him as soon as he saw her.

"Yes, I did," she answered, her smile even wider now.

"Oh, I'm so happy for you both," Helen gushed. "It's been so difficult for Steven and me to keep our mouths shut. Steven wanted to tell Charles so badly that you were going to be there today, and he knew Charles was planning to propose to you in Seattle on the weekend. It's been exhausting for us, but I'm just glad it all worked out. So I'm assuming you're not coming home tonight, or any night from now on," Helen said coyly.

"You're probably right," Tori agreed. "But I'll be there early in the morning. I don't have anything here with me so I'll want to get ready for rehearsal and probably pick up some of my stuff to bring back here."

"Okay, I'll see you when you get here. And congrats again, to you both."

"Thanks, Aunt Helen," Tori said before they hung up.

Next she called Evan. It was earlier in Seattle, so she knew he wouldn't be asleep. He also picked up immediately.

"Okay, so spill. I want to hear everything," he said as soon as he answered.

"I'm getting married," she said and Charles could hear

Evan's joyful cry from across the room.

"So when's the wedding?" he wanted to know.

"We haven't gotten that far yet," she answered. "But you'll be the first to know," she promised.

"I'd better be," he warned playfully. "Oh Tori, looks like it's working out the way it should for both of us."

"I know. I haven't come down off my cloud yet." Her face was starting to actually hurt from smiling.

"I hope you never do," said Evan. "I love you."

"I love you, too. I had to let you know as soon as I could. I told Charles about everything that happened with us and where things stand between us now, and he's totally fine with it. He said he wants you in our lives."

"I'm so relieved to hear that," he said. "I'm looking forward to finally meeting him. And tell him if he hurts you, he'll have to answer to me."

"I'll tell him," she said and they hung up a little while after.

"Evan is so happy for us," she told Charles. "But he says if you hurt me, you'll have to answer to him."

Charles gathered her in his arms and kissed her. "Tell him he has nothing to worry about," he said.

All the while she was talking on the phone, she had been watching Charles working expertly around the kitchen. "You know," she said, wrapping her arms around his neck, "I'm not gonna lie, a man who knows his way around the kitchen is a total turn-on," she said, running her fingers through his hair. "But a man who knows his way around a woman's body is even sexier, and you certainly know your way around mine. It would seem as though there's more than one room in the house where you possess superior skills."

"Wow, you're really stroking my ego. Keep this up and I'll get a swelled head."

"I can think of another swelled head I could be stroking right now," she said provocatively as she unzipped his jeans and began to fondle his growing desire.

Charles inhaled sharply and moaned. "Would it be possible for me to take my fiancée to bed now and make love to her for the rest of the night?" he whispered, nibbling on her earlobe.

"Oh, yes. I thought you'd never ask," she said, and he proceeded to demonstrate his prowess in the bedroom over and over again.

Chapter 20 – One Year Later

The *Aurora* sat at her dock in Seattle, once again, ready to begin sailings to Alaska in a couple of days. But before it would welcome passengers aboard, the ship would be hosting a very important event: the marriage of Victoria Elizabeth Stewart and Charles Edward Ryan.

When Tori and Charles began their wedding planning the previous summer while aboard the *Aurora*, neither of them could think of a more appropriate location to be wed than the place where it all began for them. They were to be married in the ballroom, which held such special memories for them, and they were spending their wedding night in the best accommodations the ship had to offer. Unfortunately, they would not be joining the sailings for that coming season, as they had a Broadway show to open in a couple of months.

Radiant in her floor-length princess wedding gown, designed and made especially for her by Kayla, Tori stood waiting for her father to arrive to walk her down the aisle, ready to commit her life to the man she had loved for two years now. Evan, her Man of Honor, and Chanel, her Maid of Honor, stood by her side, placing the finishing touches on her ensemble and making sure everything was perfect.

"Are you ready?" Evan asked her.

Tori nodded her affirmation.

"Any jitters?" asked Chanel.

"Not a single one," Tori said. She couldn't wait to become Charles' wife.

"You look breathtaking," Evan said to her with his heart

full of love for his best friend. His face turned pensive then, and Tori noticed it immediately.

"What are you thinking?" she asked him.

"Just that, in another lifetime, you would have been dressed like this to marry me," he answered.

"Does that make you sad?" she questioned. "Is there a part of you that wishes it had happened for us?"

"Maybe a little," he confessed. "But we both ended up with the people we were made to be with." He knew things were working out the way they were meant to. He was happier with Ben than he ever could have imagined, and they were now engaged to be married later that year. Tori would be standing for him at his wedding, just as he was for her now. He had seen firsthand during the past year how happy Charles made Tori, and Evan had to admit that he liked Charles a lot and had become close to him over the last year. Yet, there would always be a part of him that wondered how a life with Tori would have worked out for them. He missed her terribly since she moved to New York with Charles the previous September when they finished the cruise season, and Evan loved her fiercely. He wished nothing but a lifetime of happiness for her now as she was about to take her wedding vows.

"I know," she agreed, breaking into his thoughts. "You will always be a part of me, Evan. It doesn't matter where we live or what life throws at us. It's you and me forever."

"I love you, and I always will," he said, giving her a final kiss before her father arrived to walk her down the aisle. Chanel and Evan walked arm in arm ahead of them. Tori gave her father a final glance and he looked lovingly at her as they began their walk towards Charles, where he would give his daughter away to the man who wanted nothing more in life than to make her his wife.

Tori looked around at all the guests who were assembled to share in their joy. Her mother and stepfather had flown in from London a few days earlier and sat in the front row, beaming at her. Charles' parents, along with his sister and brother and their families also sat in the front row on the other side of the aisle. Ben sat with Marcus as they looked adoringly at their partners walking down the aisle ahead of Tori. Helen was sitting with Tori's stepmother and Chanel's mother, each of them smiling broadly as Tori walked past them. The entire company of the upcoming cruise season's shows all sat together, most of whom knew Charles and Tori already from previous years. Tori noticed Simone was there and was particularly happy to see her. She looked lovingly at Charles as she arrived at the front of the room and smiled at Andy, who was the Best Man, and Steven, who was Charles' second groomsman, standing next to Andy. Everyone she loved was there, but the person she loved the most in the world stood directly in front of her now, as she and her father finally reached him. As she stood facing Charles, she reflected upon the events of the last year that had led up to this day.

As he had promised, the very next day after they got engaged, Charles went out and got her a magnificent ring. He got down on one knee and made it official.

    The next weekend, he brought her to New Haven to meet his parents, which went very well. Tori hit it off with them immediately and thought they were as adorable as Charles had said. They were elated to see their son so happy and were ecstatic he had finally gotten out of his wretched marriage. Tori loved seeing the house and neighborhood Charles had grown up in and asked his mother to show her photos of him as a child, which embarrassed Charles, but delighted Tori. "I'm going to get you back for this the next time we're in Seattle," he said playfully.

    After the six weeks of rehearsals in New York, they flew to Seattle a few days before they set sail so that Charles could meet Tori's father and Evan. Charles was very nervous about both meetings. When he met her father, he felt like a schoolboy picking up his date for the prom and meeting her father for the first time. However William Stewart was very gracious, and while he took pleasure in making Charles sweat for awhile, he reassured him that he could see how happy his daughter was with him. He told Charles that he had had some reservations about the age difference between the two, but after seeing how much Charles obviously loved Tori, and she him, his concerns had quickly been put to rest. Then, true to his word, Charles asked to see childhood photos of Tori, and it was Tori's turn to be embarrassed.

The prospect of meeting Evan was even more daunting for Charles. He was, after all, the other most important man in her life, and he wanted to make a good impression.

They scheduled dinner with Evan and Ben at their place and the guys cooked a lovely meal of Italian food for them. Tori flew into Evan's outstretched arms as soon as he opened the door. "Oh, I missed you so much while I was in New York," she gushed. "That's going to be the hardest part for me about moving there permanently. I won't get to see you all the time."

"I know, I'm dreading that, too," Evan confessed woefully.

She introduced him to Charles then, and the two men shook hands and greeted each other warmly. "I'm so glad to finally meet you Charles," said Evan with a welcoming smile.

"Same here," Charles replied. "To say I've heard a lot about you would he an understatement."

They sat in the living room for awhile and chatted easily about the upcoming cruises, Charles and Tori's wedding, as well as Evan and Ben's plans for the summer. A while later when Evan excused himself to check on dinner, Charles took the opportunity to get a moment alone with him, and offered to help.

He followed Evan into the kitchen and helped him take things out of the oven. "Look, Evan, I... um, well, what I wanted to say is..." Charles stumbled nervously, trying to find the right words to express what he needed to say to him.

Seeing how uncomfortable Charles obviously was, Evan immediately put his mind at ease. "Charles, it's okay, we're all good," he said reassuringly, resting a comforting hand on Charles' shoulder. "I can see that you love her with your life and

I couldn't ask for more for her. Aside from her father, you're the only other man on this planet who loves her as much as I do, and I know you'll take good care of her."

Charles exhaled with relief. "I just feel really badly about the fact that she cheated on you with me. We really didn't go looking for this, but we knew it was a force greater than either of us could fight. You are right, though. I love her more than my own life. I want to spend the rest of my days cherishing her and making her happy, and I'll never do anything to hurt her."

"That's good, because if you do, *then* we have a problem," Evan said bluntly, but with a mischievous grin, letting Charles know he approved.

"Duly noted," Charles said. "I'm really glad she has you. It gives me comfort to know that she has someone who cares so deeply for her, and I'm so glad you were there for her through all the difficult times in her life. I know she'll have support should something ever happen to me. I also want you to know, Evan, that I'd like for you to be a big part of our lives. You are so important to her, so that makes you important to me, too, and I really hope you and I will be close friends as well."

Evan could hear the sincerity in Charles' voice and saw it in his eyes. "I want that, too," he said. "Besides, there's absolutely *no* chance you're ever getting rid of me."

The two men smiled at each other and continued to get dinner on the table. The rest of the evening passed comfortably, and Tori felt as though a close friendship had been forged between all four of them.

The months on the cruise were blissful for Charles and Tori. They settled in nicely to a schedule almost exactly like that of the year before. The only difference was that they were now able to be free and relaxed in their relationship, without the foreboding dread of what would follow afterward hanging over their heads, as had plagued them the previous summer.

The first thing Tori did when she got on board was talk to Kayla about whether she would be interested in designing and making Tori's wedding gown. "Are you kidding me?" Kayla shouted with glee. "Wild horses couldn't keep me away from that." The two women immediately got to work on a design that would fulfill Tori's lifelong dream of her perfect princess wedding dress.

Charles worked a lot more during the cruise this time, as he had to finish the orchestrations for Tom and Jerry's new musical. As he worked, he told Tori the details and shared the music with her, telling her he thought she should try out for the lead.

"Honestly, Tori, the more I work with this music, the more I think it's perfect for you," he told her one evening while he worked. "It would definitely fulfill your dream of playing a princess in a Broadway musical."

Tori looked at the music and agreed with him. "I know it would," she said, "but am I ready for it, Charles?" she asked, her old anxiety creeping in. "I've never even been in a Broadway ensemble. I don't think there's any chance I could land this."

"Hey, it's happened before," he said. "Sierra Boggess' Broadway debut was Ariel in *The Little Mermaid*. And look at Lea Salonga. She was an unknown in the theatre world until she landed the role of Kim in *Miss Saigon* on the West End. She won an Olivier award for that and then won the Tony for it when the show transferred to Broadway."

"Okay, okay, you've made your point," she conceded. "God, you know your theatre shit as well as I do."

Charles grinned. "All I'm saying is that you shouldn't rule out the possibility. You'll never know unless you try. I'm one-hundred percent positive you could do this Tori," he said. "Plus, how amazing would it be for us to be working on the same show together? That would be a dream come true for me."

"Oh, it definitely would for me as well," she agreed. "I'll have to give it some thought."

"Well, the way I see it, what do you have to lose by at least trying it? At the very least it would be audition experience for you at the Broadway level, if nothing else."

He had a point. Tori studied the music throughout the

cruise and became more familiar with it, just in case. The music was challenging, but incredible, and she agreed with Charles that it was perfect for her.

Chanel and Marcus were both back that season as well, and, at the end of the summer, Marcus proposed to Chanel and she accepted. There was a jovial atmosphere on board as they all celebrated their engagement. It was then that Tori got the idea to have their own wedding on the *Aurora* before the start of the next season. They brought it up to the ship's captain and Steven and they all felt confident that they could make it work. Tori and Charles thought it was the most perfect place to have their wedding, and they were elated about it.

When they returned to New York after the cruises ended, Tom Parsons contacted Charles to let him know that auditions were going ahead within only a week of their return. He told Tori and encouraged her again to try out.

"I won't be present at the auditions, and I have no say over casting," he told her, "but, like I said before, it's worth a shot if only for the experience. Oh, and guess what?"

"What?" she asked.

"The out-of-town tryouts are going to be in Seattle at the 5th Avenue Theatre in January." Tom had confirmed that information on their call. "How perfect would that be for you?"

"Oh my God, that would be amazing!" she cried.

She gave some more thought to at least going out for the audition. Charles was right, she needed to get some Broadway audition experience under her belt. She had no delusions whatsoever that she would have any chance of actually getting the part, but she decided to go anyway. And because she felt she had no chance at it, she was not one bit nervous as she channelled her inner princess and did what came naturally to her. However, she did not want Charles to know she was auditioning, so to ensure nobody knew who she was, and that she did not get hired because of who Charles was, she used her middle name, Elizabeth, and her mother's maiden name on her application, just in case anyone involved in the project had heard the name of Charles' fiancée. To her utter shock, she got a callback, and then got called back a second time as a finalist. She couldn't believe her ears when they finally called to offer her the role of Princess Aurora. She thought it was kismet that it was the cruise ship *Aurora* that had brought Charles into her life, and now she would be playing Princess Aurora on stage. She was on cloud nine when she told Charles the news. He swept her up into his arms and kissed her.

"I knew you could get this," he said, a broad smile lighting up his face. "I'm so unbelievably proud of you."

"Now I just have to hope I don't screw it up," she said, doubting herself once again.

"You're going to be outstanding. And remember, if you need encouragement, all you have to do is just look down into the pit and there I'll be."

"That's exactly what I did on the cruise ship and you have no idea how much it helped me. Even then, right from the beginning, you were a comfort to me. No wonder I fell in love with you."

"I have to admit, though, that I'm a little jealous that another guy, other than me, gets to sing 'Once Upon a Dream' with you." They had sung it beautifully together on the ship in their lounge sets.

Tori smiled adoringly at him. "In my mind, and in my heart, I'll always be singing it with you, my love," she said, kissing him.

Charles did not travel for conducting jobs as much that fall, as preparations for the out-of-town tryouts in Seattle would be in full swing by the end of October. However, he did line up one concert in Boston for the week before things got underway, and Tori planned to accompany him. About a week before the concert, Charles received an urgent call from the orchestra's panic-stricken general manager with news of a development that Charles thought might just lead to an interesting opportunity for Tori.

"So, if I remember correctly, you told me once that you'd

welcome the chance to perform *Carmen* if the opportunity ever arose," he said to her later that evening while he was cooking dinner.

"Yes," she confirmed, confused as to why he would be bringing it up out of the blue. "Why do you ask?"

"Well, I just got a call from Boston about next week's show. It's a concert of some of the most famous and well-loved selections from various operas. Anyway, apparently, the mezzo they had lined up to do the arias from *Carmen* had to bail at the last minute due to a family emergency. So now they're scrambling, trying to find a replacement, with no luck. So I told them about you, and they said that if you're available, they'd love for you to do it. I know it's really short notice, but..."

"Charles, are you fucking *crazy*? You know opera is not my strength. Do you really think I could do it?" she asked, her old self-doubt rearing its ugly head yet again.

"Baby, I wouldn't have even brought it up if I didn't think you could nail that shit out of it," he said with complete confidence in her. "How well do you know the material?"

"Pretty well, I think. I've always loved 'L'amour est un oiseau rebelle' and I performed it in one of my recitals at Carnegie Mellon. Singing in French is definitely not an issue for me."

"They'd also need you to do a few others as well. I know one of them is 'Voi, che sapete' from *The Marriage of Figaro*. How do you feel about that one?"

"Oh I adore it, and I *have* performed it, but it was a long time ago. I sang it for a vocal exam back in high school. I had to learn it by rote because I really don't know much Italian, so I'd definitely need a refresher on that. I'd really need you to work intensely with me on all of this if I have any chance of doing it in a week." She couldn't even believe she was actually considering the prospect of doing this.

"I will do everything I can to make sure you are one-hundred percent prepared. I'll work with you as much as you want. So, what do you think?" he asked hopefully.

"Jesus, Charles, I don't know," she said dubiously. "It's very short notice."

"I know, but I also know you can do this," he said with more confidence than she felt.

"Okay, I'll do it," she said before she had a chance to overthink it and let her fears take over. Otherwise, she would surely have declined.

"Excellent!" he exclaimed. "So they were just about to go to print with their programs but halted it when the singer bailed, so they'll need your headshot and bio for that ASAP."

"Okay, I'll get that ready before the night is out," she promised.

They worked tirelessly on her selections that week before heading to Boston, and as Tori watched Charles run rehearsals once they got there, she realized that she had not seen him work with such a large orchestra before. She was mesmerized, watching him take charge and lead the group with such ease and expertise.

Just as Charles had predicted, Tori's performance went brilliantly and the audience was charmed by her, as was the orchestra and its administrators.

"You were a star tonight, my love. Just as I knew you would be. There are no limits to the heights you can reach in your career," he said proudly when they returned to their room that night. She was spreading her wings and taking her talent to new horizons, and he was thrilled to have a front row seat to watch it all unfold.

"Well, you were pretty amazing yourself," she said. "I've never seen you work in that capacity before. It was incredible to watch. And I have to admit, I found it kind of sexy," she confessed.

"Oh yeah," said Charles, folding her in his arms and kissing her. "Just how sexy?"

"Really freakin' sexy," she said provocatively as he removed her clothes and made love to her.

Tori, Charles and Andy settled effortlessly into life as a

family, and none of them had ever been so happy. Andy started his senior year of high school and had applied to both Carnegie Mellon and Tisch for the next September. Charles and Meredith's divorce was final in the fall and Andy had no contact with his mother whatsoever, and didn't want any. They knew nothing about what she was doing or if she was even still seeing Aaron Leonard, and neither of them could have cared less.

They all went to Seattle for the holidays and would be staying there while the show played at the 5th throughout January. It was the most traditional Christmas Charles had had since he married Meredith, and the only one Andy had ever had. Tori, Charles and Andy, along with Evan and Ben, all gathered at Tori's father's for a warm family Christmas. Charles was comfortable with all of them by then, and they considered him part of the family.

The show opened to rave reviews in January in Seattle, and they secured their theater for a Broadway opening at the end of June, following a month of previews beginning in late May. They would not open in time for qualification for that year's Tony Awards, but would surely be nominated the next year. Charles had taken a sabbatical from Juilliard and was considering resigning entirely, depending on how the show went.

Charles and Tori redecorated the apartment as Charles had hoped they would, and they turned it into the cozy, welcoming home Charles had always wanted. They no longer needed the third bedroom that Meredith had occupied, so they turned it into an office for Charles, and he moved all of his books and personal things from his Juilliard office to his new one at home.

In the spring, Andy received acceptance letters from both Carnegie Mellon and Tisch, but decided to go to Tisch at NYU so he could stay home. His home life was so idyllic now that he didn't want to leave, and Charles and Tori were both thrilled with his decision.

Now they were taking a little bit of time off for their

wedding before the show opened, and they were excited to be back on the *Aurora*, if only for a few short days.

Charles was shaken out of his reverie of the events of the past year when he saw Tori appear in the entrance at the back of the room on her father's arm. His jaw dropped as he beheld the vision of the woman who would, in a matter of moments, become his wife.

As they stood facing each other with tears in their eyes, they knew they had come full circle. Their journey had been fraught with many challenges and they had risked everything for each other. But their love had triumphed over all of it, and now, as they exchanged rings and vows before the most important people in their lives, they knew it was just the beginning of a life filled with love and adventures they could not even comprehend.

The reception dinner was held in the most elegant of the ship's dining rooms, with an exquisite meal catered by the best chefs on board. Everything went off without a hitch, as guests were regaled by the usual toasts, well-wishes and funny, and sometimes embarrassing stories shared by loved ones about Tori and Charles.

After dinner, they all returned to the ballroom for the remainder of the evening. Charles and Tori's first dance was to their own rendition of "All I Ask of You" from *The Phantom of the Opera*, which they recorded while in the studio recording the cast album for their upcoming show. They thought it would be a nice touch to dance to it at their wedding. As they took to the dance floor, they both remembered the first time they had danced together in this ballroom, nearly two years before, when she had looked so radiant in the ball gown that matched her eyes. Yet as amazing as she had looked that night, it could not compare to the vision she was on this day.

Charles gazed into Tori's shining eyes. "The first time I danced with you on this floor," he said, "I wanted more than anything to do this." He cupped her chin with his hand, tilting her face toward him, and kissed her ever so gently. "I love you Mrs. Ryan."

A single tear fell from one of Tori's eyes and rolled down her cheek. "Hey, what's this about?" Charles said tenderly, kissing the tear away.

"I just wish I could freeze time, right here, right now. I want to savor this night forever," she said, gazing lovingly into his eyes.

"But baby, we have so much life to live and amazing things to do together. You are standing on the threshold of an awesome career, and I guarantee you that in a year from now, you'll be the toast of Broadway and everyone in the theatre world will know who you are. You're about to do incredible things and I can't wait to stand by your side and watch you do all of them. If you were to freeze time right now, we wouldn't get to live our dreams, and I wouldn't get to make love to my beautiful bride, which I hope to do very soon, if that's all right with you," he whispered seductively in her ear. "I cannot wait to consummate this union," he said with hunger in his voice.

"Me neither," she agreed, "but just let me bask in this night and this dress, and all of it for a little while longer." She wanted to commit every detail of it to her memory.

"Take as long as you need, my love. I've got a lifetime to make beautiful love to you. I can wait a while longer," he said, his eyes dancing and his face displaying all the love he felt for her. As their guests watched them dance, they could all see the intensity with which Tori and Charles looked at one another and the adoration in their eyes.

The song changed then to Shania Twain's "From This Moment On" and Tori danced with her father, followed by Evan, her stepfather, Andy, Steven, and Charles' father, while Charles danced with his mother, his sister, Tori's mother and her aunt Helen.

"Charles, I'm sure you remember how skeptical I was when Tori first got involved with you," Helen said as they danced. "I was protective of her and afraid she would get hurt.

But once I saw your devotion to her, I quickly became your biggest supporter. I can't tell you how delighted I am on this day to see you two so happy. I love you, Charles, and I couldn't be happier to welcome you to this family."

"That means the world to me, Helen," said Charles, touched by her sincerity. "You are such an important person in Tori's life and your support means everything to us both."

A little while later when Tori took a break from dancing, she finally got a moment alone with Helen. "Congratulations darling," said Helen. "It was a beautiful wedding."

Tori beamed at her aunt. "It was even more perfect than I could have imagined."

"Well, I have some news for you," Helen said with a huge smile on her face. "Steven didn't want to upstage you guys on your special day so he didn't make a big scene, but he quietly proposed to me earlier today." She extended her hand in Tori's direction to show off her ring.

Tori's mouth opened wide and she squealed with delight. "Oh my God, that's amazing news! Congratulations," she said, hugging her aunt tightly. "Tell me everything."

"It was after the wedding while you guys were getting pictures taken. He nonchalantly said, 'Helen, I have something I'd like to ask you,' and then he got down on one knee, took out the ring, and popped the question. I was completely bowled over. I did *not* see that coming at *all*, but once I got over the shock, it didn't take me long to say yes."

"Oh, that's so romantic, and you are absolutely glowing," Tori gushed. "Have you talked about a date yet?"

"No, we haven't gotten into any details yet," replied Helen. "However, there is one detail that I am *very* certain about."

"And what's that?" Tori asked.

"I am absolutely positive that I want you for my Matron of Honor. Does that work for you?" Helen asked hopefully. "We'll work our date around your show schedule."

"Oh, hell yeah!" Tori shouted. "It would be my great honor," she said with tears in her eyes.

Steven came over then and stood beside Helen, grinning like a schoolboy. Tori threw her arms around him in congratulations. "This is incredible!" she said to him with elation.

"I tried to be very discreet about it," Steven said. "I didn't want to overshadow you and Charles on your special day."

"Oh Steven, it doesn't take anything away from us," Tori reassured him. "If anything, it makes this day that much more special. Does Charles know yet?"

"I told him earlier and asked him to be Best Man, but I made him promise not to tell you anything until Helen got the chance to tell you herself," Steven confirmed.

Tori couldn't contain her excitement and made the announcement of Helen and Steven's engagement to all their guests. Everyone cheered and then watched as Helen and Steven took to the dance floor for a celebratory dance.

Charles and Tori's wedding day had surpassed their wildest dreams. They stayed and danced and visited with all their guests for another couple of hours, and before they left, Tori threw her bouquet and Charles threw her garter. Chanel caught the bouquet and Evan caught the garter. And then Charles got his wish. He carried her over the threshold of their suite and took one last long look at her in her wedding dress before pulling down the zipper and watching as the gown fell to the floor in a heap of fluffy ruffled layers. He looked at her naked body as he laid her on the bed, which was strewn with rose petals, and made love to his wife for the first time by the glow of numerous votive candles placed all around the room.

"You look thoughtful," he said after they made love. "What are you thinking right now?"

"I just never want this to change. I don't want us to become one of those couples who make love once a week or even less, and have to schedule it in their calendars, or get to the point where sex becomes a chore."

"That's definitely not something you need to dwell on, sweetheart, because I honestly don't see that happening," said

Charles, snuggling into her.

"Neither does anyone, yet it does," she said. "It happens to lots of couples once they've been married a long time. The thought of that makes me sad."

"I can't see there ever coming a day when I don't lust for you."

"But lots of nasty things happen to a woman's body as she gets older. Gravity's a bitch. What happens when I don't look like this anymore and I'm no longer desirable to you?"

Charles looked her directly in her eyes. "Not desirable to me? Baby, that's never going to happen," he announced as he gathered her in his arms. "Oh my love, don't you know by now that, for me, making love to you is so much more than just physical? When I make love to you, I'm making love to everything that is the pure essence of you: your beautiful mind, your kind heart and everything else that I love about you. I can only see that growing even deeper with time. Yes, your body is spectacular, and I'm a lucky man to get to love it every day. But when these perfect breasts are not as perky as they are now, and you get varicose veins, or whatever else happens to you, I'll still be craving your body just like I do now. That's a promise. And if we grow so old together that long nights of passionate lovemaking are only a memory, then it will be a beautiful memory that I will treasure forever," he said and kissed her tenderly. "All I want is to still be holding you and telling you how much I love you when we're old."

"Oh, Charles, that's all I want, too," she said, tears welling in her eyes from all he had said. He was such a sentimental man, and it was yet another one of his beautiful traits that she most adored.

"Besides, I'm a lot older than you. I'll probably lose my appeal long before you ever would. What happens when I can't satisfy you anymore?"

"You definitely don't need to fret over that. You're sexy as hell, and your stamina knows no limits," she said. "And lucky for you, I dig older men, so I'll probably find you sexier as you age.

But I don't care if you turn into Shrek, I'll still love you."

Charles guffawed at that. "Oh my God, there's a mental image I didn't need right now."

"Sorry baby, I didn't mean to kill the mood," she said with a giggle. "So would you still love me if I turned into Fiona?"

"Depends, are we talking the princess version or the ogre?" he asked with a devious grin.

She gave his arm a playful smack. "Asshole," she said, laughing.

Charles chuckled as he recalled the first time she had said the same thing to him on the day they had first walked through the park in Juneau. "Oh, now that's the second time in our lives that you've called me an asshole," he said, pouting as he had done on that day.

"And I'll say again what I believe I said then. 'I call 'em as I see 'em,'" she teased.

He looked deep into her eyes once more and grew serious again. "You're worrying again for nothing, my darling. Stop paying interest on that loan you haven't taken out yet," he said, reminding her of his mother's sage advice. "You needn't fear the future so much baby. As long as I'm on this earth, I'll be loving you."

"And I you," she echoed, and they made love once again.

Epilogue

Next to her wedding day, this was probably the most amazing day of Tori's life. She sat in the audience at the Tony Awards – Broadway's biggest night of the year, with Charles on one side of her and Evan on the other. And just as both Chanel and Evan had predicted, she was wearing the gown she had worn to the ball on the *Aurora*, along with the matching jewellery Evan had given her, and Charles was once again wearing the matching tuxedo accessories. She had just sat down again after giving a phenomenal performance of a number from the show. Each musical nominated every year for Best Musical always performed a selection from their show at the Tony Awards, and Tori brought the house down with princess Aurora's big 11 o'clock number, receiving a standing ovation from the audience.

Their musical had opened at the end of June the previous year, as planned, and the reviews were very favorable, especially for Tori's performance. The show was nominated for a whopping nine Tonys and had already taken five of them, including two for Charles: Best Orchestrations and Best Music Direction, for which he had been favored to win. Tori's heart raced with anticipation as her category was being announced: Best Performance by an Actress in a Leading Role in a Musical. Charles and Evan were holding each of her hands, both giving them a squeeze at the same time. Tom and Jerry were presenting the award, and as she listened while they announced the impressive list of veteran nominees that she had the great fortune of being nominated with, she knew she had absolutely no chance of winning it: not for her Broadway debut. She was floored just to be nominated in such incredible company.

"And the Tony goes to..." Tom said, opening the envelope.

"Oh this makes us very happy," Jerry said as he read the results, "Victoria Stewart-Ryan."

No, she did not just hear her name. This couldn't be right, she thought as she sat immobilized in her chair.

"Baby, you *won!*" Charles said in her ear, his eyes lighting up with pride. She jumped out of her seat and hugged Charles, and then Evan. She made her way to the stage to accept the great honor.

"Oh my God," she said, taking the award from Tom and facing the audience. "What the hell just happened here? I'm not in any way prepared for this. I was sure I wouldn't win with all these other outstanding ladies who were nominated, so I didn't even prepare a speech." She paused to gather her thoughts and forged ahead. "Um, I'd like to thank Tom and Jerry for writing the amazing music that I get to sing eight times a week, and everyone else in the company. You are all incredible, and it's like getting to hang out with an awesome family every day. To the other nominees, I'd just like to say, wow! You are all idols of mine and I can't believe this is happening right now. I'd also like to give a big shout-out to the talented lady who designed my dress and made it with her own hands, Kayla Miller. You don't know her name yet, but I guarantee you that you will. I want to thank my parents and step-parents for always encouraging my aspirations. And finally, to the two most important people in my life. My best friend Evan. Evan, you've been my best friend since we were four. You know everything about me and still love me unconditionally anyway. And my husband. Charles. You are my strength, my confidante, my one true soulmate, and you have my undying love forever and always. I'm so fortunate to be able to go to work with you every day. I feel like I'm dreaming, and if I am, I never want to wake up. Thanks everyone for this," she concluded, raising her award into the air.

By the end of the night, the musical had taken seven of the nine awards it was nominated for, including Best Original Score, Best Book of a Musical, and at the end of the ceremony, they were named Best Musical. These three big awards were considered the trifecta among the Broadway community, and it was a huge accomplishment for any musical to take all three.

"Oh my God," Tori said to Charles later at the after-party, as the reality of her achievement hit her, "I just won a fucking Tony Award!" She was still dumbfounded.

"I told you that you were going to do awesome things and that everyone would know who you are," Charles said, his pride in her beaming from his eyes. "And it's only the beginning for you."

"For us," she corrected him. "The only thing I care about is that you're by my side for all of it," she said, her eyes shining as she gazed lovingly at him.

She checked her phone a while later and smiled. "It's a message from Kayla," she said. "Apparently her web page and socials have blown up since I mentioned her in my speech. She's already got offers coming in to do costumes for upcoming shows."

This had been an unbelievable evening in so many ways, and was a glorious end to what had been a busy year for them. Not only had they opened a hit Broadway show, which was the hottest ticket going right now, they had also had three weddings since they were married a year ago: Evan and Ben, Chanel and Marcus, and Helen and Steven. And Tori had stood as Matron of Honor for all three of them. She was looking forward to a break in a few weeks, as she and Charles were finally going to take the honeymoon they didn't get to have after they were married. They were going to London to visit her mother and planned to spend a few days in Paris as well.

Charles had officially resigned his position at Juilliard, once they realized the show would enjoy a lengthy run, and he was now getting offers from all directions for future projects.

His Tony wins would only help to increase the demand for his talents. There was also talk of a London transfer of their musical, and Charles knew Tori would welcome the opportunity to open the show there and spend some quality time with her mother for the first time in years. Plus, Charles loved the idea of Tori getting the opportunity to add an Olivier Award to the mantle, along with her Tony. Their future prospects looked very promising and he was bursting at the seams with pride in Tori's success.

Later that night as they lay in bed after making love, Tori considered all they had been through since they'd met. She thought about the song, "That's How You Know," which had played such an integral role in bringing them together three years before. She smiled as she remembered all the cute things that were mentioned in the song, which Charles had done to show her he loved her. She then reflected on all the things he had done since then to prove his love. He had fought hard to find his way back to her, and demonstrated to her every day how much he cherished her. There were no words that could possibly come close to expressing how much she loved him and how grateful she was for the extraordinary life she was leading.

"What were you thinking just then?" he asked, noticing the smile on her face.

"I was just thinking about everything we're been through since we first met, and how lucky I am for all the blessings in my life, especially you."

"I'm the lucky one," he said. "The purpose of my life is to make you happy. Everything else is secondary." He was just as crazy about her as ever, if not more so. There had not even been another harsh word between them since their fight aboard the *Aurora*, and their sex life definitely had not slowed down one bit. He considered it an honor to make love to her, and thanked his lucky stars every day that she had chosen to give herself to him. They held each other, both secure in the knowledge that whatever life brought their way, good and bad, they would face it together, and that was all the reassurance they needed in an otherwise uncertain world. No matter how unpredictable life could be, they knew their love was a constant, and never questioned for a second that they would spend their lives in each other's arms, joined at the heart.

The End

Acknowledgements

When I first sat down to begin writing this novel in January of 2023, I had no idea if it would actually become anything, or if it would just be a failed attempt to fulfill a lifelong dream of mine. Therefore, during its writing, I was incredibly secretive about the whole endeavor. My husband, Rod, was the only person who knew about it during the first weeks, followed by my aunt Verna. I told no one else about it until I knew I had created something I was proud of and wanted to attempt to publish. So to Rod and Verna, who were hugely supportive throughout this process, I want to extend my most heartfelt thanks for your love and encouragement. Until now, Rod is the only person to have read this, and I want to thank him for his proofreading and for catching some minor typos and spelling/punctuation issues. Aside from these small fixes, every word you read is my own and was typed with my own hand, so to say that I feel incredibly vulnerable and exposed as I now put this baby out into the world, would be an understatement.

I want to send a huge shout-out to Sandra Verhoeff, of Signet Studio Design in Kamloops, BC for the stunning cover design. I sent her a detailed and very specific description of my ideal vision for this cover, and she completely knocked it out of the park, checking nearly every one of the boxes on my wish list. She created a cover that far exceeded my wildest expectations. Brava, Sandra! I only hope this book can live up to your breathtaking cover.

Of course, I could not have accomplished any of this without the exceptional people who raised me: my parents, Ed and Angela Benson. They have encouraged me in everything I have attempted throughout my life (and lots of things I was too scared to attempt on my own). Raising a legally blind child was not an easy task, especially in a very small town with minimal outside supports and resources, but they proved time and again that they were equal to the challenge. In my humble opinion (and yes, I'm biased), they far surpassed anyone's expectations, especially their own. They encouraged me to be a confident and independent child who would grow up to be a strong, resilient woman, and for that, I am eternally grateful.

I am also incredibly fortunate to have two more sets of wonderful parents on my husband's side: his mother, Maxine Lane and stepdad, Kevin Lane (who sadly passed earlier in 2023), as well as his father, Eric Simmons and stepmom Christine Simmons. They have embraced me as one of their own and shown me immeasurable love and support in the 30+ years I have known them. My father-in-law has always claimed to be the president of my fan club and it is a title I happily bestow upon him. I also want to thank him for the many bits of sage advice he has given me over the years, two of which have made their way into this novel. He is responsible for the "get off your own back, there's not enough room for you back there," and "worrying is like paying interest on a loan you haven't taken out yet" pearls of wisdom, which I have taken with me throughout my life. So there you go, Eric, If you thought I never listened to you, this proves beyond a shadow of a doubt that I definitely did. You are actually the most quoted person in my life, but don't let it go to your head. There's really not enough space on this planet for the enormous ego boost I'm sure this gives you.

I would like to send genuine thanks to my beloved aunt Verna for her love and support. You are definitely the co-president of my fan club, along with Eric, and you have become my very best friend (next to Rod, of course). And in case you're wondering, yes, the character of Tori's aunt Helen and her touching bond with her niece were definitely inspired by you. Like Helen, you possess an extraordinary degree of kindness and generosity, not to mention your fierce affection for those you love. I have been so infinitely blessed to have you in my life.

And finally, to my husband, Rod, there are not enough words in the English language to express to you my gratitude for your undying love and encouragement. As I said in my dedication, I based so many of Charles' phenomenal qualities on you, and as I'm sure you noticed, many of his comforting and loving words to Tori are yours. I hope my readers will fall in love with Charles, and if they do, they will have fallen in love with you as well. The day you placed a ring on my finger was the most amazing day of my life, and there is no greater privilege I could ever receive than getting to spend the rest of my days with you on this adventure of life.

About The Author

Julie Simmons

Julie Simmons has a Bachelor of Arts in English and Bachelor of Education degrees from Memorial University. She currently resides in Kamloops, British Columbia, Canada with her husband of 30 years, Rodney. Her passions in life (besides her husband, of course) include musical theatre, Disney, and Christmas. She has been the host of On The Marquee, a musical theatre themed radio show, since 2017, which is now syndicated in Canada. Julie has

been legally blind since birth and is a peer support volunteer with the Canadian National Institute for the Blind (CNIB). That's How You Know is her first novel.

Manufactured by Amazon.ca
Bolton, ON

41842859R00169